Morganna lay bewitched. The Earl's face was so close she could see tiny beads of glistening moisture forming on his upper lip. Their gazes locked. Her breathing slowed. Against her will she found herself relaxing. Dreamy-eyed she was held captive by his stare.

This was how it had been at their first meeting in the forest. Then they had been strangers with no reason for distrust. Just a man and a woman for whom no other world existed but the enchantment of the moment. Then the blast from a hunting horn brought her rudely to her senses. What was she doing?

The ground was suddenly cold and damp and she hit out to free herself from Pengarron's grasp. Her struggles increased, but each movement of her writhing body moulded them closer together. Traitorously, instead of protesting, her whole being glowed and throbbed beneath the long powerful frame covering hers.

'Let me go!' she gasped, more frightened by the compelling force which was tempting her to submit to him than of the danger of her situation.

She saw the corners of his mouth twitch in amusement. 'There's a score to settle between us. Any who dared draw naked steel against me has learnt the error of such rashness. Now, sweet vixen, you will learn that you cannot fight me and win.'

For as long as Pauline Bentley can remember, she has been captivated by history. She finds reliving the excitement of the battle of Crecy or a medieval tournament more exciting than the current news of the day. Born in Essex she was trained as a legal secretary, but always came away from visiting castles or manor houses with the desire to write about them. She now lives in Sussex and finds inspiration and relaxation during long walks over the South Downs with the family and dogs. She is married and has two children and a growing menagerie of pets. *Shadow of Pengarron* is her first Masquerade Historical Romance.

SHADOW OF PENGARRON

Pauline Bentley

MILLS & BOON LIMITED
ETON HOUSE   18–24 PARADISE ROAD
RICHMOND   SURREY   TW9 1SR

*First published in Great Britain 1987
by Mills & Boon Limited*

© Pauline Bentley 1987

*Australian copyright 1987
Philippine copyright 1987
This edition 1987*

ISBN 0 263 75806 0

*Set in 10 on 11 pt Linotron Times
04–0887–74,600*

*Photoset by Rowland Phototypesetting Limited
Bury St Edmunds, Suffolk
Made and printed in Great Britain by
Cox & Wyman Limited, Reading*

HISTORICAL NOTE

The seizing of Richard II's throne by his cousin Henry Bolingbroke in 1399 was one cause of the fifteenth-century Wars of the Roses. Though still only thirty-three, Richard had become a despot. Many nobles saw their estates threatened and so favoured Henry's IV's claim to the throne. In February, Richard died a prisoner in Pontefract Castle—whether he was murdered or starved himself to death is still heatedly debated.

Paganism, although rare, was still practised in England. Morganna's treatment at the hands of the Druids was not an uncommon form of punishment in the middle ages.

CHAPTER ONE

THE RAINSTORM STOPPED as suddenly as it had started. Lady Morganna flexed her cramped fingers encased in jewelled riding-gloves and pushed the wet hood of her cloak back from her face. Everywhere smelt fresh and clean, and the leaves of the forest splashing large droplets of water upon the domed helmets of her armed escort filled the air with a hollow, ringing sound.

Cold and stiff from long hours in the saddle, Morganna glanced about her, relieved to recognise an ancient oak severed by lightning. At last she was on her brother's land, and soon she could rest in the warmth of Daneton Castle. As they passed the oak, she saw her tiring-woman, Jocelyn, nervously touch a coral charm sewn to her cloak to ward off evil. Usually Morganna ignored her maid's superstitious ways, but today she too felt a shiver of unease as they passed the bleak place once dedicated to the worship of pagan gods.

After the rain, the hush seemed oddly sinister. The massive trees loomed like dark siege-towers around them, and the hair at the nape of Morganna's neck prickled with foreboding. She tensed, listening to the sounds of the forest as her grey palfrey stepped daintily through the puddles along the rutted track. Why did the rumble of the laden baggage-carts following the riders sound menacingly loud in the stillness?

Morganna looked back, her glance sharp and anxious as she scanned the line of soldiers and wagons. Here was plunder enough, she thought fearfully, to tempt an attack from outlaws. Resolutely she pushed aside her apprehension. Had she not travelled safely during her three weeks' pilgrimage to the holy well of St Winefride, a saint compassionate to women? Even with unrest obvious in the countryside, her armed escort of a dozen retainers had deterred attack from outlaws and Lancastrians alike. They were safe now among King Richard II's supporters.

No, her unease must be due to what lay ahead at Daneton. She was no coward, but she did not look forward to a battle of wills with her brother. Her frown deepened. Giles, proud of his newly created rank of Marquess of Radford, had summoned her, determined that his guest, the Earl of Linsdale, would ask for her in marriage. How she wished she could obey him without question, but meekness was not her way. Even for Giles she would not become a pawn in a loveless marriage.

Morganna sighed. Her first duty was to her brother. Why must Giles be so stubborn and proud? Aware of his increased importance, he was adamant that no nobleman less than an earl was good enough for his sister. How could she convince him that the rank of countess meant nothing to her? It had been different when their father was alive. He had been content with the match arranged between herself and Ralph Warrender, the second son of the Earl of Pengarron, even though her future husband would inherit no land of his own. Those days of innocence were past.

Rebellion returned to stir her. Since Giles had denounced her first betrothal, she had been betrothed twice more, and each time, fate had denied her a husband. Now, if Giles had his way, she must face the ordeal again. It was humiliating, the weeks spent bargaining over dowries and settlements—she felt like a piece of bartered property. Worse still was the knowledge that having met her proposed husband at Court the year before, she had formed an instant dislike for the man. Almost twice her age, Lord Linsdale was nothing like . . . She checked her wayward thoughts. It was time she stopped comparing every man to the one who was lost to her for ever.

As she stared back along the column of soldiers, her attention was caught by the rigidness of Sergeant Fletcher. Was it her imagination, or was the old campaigner worriedly studying the closely-packed trees on each side of the track? Then she, too, stiffened upon seeing the bloody figure dressed in her brother's scarlet and gold livery lying on the ground ahead. It was the messenger she had sent to warn the Marquess that her party approached.

Before she could draw breath to cry out a warning, dark shapes burst out of the undergrowth, hurling themselves at her party.

'To arms!' The Sergeant's bellow rang out as he snatched out his sword.

Morganna reined in instinctively. She exchanged a nervous glance with Jocelyn. Two of her escort fell to the ground, arrows in their backs. From out of the trees swarmed a score or more wild-looking men, brandishing clubs and axes. Within moments her party was surrounded. Chaos broke out around Morganna, and the forest rang to the clash of steel and the snorting of horses. While Sergeant Fletcher barked orders above the rising din, the prayers for heavenly intervention intoned by the chaplain were drowned by Jocelyn's screams. For a moment, as her palfrey twirled and pranced, Morganna froze with shock. Blood pounded in her ears, and the scene before her seemed played out with tortuous slowness. Already her escort appeared overwhelmed.

Blessed St Winefride, have mercy on us! she prayed, frighteningly aware of their fate should the outlaws kill her escort. If they were desperate enough to attack on her brother's land, they would stop at nothing short of murdering everyone—after they had had their sport with Jocelyn and herself.

A bearded man sprang forward to grab the palfrey's reins. A stench akin to rotting meat rose from his ragged clothing, jerking Morganna into action, and anger replaced her fear. How dare these peasants lay hands on her party! Ducking the nail-studded club the outlaw swung at her, she lashed out with her whip. The leather thong cut into her assailant's cheek, deflecting his blow, so that it missed her head by inches, but as the heavy club jarred against her shoulder, she cried out in pain. She almost lost her grip on the reins and had barely recovered her balance when the terrified mare reared, her hooves striking the outlaw in the chest. With a bellow of rage, her attacker raised his club to strike at the mare's head. Too far from the figure to reach him with her whip, Morganna stared in helpless fury as he prepared to deliver a death-blow.

At that moment an ear-splitting battlecry resounded like thunder though the forest, and a rush of wind passed Morganna's uplifted whip-hand. To her astonishment, her assailant's mouth gaped pinkly open. He swayed momentarily, then, eyes glazing, crashed like a felled tree, a quarrel from a crossbow embedded in his throat.

A hunting party from the castle must have heard Jocelyn's screams, Morganna thought with relief. Her escort carried no crossbows, and the outlaws were armed only with clubs and axes. But before she could think further, Sweet Eglantine shied again, whinnying shrilly at the smell of blood from the corpse which had fallen between her hooves. The pain in Morganna's shoulder numbing her fingers, she strove to calm her frightened mare. But even as her mount came down on all fours, two struggling figures fell against the palfrey's side. Snorting with fear, Sweet Eglantine plunged violently forward, wrenching the reins from Morganna's weakened grasp, and bolted back along the churned-up track they had just travelled.

Briefly Morganna glimpsed Jocelyn trying to beat

off an attacker who had dragged her from her horse. Then the thin, worried face of Father Matthew, her chaplain, flashed in front of her as he snatched at Sweet Eglantine's bridle, but missed. His flapping habit spurred the frightened palfrey to a faster pace and, her stride lengthening, she sped past the last of the baggage-carts.

There was a thudding of hooves, and from a side track on the right a troop of men-at-arms appeared to bear down upon the fighting men. Concentrating on bringing her mare under control, she gained only an impression of black-cloaked figures, their shields and drawn swords gleaming, as she was carried onwards. Showing no sign of flagging, Sweet Eglantine raced ahead. Branches tore at Morganna's cloak and gown as the sound of a fast approaching rider increased the mare's headlong flight.

Suddenly, ahead of her, Morganna saw a fallen tree blocking her way, and her already thudding heartbeat matched the frantic pace of her mare's hooves. The palfrey could never clear the barrier while she carried a rider . . . They would both be killed!

She kicked her feet free of the stirrups and prepared to throw herself to the ground. At this speed she faced certain injury, if not death, but at least there was a chance of survival. She hesitated, aware of a horse drawing level with hers. Then, before she realised what was happening, an arm seized her waist and heaved her from the saddle.

'Hold on tight!' a deep voice shouted from above her.

Too astounded to cry out, for a moment she was suspended over the ground flashing beneath her. Then, as her body slammed against a horse's side, the pleasant scent of sandalwood wafted over her, and the iron grip about her waist crushed the breath from her lungs. An equally unyielding thigh pressed against her ribs as her rescuer veered his mount into the undergrowth and drew to a halt. Through a dizzy haze of swirling greenery, she

raised her head to see a flash of white arc skywards.
Sweet Eglantine had safely jumped the tree-trunk.

The danger over, Morganna became conscious of the
indignity of her position. When she tried to move, she
found her hand was trapped against the tensed, hard
muscle of the man's thigh. The warm skin of his shaven
cheek brushed her face fleetingly, as he bent over and
gently lowered her to the ground. To her dismay, the
moment her feet touched the forest floor her legs trembled so violently that she would have fallen, had not the
supportive arm remained about her waist as the man slid
from the horse to stand at her side.

'You're safe now, my lady,' he reassured her.

Still trembling, she turned to face her rescuer. She
encountered amber eyes, piercing as a hawk's, studying
her from beneath the black hood shadowing his lean
features, and a gasp of astonishment rose to her lips. His
gaze held hers captive, as though she was indeed prey to
any will he chose to inflict upon her. But it was the
unusual colour of his bold eyes which held her spellbound. She had known only one man, then a young
squire in her father's castle, whose eyes matched the
fierceness and pride of a striking eagle. Surely it could
not be he? Not after so long!

A part of her mind warned her of danger, but movement and speech deserted her beneath the compelling
force of his appraisal. It was the shock of her brush with
the outlaws playing tricks upon her mind, she told
herself sternly. She would not allow her childhood
infatuation to haunt her. He had given no sign of
recognising her. But it had been so long—eight years.

She must be mistaken! Not even he would dare to
trespass on her brother's land. But Daneton had not
always belonged to Giles, and a stab of guilt plagued her.
Swallowing hard, she ran her tongue over dry lips before
she risked finding her voice. When it came out, it
sounded oddly breathless.

'I am indebted to you, sir.'

'The honour is mine to have been of service to so fair a lady.'

The admiration obvious in his gaze and the awareness of his arm still about her waist sent a tingle of apprehension through her. Clearing her throat, she moved restlessly.

'I am quite recovered from my fright,' she declared. To her annoyance, her voice quivered, betraying the shaking which still possessed her body.

Instantly his arm dropped to his side, but the corners of his eyes crinkled with amusement as he continued to regard her steadily.

'Your courage is matched only by your beauty. With respect, my lady, I had no wish to offend.'

As the stranger bowed formally, her glance took in his tall, slim figure. Though the long black cloak bore no insignia, it covered broad shoulders and fell to his ankles, where golden spurs over his pointed riding-boots proclaimed his knighthood. When he straightened, he tossed the cloak back over his shoulders, revealing a sable-trimmed black velvet surcoat, with a jewelled sword-belt about his hips. From the gold-embossed black leather baldric across his chest hung two daggers and a pouch.

Again Morganna found herself caught by the power of the knight's assured scrutiny. To her chagrin, his features remained partially shadowed by the hood, but she guessed him to be no older than his late twenties, though there was about him a calm self-possession given to few men of even more advanced years. Only as his full lips parted in a smile, which became both a challenge and a sensual promise, did she look away, blushing, aware that she had been staring.

Acutely conscious of the knight's gaze upon her and of the sound of approaching riders, no doubt her own escort, Morganna glanced sidelong at her rescuer from beneath the long peak of her felt hat. The wild pounding of her heart responded treacherously to the admiration brightening his eyes. Those eyes—disconcertingly familiar . . . Were there any to equal their piercing brightness in all England?

Without turning, the knight called for her mare to be captured by the riders who had drawn to a halt behind them. Even after Morganna heard the horses ride off, she was still powerless to drag her eyes from his bold gaze.

'Do you travel far, my lady?' he asked with obvious interest. 'Perhaps my men should join with yours.'

'I would not inconvenience you further, sir. I am almost at my journey's end.' Her voice fortunately sounded unruffled, despite the wild beating of her heart. 'Though, if your men are tired, my brother would scold me did I not offer you his hospitality for the night.'

Did she imagine it, or was there a flicker of suspicion in his eyes? As quickly, it was gone.

'I regret I must decline the offer. I have business elsewhere which must be dealt with before nightfall.'

His stare displayed none of the reverence she had become used to during her year at Court. A ripple of excitement flowed through her veins. This was no simpering courtier to beg favours. There was a ruthlessness in that amber gaze which proudly proclaimed that he would allow nothing to stand in the way of what he wanted.

Morganna managed to look away. His imperious hawkish features were too near, too commanding, for her peace of mind. It was on the tip of her tongue to demand his name, when at that moment he pushed back the hood of his cloak. As she gazed into his handsome countenance with the sunlight enriching the sheen of his dark shoulder-length hair, she knew him. It was the man she was once to have wed. Sir Ralph Warrender had returned!

The knowledge stabbed agonisingly through her. With relief she heard the sound of riders approaching, and looked up to see Sweet Eglantine being led forward by a panting page.

'I must bid you Godspeed, sir,' she said softly, a catch in her voice.

She moved towards the mare, but as she turned to put her foot in the cupped hands of the waiting page, the lad was pressed firmly but gently aside. Before she could protest, a hand grasped her waist and she was lifted up to the saddle by the knight. Unrepentantly, he grinned up at her.

'Until we meet again, my lady.'

The ominous chink of armour warned Morganna that her escort had ringed about them, and her eyes widened in momentary alarm. If they recognised him, they would take him prisoner. She could not let that happen. Had he not saved her life? Even so, her conscience pricked her. Sir Ralph Warrender was her brother's sworn enemy.

Suspicion again darkened the knight's eyes, but he cast no more than a cursory glance over his shoulder at the grim, hostile faces. Morganna saw him stiffen slightly as he regarded the flamboyant scarlet and gold livery of her brother's retainers. When next he regarded her, the challenge was unmistakable in the sardonic twist of his lips.

'Even in France, my lady, the troubadours sing the praises of the fair Morganna Barnett! For once, they do not exaggerate.'

His eyes glittered with a cold amber light, then their expression became guarded, and he smiled. The change was disarming, leaving her light-headed and wondering if the autumnal bleakness, so fleetingly glimpsed, had ever been.

'So, Radford, arrogant after his rise to marquess . . .' a dark brow lifted, condemningly, 'looks higher than a mere knight for the hand of his sister.'

The gauntlet was flung down openly between them. He must know she had recognised him, and was daring her to betray him. With a calmness she was far from feeling, Morganna lifted her chin and met his chilling glare.

'You are insolent, sir knight! Ride quickly before Lord Radford learns who trespasses upon his land.' She quailed before his blazing fury, but continued her defiance as his own men-at-arms galloped into view. 'I am indebted to you for my life. Therefore go in peace.'

Abruptly he spun on his heel and strode towards his horse, the fierceness of his angry glare causing even the most stalwart of her men to step back as he approached. With lithe, effortless grace he swung into the saddle, and his black gelding side-stepped towards Morganna as he delivered his parting shot in silky tones.

'The Earl of Linsdale is not for you, my lady!'

Struck speechless by his audacity, Morganna watched him ride away. She saw that Sergeant Fletcher was not present among her escort, and, hoping the old retainer was not wounded, she felt a measure of relief that he had not seen her rescuer. He would have recognised Sir Ralph, and betrayed him to her brother. Morganna's head began to throb. Should she not inform Giles of the danger that could threaten his land? Land which had once belonged to the Warrender family, before King Richard had sent the old Earl of Pengarron into exile and confiscated his English estates.

And how had Sir Ralph known of her intended betrothal to Lord Linsdale? Were there spies among the old servants at Daneton? Her unease grew with each unanswered question. What was Sir Ralph doing here? Whatever his reason, it was bound to stir up trouble for Giles.

Morganna shivered despite the increasing warmth of the sun, as she recalled the unrest she had witnessed during her pilgrimage. Many people believed King

Richard's second marriage, to a child-bride, was disastrous for the good of England, especially since his first wife, Queen Anne, had died without giving England an heir. Since his majority, Richard II had indulged his extravagance at the expense of his people's suffering, until even his nobles were growing discontented. Only a favoured few had risen high—her brother among them.

Over the years since Giles had ended her betrothal to Sir Ralph, Morganna had continued to learn all she could of the knight she had idolised in her girlhood. He had become the close companion of the King's cousin, Henry Bolingbroke. When Bolingbroke had been exiled, he had joined him in France. Why, then, had Sir Ralph returned? The old Earl of Pengarron had died in exile. If Sir Ralph was in England, it was for a purpose. Did he mean to take up his elder brother's cause and to win back the Earl's lost estates—Daneton included?

As the baggage-train came into view, the devastation that greeted Morganna pushed all other thoughts from her mind. She was shocked and angered, and gave no more than a glance at the dejected and battered group of prisoners. One of the carts had been overturned, spilling bed-hangings and silver plate over the muddy track, but worse was the sight of the dead and wounded. Three of her own escort were dead, and several of the outlaws. She could see none of Sir Ralph's men among either the dead or the wounded, and for that she was grateful, but four of her escort were slumped on the ground, their wounds being attended to by Jocelyn and Father Matthew.

Scanning the littered track, her frown deepened at seeing Sergeant Fletcher limping towards her, the bandage on his thigh already covered in fresh blood.

'You should be resting that wound, Sergeant.'

'When you are safe at Daneton, I shall rest. I failed you, my lady.'

Morganna smiled fondly at the gruff, battle-scarred

countenance. 'We were outnumbered. Your men fought well.'

'Lord Radford will not think so!' the Sergeant pronounced harshly. 'And rightly. If we had not been aided by those cursed Lancastrians, we would all have met our Maker this day.'

'Then we have much to be grateful for.' Relieved that her voice betrayed no sign of the erratic pounding of her heart, Morganna prompted cautiously, 'By Lancastrians, you mean that they wore Henry Bolingbroke's badge? You forget, Sergeant, that when John of Gaunt, the Duke of Lancaster, died, the King seized his cousin's lands, so there is no Duke.'

'Ah, my lady, they wore Bolingbroke's badge all right! And that makes them no friends of my lord Radford.'

Morganna felt herself grow pale. 'Did you learn their leader's name?'

Upon seeing the old veteran's glower, she added quickly, 'I was so shaken after my mare bolted that I scarce noticed his device. I would inform the Marquess that such men, as well as outlaws, roam unhindered across his land. More patrols must be sent out to protect our people.'

Sergeant Fletcher eyed her narrowly. He had served under her father, and in recent years had always been in charge of Morganna's escort whenever she journeyed abroad.

'Strange that the knight did not reveal his name to you. The men say he wore no device.' Sergeant Fletcher rubbed his gnarled hand across his chin thoughtfully as he spoke. 'There's much about this day which smacks of treachery, my lady.'

Morganna lowered her gaze, fearing that his sharp eyes would discover her evasion. 'Send a rider ahead to warn Daneton that we approach with prisoners.'

Dismissing the Sergeant, she dismounted, and was

immediately confronted by Father Matthew. Morganna suppressed a sigh. There was a strained, taut expression on the priest's face, which usually meant he was about to lecture her on some point of her conduct.

'Blessed Mary be praised, you are unharmed, my lady,' he began, then looked pointedly back along the track. 'And where are our knight-errants? Have they departed? Shame on you, Lady Morganna, for not offering them Lord Radford's hospitality.'

Morganna flushed. 'Daneton's hospitality was indeed offered to them, Father. They were Bolingbroke's men, and declined to accept.'

The priest's grey, lashless eyes seemed to probe her soul. Usually there was little he missed. Did he guess something of the truth?

'These are sad times, my lady.' He looked about at the carnage as he spoke, clearly too disturbed to pay much heed to her heightening colour. 'If you will excuse me, I would return to the injured.'

Morganna walked with him and, discovering that the soldiers' wounds were already dressed, she moved among them offering what comfort she could. Unmindful of the mud clinging to the hem of her kirtle, she praised each man in turn for his bravery, unable to check her tears of concern at the sight of their bloodstained bandages.

When the baggage-carts were reloaded and room made on them for the more seriously wounded, they resumed their journey. Morganna was impatient to be reunited with Giles, worried at the outlaws' attack upon her brother's land.

A vision of Giles's tall, laughing figure warmed her. She had missed him these past months when duty had taken him from Court. Soon he would leave her again. But was it wise of him to be setting out with the King shortly on an expedition to Ireland, if the mood of the people was uncertain? Not that Giles would pay much heed to her advice. Their meeting was bound to be stormy, for all she loved him dearly.

As they travelled on through the forest sparkling in the aftermath of the rainstorm, Morganna was troubled. Aware of Jocelyn's questioning glance upon her, but bedevilled by emotions too raw, too poignant, to be laid bare to another, she avoided looking at her maid. She sat stiffly in the saddle, scarcely noticing the ache in her back and legs, as guilt swept over her.

In an unguarded moment, when she had been almost witless with fear, she had forgotten all her years of training, first under the nuns of the local convent and then, as her brother had risen in favour at Court, under the exacting guidance of Lady Luttrell. All her life she had been schooled in obedience. Although at times her wilfulness made her resent the submissive role she must play, she strove to overcome it in her devotion to Giles. Her loyalty to him was fierce, adding to her growing unhappiness. It seemed impossible to reconcile herself to marriage with Lord Linsdale.

Throughout her teenage years she had carried the image of her lost suitor with her. He had been a squire in her father's household only a few months before he had left to join the Duke of Lancaster's entourage. But even as a young man, Ralph Warrender had stood taller than his companions and had won acclaim for his skill in the lists against the younger knights. Morganna herself had been no more than ten when she had stolen out to watch him practise at the quintain, and the handsome squire had captured her heart.

As they neared Daneton, she could see, above the trees, her brother's standard flying from the highest turret, and her feelings of remorse weighed heavier. She could never look at Daneton and not remember that, once the ancestral home of the Warrenders, it had been given to Giles as a token of the King's friendship.

With an impatient shrug at the gloominess of her

thoughts, Morganna urged Sweet Eglantine to a faster pace as the square keep and round-domed turrets of the castle rose before her. Against a backdrop of black stormclouds gathering on the horizon, a shaft of sunlight turned the white-painted walls of the battlements to a rich gold. The power and majesty of Daneton Castle had never been more beautiful—or more threatening.

She pulled her thoughts up with a start. Tiredness really was making her fanciful, and she was allowing herself to become as superstitious as Jocelyn! As she rode between the double row of thatched cottages of the village, her stomach tightened with hunger at the smell of baking from the communal oven, which mingled with the tang of woodsmoke from the forge. She waved and returned the smiles of the younger villagers, yet noticed that some of the older ones remained sombre faced. Was there an air of expectancy, a cautious lowering of the older tenants' eyes when her gaze fell upon them?

Morganna dismissed the idea as absurd as they clattered over the lowered drawbridge. Observing the jagged spikes of the raised portcullis, she noted with relief that once the iron barrier was lowered, Daneton was impregnable.

CHAPTER TWO

THE NOTES OF the herald's trumpet died away as Morganna's entourage rode out of the darkness of the Gatehouse Tower, and she blinked against the sun's brightness. Before her, the courtyard bustled with activity: lackeys were unloading two cartloads of provisions; a swineherd, accompanied by several jeering soldiers, ran across her path, chasing a squealing pig which seemed determined to escape the butcher's knife. In a far corner, a human tower of five tumblers somersaulted to the ground in front of a dancing bear and its trainer. She had little chance to notice more. The moment they halted by the stone steps leading to the first-floor entrance of the Great Hall, they were surrounded by the pages and grooms who ran forward to hold the horses' heads.

'God's greetings, Anna!' boomed a familiar voice from above her.

'Giles!' she answered with a laugh as her brother, dressed in his favourite colour of scarlet, strode down the steps towards her.

The scalloped points of his trailing sleeves swept the steps behind him when he paused on a level with herself. Without warning, his arms were about her waist, lifting her from her palfrey. As he impatiently brushed a hovering groom aside, his gesture was an echo of Sir Ralph Warrender's boldness, which she was trying to forget.

His black eyes sparkling with devilment, Giles set her down at his side and, for all her resolution, she could not stop herself thinking how alike in temperament were her rescuer and her brother.

'Thank God you're safe, Anna!' Giles proclaimed. 'I have sent out a patrol to scour the district for those outlaws. The prisoners taken will hang, as an example to others.' His swarthy countenance tightened in anger. 'All must learn that I am master here.'

As Giles slid his arm about her waist and escorted her up the steps, Morganna lowered her gaze, fearful lest he suspect she was hiding something. She would give Sir Ralph until nightfall to ride far from her brother's land; then she would warn Giles of the danger. It was with him her loyalty lay; her handsome rescuer could have no part in her life. Did not Daneton stand between them?

'You should have seen Linsdale's face when your messenger told us of the attack!' The excitement was evident in her brother's voice. 'We have him, Anna! Before the week is out, he will ask for your hand, I know it. Come and make haste—Lord Linsdale awaits you in the solar.'

Morganna swallowed against her rising panic. She could not face Lord Linsdale yet, and her step faltered. Instantly Giles's hand tensed upon her shoulder, his expression searching as he turned her face to him.

'What's amiss? Not second thoughts, I hope,' he began teasingly, but his indolent lips compressed as though sensing her withdrawal, and his voice sharpened. 'We need this alliance.'

Releasing her, he paced before the entrance to the Great Hall. 'My enemies have grown. There are many who are suspicious of anyone close to the King. They cannot see that, in his need for money, his Majesty could seize any land—even mine. Few nobles trust King Richard since he disinherited Bolingbroke and took the Lancastrian estates for himself. There are rumours that Bolingbroke plans to return from exile and lay claim to his inheritance. Should he succeed, others such as the Earl of Pengarron will follow suit. But with Linsdale's troops to support us, I can hold Daneton from any force

Pengarron may send against us.'

Morganna's mind reeled at the seriousness of his words. Was that why Sir Ralph was here—to attack Daneton? She dismissed the notion at once, for Sir Ralph had few men. Wherever she looked, she saw the blue and white tunics of Lord Linsdale's followers mixing with her brother's soldiers.

'His Majesty will not allow such an act of aggression,' she suggested, more to reassure herself than Giles.

'The King is weak!' Giles declared. 'The people are turning against him.'

'Have they forgotten how his Majesty faced the rabble during the Peasants' Revolt? Why, when Wat Tyler was struck down, his Majesty declared himself the people's leader. They loved him for it.'

'That was in his youth!' Giles shrugged, his tone embittered. 'Then Richard showed himself a true son of the Black Prince, the hero of Crecy. Now he's middle-aged and self-indulgent. This last year has shown him as a tyrant—a despot with a long and vengeful memory. He intends to destroy any who thwarted his wishes during his minority.'

Warm brown fingers closed over Morganna's hand, and her concern grew at the ambition she saw blazing in Giles's eyes.

'You'll not fail me, Anna? We need the strength of Linsdale's support if we're to survive.'

'You sound as though there's to be a war!' she said, horrified.

Giles looked at her in astonishment. 'Nay, Anna, it'll not come to that—Richard is our anointed King! Who would be his successor? But I have risen high . . .' He sighed, his proud features setting cynically. 'The higher we rise—the harder we fall.'

'Oh, Giles, how can you jest upon such a matter?'

Fear clutched at Morganna's heart. Too many of the great had fallen from the King's favour recently. The possessions heaped upon Giles by the unpopular monarch had won him enemies. Again, the discontent she had seen among the people during her pilgrimage nagged at her. This closing year of the fourteenth century had been one of harsh taxes levied to pay for the lavishness of the King's Court and entertainments. Would next year, with the promise of a new century, see an end to the depotism that was turning nobles and peasants alike against their sovereign? From what she knew of the pompous King, Morganna doubted it. After so many years of suppression by his counsellors during his minority, the grandson of Edward III was too immersed in pleasure-seeking to show temperance and wisdom. Moreover, Giles seemed to share the King's outlook and to scoff at signs of trouble. Foreboding seized her. She could not rid herself of the notion that one day it would end badly.

As she studied him, his lips twitched mockingly, and she was comforted by the devotion mirrored in his eyes. Ten years younger than Giles, she had been dazzled from her earliest years by his easy, teasing charm and sharp wit, which had later won him the King's favour. No one could measure up to him—except . . . a forbidden thought treacherously whispered . . . a golden-eyed knight in black.

Since the death of their father when she was nine, Giles had been her mentor, hero and guardian. Despite the difference in years, there was a closeness between them, the only two of their parents' five children to survive infancy.

Now she could sense his impatience, as if he suspected her of holding back. Unwilling to confront him and spoil their reunion, Morganna admonished him gently, 'Would you have me meet the Earl of Linsdale covered in travel-dust? Allow me to bathe and change. If, as you say, his lordship is so eager for my company, an hour's wait will give an edge to his ardour!'

Giles looked down at the muddied hem of her kirtle, and relaxed. 'I'll give you an hour—no longer. Even Linsdale's ardour will not wait for ever! But first tell me of the attack,' he said, guiding her to the archway leading to her apartments in the South Tower. 'Whose troop came to your aid on my land?'

To her consternation, Morganna felt the colour rising to her cheeks, and to avoid his sharp stare, she focused her attention on walking up the steep spiral steps. 'Their leader wore no insignia, but from the badges on the tunics of his men it showed them to be Lancastrians.'

She skimmed over her incident with Sir Ralph as of little importance, and told him what she could of the outlaws' attack. They had reached her chamber by the time she had finished. When Giles remained silent, she was alarmed to see white lines of fury etched into his eyes and mouth.

'The unrest in growing. I would see you married and safe before I set sail with the King to Ireland. I have made enemies, Anna. Many would see me dead. Linsdale can give you protection.'

A growing fear for his safety churned her stomach. 'You must not talk in that way!'

His broad smile did not lessen her worry. It was two months since she had last seen Giles, and his deep anxiety showed in the dark shadows about his eyes. During the last year, he had changed much. Often, when she had been in his company at Court, his once care-free laughter had sounded forced and unnatural. It was not fear of any man which haunted him, for his prowess in the Court tourneys proved he was no craven. If he feared anything, it was obscurity. The need for power was hardening him, she reflected sadly. He had shown no remorse when Sir Robert, her former betrothed, had been fatally wounded in the lists during the last Twelfth Night celebrations. Within a few days Giles had been scheming to make an alliance with Linsdale.

But, then, was she any different? Apart from a sense of regret at the death of Sir Robert and also for Sir Percy, her other ill-fated suitor, who had succumbed to the pestilence, her heart had remained unmoved by any of the prospective husbands after Ralph Warrender.

She shivered in the warmth of the burning log fire. Its rosy glow mellowed the gaudy blues and golds on the painted canvas hangings, and they merged into a green-ish blur. In an effort to dispel the suspicion that still narrowed Giles's eyes at her long silence, Morganna turned the conversation, asking brightly,

'How is the Lady Elizabeth? Her time is close now, is it not?'

Giles grinned. 'My wife is well enough, but she is disappointed she must miss the feasting this week. That's why I chose Daneton, so that she could rest in the quiet of Surrey, now she is large with child.'

'It will be a son this time, Giles,' Morganna pro-claimed, knowing how he yearned for a male heir, for all he doted on his four raven-haired daughters.

Giles took her hand. 'I pray only that Beth and the child are healthy. God willing, she will be delivered before I set sail with the King.'

'You are blessed with a good marriage,' she said fondly. 'Father chose well for you.'

'As I have chosen well for you!' The suspicion was back in his voice as he strolled to the door, and warned her, 'Linsdale is a good match. It will make you mistress of one of the largest estates in England!'

Morganna closed her eyes wearily. She was used to Giles's stormy flashes of temper, but of late they were more frequent and violent, a sign of the strain he was under. It was going to be worse than she feared to tell him she could not marry the Earl of Linsdale. A vision of hawk-like features filled her mind, and her eyes flew open. It was time she freed herself from her childhood dream. If only Sir Ralph had not been so handsome, so much more of a man than his peers, it would be easier to banish his memory!

An hour later, the sound of music and laughter drifted to Morganna as she descended the stairs. Beset with an unaccustomed bout of nerves, she touched the Saxon cross hanging from a chain about her neck. The familiar smoothness of the gold and enamelled design eased some of the tension within her. How often had she seen her mother make the same gesture when she was troubled. If only the Lady Edith were here now! But she had been dead for over a year, and the only comfort Morganna had left was the cross she always wore. For once, its touch gave her less than complete reassurance.

She hesitated before entering the Great Hall, and glanced towards the chapel. She needed advice before she joined Giles, as it was likely he would question her further about the knight who had rescued her. And Linsdale – she would have to face him, too. But first she would speak with Father Matthew.

Beckoning to a passing page, she ordered him to fetch the chaplain to her in the chapel. Suddenly she was surprised to see Jack of Tewkesbury, the bailiff, detach himself from the shadows and approach her.

'My lady, do you not join the feast?'

'Later. But what of you? Is something wrong that you are not at the feast?'

'No, my lady. A small problem the reeve called me to attend to.'

She smiled at him absently, dismissing him. Too preoccupied with her troubled thoughts to pay much heed to the bailiff, she entered the high-vaulted chapel and lit a candle, placing it at the foot of the image of the Virgin and Child.

A soft footfall behind her made her turn, as the wiry figure of Father Matthew approached.

'You are troubled, my lady?'

'Will you hear my confession, Father? And there is a matter upon which I must have your advice.'

'Is it so important that you must miss the banquet? Lord Radford grows impatient at your delay. He ordered you to join him at once.'

'I have such a burden on my conscience, Father, that truly I do not think I can bear it.'

'Come, my child, speak your mind. Then I will hear your confession.'

A woman's voice, soft and low, carried to Ralph Warrender as he paused at the exit of the tunnel leading from the forest into the heart of Daneton Castle. Someone was in the chapel. In the darkness he folded his arms and leaned against the rough stonework to wait. From the number of undisturbed cobwebs he had encountered along the length of the passage, it was obvious that Radford knew nothing of its existence.

Warrender tensed, certain he had heard the woman in the chapel mention his name. He put his ear to the wooden door, recognising Lady Morganna's voice, but her words were muffled. Was she betraying him? What else should he expect from Radford's sister? He had been a fool to come. What if the meeting with Jack of Tewkesbury were a trap? Daneton's bailiff had served his old master well over the last years, keeping the Earl of Pengarron informed of what was happening on the estate. But had he changed allegiance?

The low sensuous voice continued, but few of Lady Morganna's words were clear enough to hear. It sounded as though she was upset about her forthcoming betrothal, and again his name was mentioned. He frowned, against his will finding himself curious. There was silence now from the far side of the door. Waiting a few minutes more before leaving the tunnel, Warrender raised the lever, and the well-greased section of the rood screen silently opened. Lifting up the silk hanging that concealed the entrance, he stepped silently into the chapel and froze in the shadows. In the light from the dozen burning candles Lady Morganna knelt, her head bowed in prayer.

Struck afresh by her beauty, his gaze travelled over her slim graceful figure, lingering appreciatively on the swell of her hips and full breasts. She was gowned in white, and the elegant sweep of her gold-and-pearl-studded butterfly headdress added to the grace and angelic purity of her image.

Pure, but not such an angel! He smiled, remembering the way her eyes had flashed in answer to his challenge in the forest. And before that—before they had known each other's identity—a spell had seemed to weave about him as he stared into her violet eyes. Beauty and spirit—rare qualities. And she was once destined to be his—as was Daneton! Had he not returned to reclaim his birthright?

He watched her rise and stare up at the Madonna, her delicate, almost elfin face drawn with sadness. What troubled her? Was it possible that she, too, remembered that moment's madness? Would that this was any place but Daneton, and this woman any but the sister of the Marquess of Radford!

As though sensing that she was not alone, Lady Morganna looked in his direction and gasped, 'You!'

Before she could rouse the guards, Ralph Warrender closed the space between them, blocking her retreat and trapping her against a stone pillar.

'What are you doing here?' she demanded, showing no sign of fear.

Ready to silence her if she cried out, he placed his hand on the pillar at the side of her head. The freshness of her skin—like roses, but more subtle and seductive —wafted over him. The pale column of her neck was temptingly close, but he resisted the impulse to touch its scented softness. 'After what passed between us today, fair lady, did you doubt I would seek you out?'

A light flared, amethyst bright, in her large eyes and was quickly doused, her tone reproving. 'Nothing passed between us, and your presence in Daneton speaks of treachery. I owe you my life. I repay it by giving you yours. Go at once, before I summon the guards and have you arrested!'

He chuckled, reluctantly admiring her fierce pride and defiance. Was his meeting with Jack of Tewkesbury the only reason he had come to Daneton tonight? He could easily have sent another in his place.

His ears long attuned to approaching danger, Warrender heard the light tread along the corridor. Had the priest returned? Over Lady Morganna's head he glimpsed a tall scarlet-clad figure wearing a gold circlet. It could only be Radford, and from the sound, he was alone.

Warrender bent his head towards the woman, her parted lips tantalisingly close. The temptation to kiss her proved almost too much for his self-restraint; it would be all too easy to take advantage of her. But, strangely, his desire for her was tempered by respect. A brief stolen kiss was not for him. When he tasted the sweetness of her lips, as he vowed he would, it would be a joy to be savoured.

''Ods wounds—Anna!' Radford fumed, misinterpreting the scene and the closeness of the two figures, as Ralph had intended he should. Why then did an unexpected twinge of guilt stab through him at seeing Lady Morganna's eyes widen in dismay?

'Anna! You bring shame upon our house!' Radford rapped out. 'Who is this knave? Your lover?'

Ralph moved away from Morganna, but kept to the shadows as he saw Radford's hand move to his dagger. To his surprise, instead of denouncing him, Morganna ran to her brother, putting a restraining hand upon his arm.

'This knight saved my life today.'

'And, from the look of things, he was taking full advantage of your indebtedness to him!' Radford angrily shook off his sister's hold and glared at Ralph. 'Who dares to dishonour my house?'

Ralph stepped into the candlelight. 'Your house, Radford?'

'Warrender!' He growled, his eyes narrowing murderously.

'It's Pengarron now,' Ralph corrected. 'My brother is dead. The time has come for the reckoning to be settled between us.' His gaze pointedly swept the chapel, and as it came to rest upon the pale figure of Morganna, he delivered his challenge. 'I intend to have all that was once mine.'

'Then die for your insolence, dog!' Radford spat as he lunged forward, drawing his dagger.

Ralph leapt sideways. Tossing his cloak over his shoulder, he drew his sword and began to circle his attacker, his voice taunting. 'I'll not fight you dagger to sword, Radford. Meet me on the tourney field tomorrow at midday.'

'And have my sister's dishonour proclaimed before Lord Linsdale? I think not, Pengarron!'

'Stop, Giles!' To Ralph's astonishment, Morganna flung herself between his sword and her brother. 'Lord Pengarron is deliberately taunting you. He would see an end to your alliance with Lord Linsdale. If you fight him now, you play into his hands. Linsdale is bound to learn of the incident.'

'You would have your lover go free, sister, but this cur's head shall rot on the Gatehouse come dawn!' Radford roughly pushed his sister away, shouting, 'Guards! Guards, to me!'

Even as Ralph parried the dagger, sending it flying across the chapel floor as he disarmed the Marquess, he felt a strange tightening in his chest at the sight of

Morganna's eyes sparking with hatred. The heavy stamping of feet warned him that the guards were about to burst into the chapel. Running towards the rood screen, Ralph lifted the silk hanging, but was unable to resist looking back at her.

'I shall return, my lady!'

The Earl of Pengarron's parting words rang in Morganna's ears when he disappeared from sight just as the guards clattered into the chapel.

As the hanging fell into place, Giles pointed to the concealed exit, bellowing, 'That way—an intruder. Take him alive!' Rounding on Morganna, he raged, 'Your lover will not escape!'

Pain twisted in her breast. How could Giles believe such ill of her? She had tried to stop the fight out of a sense of honour, not because she cared for Pengarron. If her pulses had raced when he had vowed to return, it was because she despised him. He had shamed her. He had deliberately sown the seeds of distrust between Giles and herself.

'He's not my lover,' she answered wearily.

'Go from my sight, Anna!' Giles snapped, in a tone he had never used to her before.

She staggered back from him, aghast. He looked through her, not at her. How many times at Court had she seen the proud, untouchable Marquess of Radford so regard an unwelcome petitioner.

'Radford! What's amiss?' Morganna turned, recognising Lord Linsdale's voice as he sauntered towards them. 'I heard the guards called out.'

'It's nothing of importance,' Giles answered smoothly, all signs of his anger wiped from his face as he regarded Linsdale with a smile. 'Lady Morganna saw a man lurking in the shadows, but he ran off when she challenged him. I ordered the guards to search the castle.'

Lord Linsdale bowed to Morganna. 'You have had an eventful day, my lady. Should you not have summoned the guards before you confronted the stranger?'

Conscious of his scrutiny, she sank into a curtsy, her eyes lowered to hide her resentment at Linsdale's condescending tone. Her hand was taken in short square fingers as she was raised up. Determined to regain Giles's approval, she replied smoothly, 'I was in no danger. The guards were close at hand.'

When she tried to pull her hand free, it was held fast. Unaccountably, her flesh cringed, although she could not understand why she should be so revolted by Linsdale's touch. At forty, his soft, roundish features were not unhandsome. His dress was immaculate, his short-cropped blond hair and pointed beard only just beginning to show threads of grey. If she was honest, though he was some inches shorter than Giles, his stance was both commanding and dignified. The long blue velvet gown he wore lent grace to his thickening figure, and the smooth pink and white complexion was unravaged by disease. Yet there was something behind those pale heavy-lidded eyes which made her uneasy.

Giles took her arm, shooting her a warning look before guiding her forward. 'Let us return to the feasting.'

Clearly he remained suspicious of her. Morganna's anger returned at the way Pengarron had manipulated her, and shame burned through her. Hating him as she did now, it seemed incredible that she had actually been waiting for—no, wanting—him to kiss her. If they ever met again, Pengarron would learn she was not a woman to be so abused! For a moment she savoured the vision of putting him firmly in his place, and a thrill of excitement warmed her. That would prove a challenge indeed! He was not a man to fawn at any woman's feet, and would not her greatest triumph over him be her marriage to Linsdale?

Her duty to Giles was clear: she must succeed in achieving this alliance he sought with Lord Linsdale. Daneton must be safely garrisoned when the Marquess rejoined the King.

They were seated at the high table before Morganna recovered herself with a start, realising that Lord Linsdale was addressing her. She smiled sweetly. 'Your pardon, my lord, what were you saying? The noise from our two households is deafening after the quiet of the chapel.'

'Your beauty and grace match your courage! You appear no worse after your ordeal with the outlaws.'

Morganna shrugged. 'Why should I? I was unharmed. The best way to forget an unpleasant incident is to enjoy the company of relatives, friends and guests. My brother has long looked forward to this moment, my lord. I would not disappoint him.'

'It is I who would have been devastated by your absence, dear lady.'

At the way his heavy-lidded gaze rested upon the swell of her breasts, Morganna tensed, and conscious of her brother's watchful eye upon her, her smile grew strained. Obviously Linsdale was as eager as Giles for the match. Why, then, after her resolution of moments earlier did she feel no elation? Instead, she felt trapped.

Throughout the endless procession of dishes brought to them amid an accompanying fanfare of trumpets, Morganna endured Lord Linsdale's attentions. But it was to another that her mind kept straying. Had Pengarron been captured?

The brightly-clad figures of the tumblers and jugglers became a hazy blur and, as the feast continued, the shrill notes of the minstrels' pipes grated upon her taut nerves. Through the haze of smoke from the dozens of burning torches and the central fire, she saw the Captain of the Guard approach the dais. From the grimness of her

brother's expression as the Captain spoke to him, she
knew Pengarron had escaped.

She was unprepared for the immense relief that
flooded through her, and looked down the line of trestle
tables to cover her confusion. Her attention was suddenly caught by the behaviour of two of the ushers, who
kept glancing towards the Marshal of the Hall. When the
Marshal turned his back on them to supervise some
pages, the ushers beckoned to Jack of Tewkesbury, and
all three men hurried out. Why did their action strike her
as sinister? If she recalled correctly, Jack of Tewkesbury
had been bailiff here when Giles took possession. Was it
just her imagination, or were they acting furtively? What
had the bailiff been doing outside the chapel? Had he
been waiting to meet Pengarron?

Morganna closed her eyes and raised her hand to her
throbbing temple. The headdress pressed down upon
her brow, preventing her from thinking clearly. Too
many conflicting emotions jostled through her mind: she
was nervous and edgy without reason.

'Are you unwell, my lady?' Lord Linsdale enquired.

Opening her eyes, Morganna forced a smile. 'It's the
heat and the noise, my lord. I fear I am poor company.
The ambush and the long journey must have tired me
more than I thought.'

She saw Giles frowning at her words, and was grateful
when Linsdale suggested that she retire. His next words
were not so comforting. 'Since the Lady Morganna will
leave us, my lord Marquess, might I suggest a private
word with you in the solar?'

As she curtsied to her brother and Linsdale, Giles's
wink of approval did not lighten the heaviness that had
settled over her heart. Linsdale's request could mean
but one thing: he intended to ask Giles for her hand
in marriage. She had succeeded in her plan, but why, as
she left the Great Hall, could she not rid herself of
the impression of golden eyes mocking her from the

shadows? Who was the knave, anyway? she thought vengefully. He might call himself Earl of Pengarron, but he was lord only of a remote Welsh castle bearing his name.

Upon entering her rooms, Morganna hid her misgivings when Jocelyn hurried forward.

'Oh, my lady, was it not a mercy the guards did not catch him?' her maid babbled excitedly. 'To think that the Earl of Pengarron was here! Did you see him?'

Startled that Jocelyn knew so much, Morganna remembered the furtive glances the servants had exchanged at the banquet. How many knew of Pengarron's visit? Or at least that he was close by? The thought was unnerving. Many of the servants had once served his father, and until now they had proved loyal to Giles. But would they remain so? For a long moment Morganna stared at her maid, wondering how much to tell her. Jocelyn had served her faithfully for ten years, and there was little she did not know of Morganna's hopes and fears.

'What exactly have you heard, Jocelyn?' she asked, thankful that the maid seemed not to notice the catch in her voice.

'That he came in by a tunnel.' Jocelyn looked towards the figure of an old woman dozing by the fire. 'Helewise saw it in the runes. She says there are several such secret places—but surely that's usual in an old place like this. Lord Pengarron rescued you in the forest, didn't he, my lady? It's just like the old tales of chivalry and romance! A single meeting, and your first betrothed risks his life to see you again. Is he as handsome as they say, my lady?'

'That's enough, Jocelyn!' Morganna cut through her maid's chatter. 'You forget yourself, and spend too much time listening to Helewise. If Lord Pengarron set foot inside Daneton, it was not to meet me but to spy on my brother. Do you forget why Lord Linsdale is here?'

Jocelyn lowered her eyes at the sharpness of the

rebuke, and realising she was taking her fears out upon the maid, a guilty heat stung Morganna's cheeks.

'Whatever the reasons you believe Lord Pengarron came to Daneton, my lady,' Jocelyn persisted as she removed the headdress and began to unbraid Morganna's silvery-gold hair, 'he was a brave man to risk so much! A truly courageous knight. They say he's as fearless as the golden eagle he has taken for his device—and just as dangerous.'

'Jocelyn!' Morganna warned. 'I have no interest in Lord Pengarron. That part of my life is over.'

'As well it should be, my lady,' Helewise said from her place by the fire. 'But you cannot change what fate wills.'

Knowing that Helewise commanded a position of respect from the servants by her dabbling in prophecies, Morganna felt a tingling of unease at the dark words. Was her duty to Giles not clear?

'If Lord Linsdale asks for my hand, I shall marry him,' she said firmly.

The stooped figure rose stiffly from the chair. 'Then let it be done quickly. The runes tell of a change to come to Daneton.'

'I do not believe in superstition, Helewise.' Morganna's voice softened as she affectionately regarded the woman who had been her wet-nurse. 'But I would know whether the servants—the ones who have always served Daneton—speak much of their old master?'

'There are always those who speak of the old days, though I have never heard them speak ill of my lord Radford. The old Earl of Pengarron was loved and respected, but the old Earl is dead. You should not mock the runes, my lady. They foretell change. And danger.'

Jocelyn gave a frightened gasp.

'We live in uncertain times,' Morganna reasoned, and turned to her maid to add soothingly, 'Lord Radford is high in the King's favour. For all the Earl of Pengarron's proud boasting, it will serve him nothing. Daneton was given to my brother as a gift. It was not taken by force.'

'Then we shall not be murdered in our beds.'

Despite her own misgivings that Pengarron would stir up trouble, Jocelyn's words were so absurd that Morganna could not help laughing. 'Certainly not! Had Lord Pengarron wished to harm us, he could have done so in the forest this day. We were at his mercy.'

Apparently satisfied, Jocelyn fell silent. Helewise shook her head and hobbled towards the door.

'The runes do not lie, my lady!' she insisted again.

CHAPTER THREE

THROUGHOUT THE NIGHT, Morganna tossed and turned in her large canopied bed, unable to forget Helewise's prophecy. Why could she not put Pengarron from her mind, or stop comparing Linsdale so unfavourably with him? Duty pulled her one way—an indefinable restlessness another. Despite her defiant words to Jocelyn, she had little inclination to marry Linsdale.

As she lay listening to the muffled noises of the castle, which was never silent, she no longer believed Daneton to be impregnable. Pengarron had proved how easily its defences could be breached, and how many of the household could be trusted? Clearly Jack of Tewkesbury needed to be watched, for his position as bailiff made him a man of influence with the lower servants. She would speak with Giles about the matter on the morrow.

When she did, Giles curtly dismissed her warning, and for a week he refused to listen to her fears. Tackling him yet again, she realised from the stubborn tightening of his lips that it was in vain. One leg bent, his long pointed shoe resting on the silk cushions of the window seat, he stared out of the oriel window for some moments before turning back to her.

'Let's talk no more of Daneton's defences, Anna.' He lightly dismissed her arguments. 'The tunnel by which Pengarron entered is well guarded. Tomorrow, when the masons arrive from Kent, it will be filled in and bricked up. I have doubled the sentries, and the troop sent out to search the estate report no sign of Pengarron or his men.'

'But, Giles, you heard his words!' she persisted. 'Lord Pengarron vowed to return. In less than a month you leave for Ireland, taking most of your men with you. Can you not stay at Daneton and join the King later?'

His hand patted her shoulder, and he grinned wryly. 'Spoken like a woman! Would you have me deny my Sovereign?'

'Pengarron did not strike me as a man to make idle threats, Giles,' she answered earnestly. 'Should he take possession of Daneton, he'll fight to the death to defend it.'

Giles shook his head, confident that he could not fail. 'Tonight the marriage contract will be signed. Before I leave for Ireland you will be Countess of Linsdale. The Earl is determined that the wedding should not be delayed. He has agreed to garrison a troop here until I return.'

At the mention of her betrothal, Morganna fought against a wave of panic. It was no good. Hard as she tried to accept her brother's arguments that Linsdale would make a fine husband, her dislike had intensified. There was something more disturbing than Linsdale's leering gaze mentally disrobing her whenever they met which filled her with revulsion. In desperation, she blurted out, 'What if there was no betrothal?'

The smile froze upon Giles's face. 'Nothing can prevent it!' he said, his black eyes gleaming with a fierceness that alarmed her.

Loath as she was to rouse his anger and distrust, the price he demanded of her loyalty was too high.

'I cannot wed Lord Linsdale!' Though softly spoken, the words rang like a death-knell.

Giles paled, and stared at her in disbelief. Then his lips curled back disparagingly, his voice emotionless. 'You will marry Linsdale. It is all arranged.'

Hurt by his callousness, Morganna glared back at him. 'Would you have me wed a man who repels me?'

A long condemning silence stretched between them. Tense and unyielding, Giles removed his foot from the cushion at her side, to stand tall and forbidding as she continued to hold and match his angry glower.

'Anna, what madness is this?' he said at last, but there was no gentleness in his tone. Rubbing his hand along his jaw, he paced the solar. 'My word is given. You will marry within the week.'

The finality of his tone forbade further discourse, but Morganna outfaced him, determined to have her say. 'Lord Linsdale treats me like a child. He was horrified when he learnt that not only could I read and write, but was fluent in Latin as well as in English and French. You saw how he scoffed when I beat you at chess last evening! What do you think he would feel if he knew of the hours you had spent schooling me in the use of a dagger? The man would have an apoplexy! As his wife, I would be regarded as his chattel, little more than a slave to do his bidding, allowed no mind of my own.'

Giles stopped pacing. 'You exaggerate! You've had too much freedom. A week in your room, fed only on bread and water, will teach you your place.'

Morganna looked at him with horror. She could not believe Giles could utter such a threat. He had always encouraged her to speak her mind, to fight for what she believed right. 'I am what you've made me, brother! I cannot change now.'

Giles rounded on her. 'Do you think I don't know what you're about? I have not forgotten the scene I witnessed between you and Pengarron in the chapel.'

'Have I not been trying to convince you that Pengarron means us harm?' She threw up her arms in exasperation. 'He has spies within the castle!'

'By the Rood, woman, I'll not have you destroy everything I have worked for because of a maidenly whim! The matter is decided. Tonight, after the Angelus bell has rung, the marriage contract will be signed.'

'And if I do not accept your terms, brother?'

Instantly Giles was at her side, his cheeks flushed with

anger. 'You will be Countess to a goodly part of three
shires, mistress of seven castles and some score of manor
houses. Why should you not accept—unless . . .' He
grabbed her arms and gave her a slight shake. 'It's
Pengarron who's behind this! He's always fascinated
you. By God, Anna, I thought you long over your
youthful infatuation! Pengarron has but a single castle,
and that a partial ruin. I'll see you shut away in a convent
before I allow that upstart to marry you.'

'You're blinded by your hatred. It's not me Pengarron
wants—it's Daneton!' Morganna's voice cracked as her
anger rose. 'Of late, my proud Lord Radford, you have
become a stranger to me. You are obsessed with ambition. Is power so important to you that my feelings
count for nothing?'

'How can you say that? I have spent months and a
goodly fortune to win Linsdale for you. Your future and
safety will be secured.'

Numbed, Morganna backed away from him. Giles
had never patronised her before. Or was it distrust which
made him act as he did? She touched the Saxon cross
about her neck, striving to control her rising temper. She
should not have to convince him of her loyalty. Giles had
changed—grown harder—but, even so, she could not
believe his bitterness was against her herself; it stemmed
from something deeper. It was Pengarron's fault there
was now this rift between them.

Yet even as she reviled Pengarron, her conscience
pricked her. Giles had insulted Sir Ralph by renouncing
the marriage contract, scathingly in declaring the
knight too lowly for her. As a younger son, Ralph
Warrender should have entered the Church, not been
set on the path for knighthood. The ties of friendship
between her father and the old Earl of Pengarron had
been strong, and they had wished their two families
united. The bond would be further strengthened when
she inherited her grandmother's estate on the Welsh

borders. Both men were content that Ralph Warrender should take control of these.

Morganna glanced across at her brother as he paced the solar like a caged beast. She thought again how alike Pengarron and Giles were: both were acclaimed for their prowess in the lists; neither would concede a fight; both now stood high in rank. Too alike, perhaps! At the sight of Giles's haggard expression, she admitted he believed she would find happiness with Linsdale. Somehow, she must convince him otherwise.

'You paint a dazzling picture,' she said heavily. 'But I am not ambitious for myself. If I cannot have a man's love, I would at least have his respect. If I were blessed with both, then nothing could content me more, even if I were to live in obscurity.'

'I have only your best interest at heart. How can you doubt me?' he answered stiffly. 'Go to your room, Anna. I ride out to hunt with Lord Linsdale. When I return, I shall expect you to act dutifully, as befits the daughter of a great house.'

Wide-eyed, she stared at her brother, the bright scarlet of his surcoat emphasising the pallor of his complexion. Had he slapped her, he could not have shocked her more. He stood rigid, arms folded, tyrannical and without compassion. Her nails gouged her palms, the pain unheeded, as she strove to master her fury. In his present mood, he was capable of having her locked in her chamber, and then she could do nothing. But his words had already given her a plan, and she was desperate enough to attempt anything to avoid marrying Linsdale.

Whirling, she fled from the solar. As she neared her rooms, she knew there was only one course left to her, and she considered it carefully. It was drastic—even dangerous. Giles would be furious, yet she could not marry Linsdale. Her mind cringed with revulsion at the thought. There would be time enough while Giles and he were out hunting to put her plan into effect.

Once in her room, she gave Jocelyn her orders, silencing her protests with a quelling look.

'What is there to fear, Jocelyn?' she chided. 'We ride but two miles to the Priory, taking alms and food for the poor, as we have done countless times in the past. Once we have been admitted, even Giles will not drag me from the nuns by force. It's just for a few days, until my brother realises he cannot force me to wed a man I despise.'

The sound of horses clattering over the drawbridge made her rush to the window. Giles and Lord Linsdale rode at the head of a long column of retainers towards the forest. When the last of the horses disappeared beneath the Gatehouse Tower, the inner bailey was strangely quiet. Morganna noticed Father Matthew's grey habit among the dispersing grooms, and watched him cross to the far side of the courtyard, where he entered one of the outbuildings. It would be some time before he emerged from grinding the dried herbs and preparing the unguents he used to heal the sick.

'My lady, what of the outlaws?' Jocelyn said, pausing in gathering Morganna's belongings.

'They have long vanished from this district.' Morganna reasoned, gesturing to the maid to hurry with the packing. 'The Priory is on my brother's land. If you've finished collecting what we need, tell Sergeant Fletcher to summon an escort to accompany us.'

Alone in her chamber, Morganna quashed a moment's unease. She hated going against her brother in this way, but what choice had he left her?

'My lady!' Jocelyn cried, as she returned, her face red with indignation. 'Sergeant Fletcher says he's been given orders that you are not to leave the castle.'

So, Giles did not trust her! Morganna fumed. At least he had not put a guard outside the door. Her eyes narrowed with cunning, an idea forming as her fingers touched the smooth contours of the cross about her neck. With a slow smile of devilment, she waved aside the velvet cloak Jocelyn had picked up and pulled the low hennin headdress from her head.

'A veil and circlet, Jocelyn, and a plain woollen cloak with a hood. We shall go to the Priory on foot.'

'But, my lady, the danger . . .'

'If you are afraid, you may stay behind. I cannot remain.'

'I would never desert you, my lady. Never!'

The quiver of her maid's lips betrayed her hurt pride, and impulsively Morganna hugged her close. 'Let's hope your fears are unfounded!'

Releasing her, Morganna opened a small casket. She took out a jewel-handled dagger, tested its weight in her hands, then placed it in the sheath and attached it to the leather girdle about her waist. With a nod to Jocelyn to bring the bundle of possessions, Morganna drew the cloak together to conceal the gold-embroidered hem of her blue surcoat. Cautiously she eased the door open and peered out.

The corridor was deserted. Hurrying through the castle towards the chapel, Morganna felt her heart thundering loudly each time they had to hide in alcoves or behind stone pillars to avoid servants and guards. In the doorway of the chapel, she froze, and, drawing back, pressed her body flat against the wall.

'The guard,' she whispered to Jocelyn. 'I'd forgotten the guard within.'

Her mind racing, Morganna removed her cloak and handed it to the maid. 'Stay out of sight. When the guard comes, bring a lighted flambeau.' She entered the chapel with a composed expression. 'Oh, is Father Matthew not here?' she said to the guard in pretended surprise. 'I must pray and make my confession before the ceremony this night. Go and fetch him.'

At her command, the guard, as she expected, shifted

nervously, and she gave him a winning smile. 'It's broad daylight. I doubt any intruder would dare invade Daneton at this hour. Besides, I cannot make my confession while you are in attendance. Go now, before I am forced to speak with Lord Radford of your disobedience.'

Reluctantly the guard withdrew. Knowing she had little time, Morganna ran forward and drew back the silk hanging behind which Pengarron had disappeared. The carved panel looked much the same as all the others. Her fingers shaking with frustration, she prodded and poked its ornate edges for some kind of a catch to open it. By the time Jocelyn arrived, it had still refused to move.

'I can hear the guards,' Jocelyn whispered. 'Come away, my lady, before we're discovered!'

Morganna hit out at the panel in vexation, her knuckles scraping as they struck a cherub's head. 'Oh, devil take the wretched . . .' Her oath dissolved into a sigh of relief as the door swung silently open.

Signalling for Jocelyn to pull the hanging into place, Morganna took her cloak and the lighted torch and edged forward along the dark tunnel. The air was musty, tomblike, the blackness suffocating. She could not breathe as chill terror gripped her. She had never liked confined spaces. A spark from the torch burnt her skin, checking her panic. She had not expected it to be easy, but they had come too far to turn back now.

As they descended the slippery slope, Morganna held her breath, biting back a scream as her hand touched something cold and slimy upon the wall. Holding the torch high, she laughed nervously at discovering her hand had encountered nothing more sinister than a growth of fungus.

''Tis the devil's lair, this place, my lady,' Jocelyn whimpered.

Unable to shake off the pressure stabbing at her temple, Morganna wondered if for once her superstitious maid was not right. At each step the darkness became more menacing, and Jocelyn's mumbled prayers to several saints jarred Morganna's tense nerves. She gulped for air, feeling that the breath was being crushed from her lungs by an invisible weight.

'My lady, what ails you?'

Jocelyn's cry jolted Morganna to her senses. What was happening to her? It was only a tunnel. There was plenty of air. Why should this fear grip her?

'I am all right,' she answered, forcing herself onwards. When the tunnel widened into a cave, its entrance covered by leaves, her breathing returned to normal.

Stubbing out the torch on the hard-packed earth floor, Morganna stiffened. Close by was the sound of men's voices. It must be her brother's guard. She edged forward and peered through the concealing foliage. There were eight of them, and it would be impossible to leave the cave without being caught. Her mind worked furiously. It was now noon, and they had been on duty since dawn. Probably they were tired and bored, and they could become careless. Fretting at the delay, she strained her ears, listening. At last she heard them move further away, the unmistakable rattle of bones audible in an expectant silence telling her that they were absorbed in a game of dice.

She eased apart some of the leaves over the entrance, and saw them squatting some distance away, their backs still towards the cave. She judged that more than an hour had passed since Giles rode out to hunt. Something had to happen quickly, or he would return before she reached the Priory. Abruptly the tone of the guards' voices changed. They were arguing. Suddenly her chance came. Two of the men sprang to their feet, voices raised in anger. One lashed out, knocking another to the ground, and the two grappled as the rest watched, laughing and jeering.

Gesturing to Jocelyn to keep close behind her,

Morganna began to push her way through the overhanging branches, surprised to discover they moved at her touch. They were not rooted, but freshly cut to disguise the entrance. Crouching now, her gaze fixed on the guards, she crept through the undergrowth. Another ten paces, and a large boulder would hide them.

She started violently at a loud snap behind her. Jocelyn had trodden on a dry twig. Throwing herself to the ground, she caught the hem of her maid's cloak and pulled her down beside her. Above the frantic pounding of her heart, she listened for sounds of pursuit. Nothing happened. If anything, the guards' voices were louder than ever. With a warning glance at Jocelyn to take more care, Morganna straightened, her pace increasing as soon as they were out of earshot of the men-at-arms. Now the fear of discovery was behind her, she paused to scan the forest, but could distinguish no landmark. The sun was behind them, so if she kept it on her right, they would come to the main track leading to the Priory.

They had walked some distance when a dozen fallow deer bounded across their path and disappeared into the closely packed trees, the young fawns close to the does' sides. After the tension of the last hour, the sight calmed Morganna. She was used to riding through the forest, and now it all seemed so different, so undisturbed and natural. The ground was dotted with patches of bluebells. Rabbits, frightened by her unexpected approach, bolted into the undergrowth. But there was also danger as well as beauty. Near by, a disgruntled snort warned of the presence of wild boar; a man from the village had been gouged to death by their vicious tusks last summer. The sound of a horn from a great way off reminded her there was still a mile to travel before they reached the safety of the Priory. It would be disastrous should the hunting party veer in this direction.

Already her feet ached; the soft leather of her shoes

was little protection against the rough ground. As they skirted a charcoal-burner's hut in a clearing, Morganna paused to rest. She stared, fascinated by the pale grey woodsmoke rising to cling like thistledown over the burning mound of a kiln.

Suddenly a tall figure emerged from the hut, and she drew back behind a tree-trunk. His loose-legged stride was disturbingly familiar as he crossed the clearing, but there was nothing remarkable about his homespun tunic with its plain green hood, or his thick woollen hose. Her heart fluttered. Could it be Pengarron?

No, surely not, she reasoned. Giles was certain he had left the district. Most likely it was the reeve; he was tall. She stared harder, but already the man had disappeared into the trees. With a shrug she dismissed her fancies. He was probably a charcoal-burner or perhaps even a forester.

Still a nagging doubt refused to ·be dismissed. She could hear several different voices within the hut. Who else was with him and his family? A charcoal-burner's work usually kept him in isolation from the villagers. She shivered, the beauty of her surroundings dimming. She could almost smell conspiracy.

'Take care, my lady, there's . . .' Jocelyn's whispered warning ended in a shriek that was abruptly muffled.

Spinning round, Morganna saw her tiring-woman struggling with a thickset figure, his hand clamped over her mouth. Two other men were advancing towards herself. Instinctively, her hand reached beneath her cloak to clasp the dagger-hilt.

Behind her, a command was rapped out, and the men fell back. She tensed at the sound of that voice, and turned to find her retreat blocked by the green-hooded figure. It *was* Pengarron!

She must escape! Her hood was low over her face, and it was possible he had not recognised her. At all costs she must get free. Pengarron would not hesitate to use her as a hostage to act against Giles, she was certain. Quickly she assessed her chance of getting away, and made a dash to one side of her enemy, but before she had covered more than a few yards, she was caught round the waist in a punishing grip.

'Not so fast, wench!'

Kicking and wriggling, Morganna fought to free herself from his hold. It was hopeless. His iron grip tightened. One of her hands still held the dagger, and with her other fist clenched she pummelled his arms.

'Let me go, you great oaf!' she raged, noting with satisfaction his sharp intake of breath as her foot made contact against his shin.

'Hold still, you little hell-cat! I'll not harm you.'

Pengarron twisted her round to face him, and her hood fell back. He looked at her in astonishment. Then, as his eyebrows curved upwards mockingly, her temper snapped, and she thrust the dagger upwards. He moved swiftly, deflecting her blow to his body. As he jerked her against him, she saw a trickle of blood running down his cheek where the point of her dagger had nicked him.

Defiantly, she held his furious glare. His eyes glinting amber shards, his bare fingers clamped her wrist, and the dagger fell to the ground. She was defenceless against him and the anger blazing in his eyes . . . She knew that, this time, she had goaded him too far.

Behind her, Jocelyn sobbed quietly, adding to her own despair. She had been selfish to place her maid's life in danger. She might have acted unwisely, but she refused to let Pengarron see her fear. Or worse, that the hard contact of his body and the pressure of his arm about her waist were making her heart beat alarmingly.

'Release my tiring-woman,' she said icily, 'and take your hands off me. Giles will have your head for this outrage!'

Pengarron's lips twisted sardonically. 'What is

Radford about, allowing you to roam these woods unescorted?'

Morganna bristled at his insulting tone. To her prejudiced gaze, the man before her bore little resemblance to the bold knight who had rescued her from the outlaws. Shadowed by the hood, the hawk-like features were no less handsome, except that now she knew that behind them lay a cold, calculating mind that would stop at nothing to bring Giles down. She looked scornfully at his arm encircling her waist. To her surprise, he released her.

'Your eyes flash fire, my lady, yet you say nothing,' Pengarron scoffed. 'I saw Radford and Linsdale ride past less than an hour since. Should you not be preparing yourself for the betrothal feast this night?'

While his sarcasm lashed her, she stood her ground, incensed. She would make no excuses to him. 'Let me pass, sir. I am on my way to the Priory.'

Without moving back, he angrily pushed the hood from his head, his voice low and taut. 'Only a fool, or a desperate woman, would risk her life in these woods unprotected. Why do you go to the nuns?'

His amber stare seemed to probe her soul during her continued silence. Then his eyes crinkled at the corners with amusement, and something more, which caused her heart to thump painfully. Could it be admiration?

'Is the match with Linsdale not to your liking, my lady?'

How accurately he had judged her. Devil take him! Let him think what he liked! Glaring at him, Morganna swept aside her gown and made to brush past him, but was brought up short by the gravity of his tone.

'You're no fool, Lady Morganna. Your plight must be desperate.'

He stood, legs planted arrogantly apart, his gaze slowly raking down her body to her feet and then up again to her flushed face. She was humiliated that he should see her with her cloak muddied and torn like some peasant girl. As he masked his expression, concealing his thoughts from her, her hatred gnawed deeper. Did he think to take her hostage? She was not about to be used by any man, especially by him! Had she not escaped the vigilance of Daneton? Here in the forest it would be easier.

As the volume of Jocelyn's sobs increased, Pengarron whirled on his men, snapping, 'Silence the wench!'

Morganna seized her chance, with his attention momentarily diverted, and, picking up her skirts, she fled.

'Stay with the maid!' The sound of his voice was uncomfortably close behind her.

Already her breath burned her throat, her flight hampered by the flapping folds of her kirtle. By wending and turning, she evaded capture, but his footfalls remained disquietingly close. The square bell-tower of the Priory was visible ahead through the thinning trees, and the sight heartened her, giving strength to her exhausted legs. She felt Pengarron's hand glance off her shoulder as she swerved. A branch caught at her flying veil, snatching it and the fillet from her head as she ran on.

Moments later, a steely arm closed round her waist. She cried out and twisted round, striking hard with her fists as her skirts tangled about her ankles and unbalanced her. Tree-tops spun crazily round her as she toppled backwards, and agony shot through her head as it thudded on the ground. The air was knocked from her lungs as Pengarron fell across her.

Dazedly, she was conscious of a sharp pain at her side where his dagger-hilt dug into her hip. The dancing confusion of coloured lights slowly cleared from her sight, though the drumming of her heartbeat continued to vibrate through her body. Then, to her shame, she was potently aware of the masculinity of the figure lying over her. The smell of woodsmoke mingled with sandalwood clung to his body. Her breasts tingled where they were crushed against his hard chest, the touch of his muscled thigh alarmingly intimate as it lay between her parted legs. Pengarron shifted his weight very slightly, so that it no longer crushed her, but he made no attempt to roll away.

An erratic pulse throbbed at the base of his throat, and raising her eyes, she encountered a honey-gold gaze, curiously tender. He was looking past her, at the ground where her hair, loosened by her flight, was spread like a mantle about her. When she tried to lift her head, the wild mass of tresses beneath her shoulders kept her trapped.

Pengarron, too, still lay motionless. Tiny islands of azure sky could be seen through the foliage above, and a golden ray of dust-misted sunlight filtered through the tree-tops to bathe them in warmth. The young leaves, glowing like emeralds against the dark branches, turned the forest into a fairy glade. Morganna felt almost bewitched. His face was so close that she could see tiny beads of glistening moisture forming on his upper lip. Their gazes locked. Her breathing slowed. Against her will, she found herself relaxing. Dreamy-eyed, she was held captive by his stare.

This was how it had been at their first meeting in the forest. Then they had been strangers with no reason for distrust—just a man and a woman for whom no other world existed but the enchantment of the moment. Again the strange languor his presence always created swept over her. She moved restlessly, breathing in the seductive scent of the bluebells, until a blast from a hunting-horn brought her rudely to her senses. What was she doing?

The ground was suddenly cold and damp, and she hit out to free herself from Pengarron's grasp. Her struggles increased, but each movement of her writhing body moulded them closer together. Traitorously, instead of protesting, her whole being glowed and throbbed beneath the long powerful frame covering hers.

'Let me go!' she gasped, more frightened by the compelling force which was tempting her to submit to him than of the danger of her situation.

The corners of his mouth twitched in amusement. 'There's a score to settle between us. Any who dared draw naked steel against me has learnt the error of such rashness! Now, sweet vixen, you will learn that you cannot fight me and win.'

His hand shot out, his dagger flashing in the sunlight. Convinced that her last moment had come, Morganna was astonished when he eased slightly back from her, a long silvery tendril of her hair dangling from his fingers.

'I was your champion against the outlaws. A champion always wears his lady's favour. Would you deny this rejected suitor what was his by right?'

She dared not move, lest she enflame him further. He replaced the dagger in his belt and, tying a knot in his stolen trophy, thrust it inside his jerkin. Unaccountably, her heartbeat slowed to a painful thud, and she saw his lips draw back in a mirthless smile.

With the swiftness of a striking eagle, his mouth swooped down upon hers, mercilessly but somehow possessively. She had been kissed by her suitors – kisses persuaded or pleaded for, which were meek and respectful. Never were they as bold as this! His mouth was demanding, forcing her lips apart until they were scorched as though touched by a burning ember. Morganna trembled with shock when his tongue flickered over her teeth to invade her mouth. Then an involuntary moan escaped her as his insistence drew an answering response. The ground appeared to revolve beneath her.

Dizzy and near fainting, she pushed against him, knowing that what they were doing was wrong. But her hands were caught in his and forced back over her head, her body arching against his hard frame. Suddenly the pressure of his kiss gentled, but instead of releasing her, he moved his mouth tantalisingly over her bruised lips and her body pulsated with new and unimagined delights, its glowing warmth bursting into flame with a hunger that seared her whole being. His lips blazed a trail along her neck, burying themselves in the hollow at the base of her throat. Blessed St Winefride, help me! an inner voice screamed at the madness which possessed her. A tremor rippled through her body, and she found the strength to sob, 'No!'

Instantly he let her go and leapt agilely to his feet, his expression grim and his breathing ragged as he glowered down at her. Ignoring his hand outstretched to assist her, she rose, still trembling, to outface him.

'So, Linsdale is not of your choosing,' Pengarron announced, hooking his thumbs over his belt. 'It was sanctuary you sought at the Priory. Radford will see that as a betrayal!'

Morganna flinched at the brutality of his words and, to cover her pain, began to rebraid her hair.

'You risk much,' he continued. 'Death awaits the unwary traveller in this forest. I shall escort you for the remainder of your journey.'

Thrusting her hair into the confines of her hood, Morganna stared at him in amazement. Why should he offer his protection? Suspicion narrowed her eyes. The steely edge to his voice warned her that his offer had nothing to do with chivalry. Of course, the alliance with Linsdale would ruin any plans he had for reclaiming Daneton, and that was why he would help her.

'Why should I want your protection', she answered stiffly, 'especially since you—you attacked me!'

'You attacked me first.' He touched the dried blood upon his cheek, the gleam in his eye sardonic. 'I never back down from a challenge!'

'Oh!' her breath expelled in fury. 'Of all the conceited oafs! Why, I . . .' She broke off at the sound of the hunting-horn, much closer. 'That's Giles! I must find Jocelyn and reach the Priory before I am discovered.'

She hurried back along the path of her flight, refusing to look at Pengarron as he fell into step beside her. Just ahead, a horse whinnied. She had time to notice several riders clustered round the place she had left Jocelyn, before her arm was roughly grabbed and she was dragged behind the wide trunk of an oak.

'Those are Linsdale's men, not Radford's!' Pengarron whispered.

Then a sharp cry that could have come only from a woman startled Morganna. Dear God, what were they doing to Jocelyn? She must go to her.

'I cannot let you go.' Pengarron's fingers tightened warningly as he sensed her decision. 'If your maid speaks of us and my men are taken, I must remain free to rescue them.'

'My maid is in danger. Those men will not harm me,' she responded sharply. 'I shall not betray you.'

'You have cause enough to wish me dead.'

'I wish no man dead, my lord.' She returned his glare steadily. 'Our fathers were friends. The past cannot be undone, but out of reverence to their memory, I shall not betray you—this day.'

His eyes glowed amber, merciless as a hawk's. 'If I let you go, you will be forced to marry Linsdale.'

'That is a chance I must take. If so, I shall endure, as other women have before me.' She moved restlessly as Jocelyn cried out again. 'My wilfulness has endangered my maid, and I must go to her.'

Pengarron nodded curtly, a flicker of an indefinable emotion crossing his face. His voice was gruff as he released her arm. 'Go, then. Your loyalty deserves better than Linsdale.'

'Look to your own safety, Lord Pengarron,' she found herself saying and meaning, before she turned her thoughts to the plight of Jocelyn. Taking care to circle away from Pengarron first, she approached the hunting party.

Jocelyn screamed again, the sound choked off in a shrill note of terror. At first Morganna could not see her, but then, on the ground between the legs of the men, she saw the paleness of a kicking limb. Dear God, they were about to rape Jocelyn! Morganna's hand sought her dagger. To her dismay, the sheath was empty. A murrain on Pengarron for taking it! she cursed savagely. Without thought of her own safety she ran forward, her voice sharp with outrage.

'Release my maid!'

Some of the soldiers fell back in astonishment, but one, grinning lewdly, grabbed at her. Immediately he paled, and shouted. ''Tis the Lady Morganna!'

An embarrassed silence followed his words, broken by Jocelyn's sobs, and all heads turned towards the man kneeling astride the maid. Arms and legs held by two men, Jocelyn lay pinned to the ground, her eyes bulging with terror. Lord Linsdale still clutched at the remnants of her bodice where he had ripped it to the waist.

Sickened at the sight before her, Morganna burst out, 'At Daneton we do not violate those who serve us faithfully! You have abused my brother's hospitality, Lord Linsdale, and shown yourself unworthy of his trust.'

Shamefaced, the two men holding Jocelyn released her wrists and ankles, but to Morganna's further disgust, Lord Linsdale showed no sign of embarrassment. Obviously this was not the first time he had indulged in such vile sport . . . And Giles would have her wed to such a monster!

'I answer to no woman for my actions!' Linsdale's pale eyes were cruel with thwarted lust. 'Rather it is I who should demand of you what you are doing in the forest.'

Morganna ignored him and, with a look that would have flayed the conscience of a more sensitive man,

hurried to Jocelyn's side. Assisting the sobbing woman
to her feet, she drew the maid's cloak about her half-
naked body, and to her relief saw that she was more
frightened than hurt. She placed her arm comfortingly
round her shoulders, and glared across at the Earl of
Linsdale.

'The Marquess shall learn of this outrage,' she said
coldly. 'There shall be no marriage between us.'

'There you are mistaken, Lady Morganna.' Linsdale
spoke quietly, though each word was laced with venom.
'I am not about to lose your dowry over a trifle such as
this! It's time you learned humility.'

'You were about to rape my maid!' Morganna stated.
'A freeborn woman—and you talk to me of humility.
You disgrace your knighthood!'

She felt Jocelyn flinch at her words, but now that
her maid was calmer, Morganna studied the group
of soldiers contemptuously. There was no sign of
Pengarron's men. At least that was one less complication to deal with.

'It's no good to look for your brother,' Linsdale
wheezed cruelly. 'He's far from here! Now, my pretty,
having denied me the pleasures of your maid, you shall
take her place. Afterwards, you'll be content to wed
me.'

Morganna swallowed, her mouth drying with fear as
Linsdale sauntered towards her. What chance did two
unarmed women stand against this brute and a dozen of
his men?

Eyes blazing, Morganna stood uncowed, drawing
Jocelyn's trembling figure protectively behind her.
Linsdale was breathing heavily, and as her stomach
churned, she coiled her fingers into talons. Without her
dagger, they were her only weapon. That, and her wits.
Edging away from Jocelyn, she believed Giles could not
be far away, whatever Linsdale had said. If she could
just gain a little time for herself!

'The Marquess will kill you for this!' she raged.
Despite her bravado, her movements became jerky
from limbs seemingly carved from ice.

'You can't escape me, my pretty,' Linsdale chortled,
moistening his lips as he lunged clumsily at her.

Morganna nimbly side-stepped, her heart hammering. Growing nausea threatened to choke her, as she
dared not take her eyes from Linsdale's bulky figure.
Hands raised ready to claw at him at his next attack, she
dimly heard a crashing in the undergrowth behind.

Merciful St Winefride, she prayed, let it be Giles!

CHAPTER FOUR

'LINSDALE!' a husky voice rapped out. 'Take another step towards the Lady Morganna, and you die!'

Morganna looked over her shoulder to see Lord Pengarron, not Giles, standing at the edge of the clearing. He was not alone. Some twenty men accompanied him, several of whom had crossbows levelled at Linsdale and his retainers. But where had they come from?

Why could it not have been Giles who came to her aid? How could she hate Pengarron if he always seemed to rescue her in the nick of time? He was infuriatingly unpredictable!

'God's beard!' Lord Linsdale fumed, obviously taken aback that he had been challenged by a woodsman. Then he glared at his antagonist, and paled. 'Pengarron! What the devil are you doing back in England? No need for such a fuss . . . I've no fight with you. A lovers' tiff, no more. The wench will be my wife before the week's out.'

Pengarron took a sword from one of his men, and his voice rang out with a possessiveness that set Morganna's pulse racing. 'Any man who wishes to claim the Lady Morganna as his bride must first answer to me. I yield nothing of what is mine by right! By Holy Law, while I live, the Lady Morganna remains bound to the contract signed by our fathers.'

Astounded, she glared at Pengarron, and was about to scream out her denial when Linsdale's enraged bellow drowned her speech.

'By Our Lady, that's a lie! The King himself has agreed to my suit.'

'Then you have but to kill me, and the Lady Morganna is yours,' Pengarron challenged.

And what a challenge! Morganna could not believe her ears as she watched Pengarron stride forward, sword poised, his lips drawn back in a taunting grin.

'Acknowledge the Lady Morganna as my future bride, Linsdale,' he declared, 'and leave Daneton within the hour. Then we have no need to fight.'

'Insolent whelp!' Linsdale spat, but made no move to draw his sword. 'I'll see you rot in hell before I forfeit my right to her dowry.'

'Ah, the famed bride price!' Pengarron's voice hardened. 'Rumour has it that Radford would look on no one less than an earl to claim the hand of his beloved sister. Is it true that he offered you a dowry worthy of a princess?'

Morganna went cold with fury, understanding his motive for what it was. He did not defend her out of chivalry, but as a mercenary. For an instant she had lowered her defences, allowing herself to believe that he, too, had felt the strange attraction forged between them at each encounter, but this cold-hearted warrior had felt nothing. It was not her he cared for. This was his chance to recoup his fortune at her family's expense. Well, he would learn that the Barnetts were not so easily used! If his bravado deterred Linsdale's unwelcome suit, all to the good, but that would be the end of the matter. She would never become a prize in a contest of arms.

Her hatred deepened as she stared at Pengarron standing tall and proud awaiting Linsdale's answer. Yet, even despising him, she watched, fascinated, when with cool assurance he took up a stance in readiness to fight. He moved with the easy grace of a predator, looking more like an outlaw than a knight, with the sun highlighting his long dark hair with coppery streaks.

Linsdale's face worked in fury, but he was clearly unwilling to fight. Backing away, he shouted, 'Mount up, men. Run these dogs into the ground!'

At an angry cry behind her, Morganna had no need

to turn; the sound of Linsdale's scattering horses told her that Pengarron had outwitted him. Some of his men must have circled behind them and loosed the animals, and both sides were now on foot. Though they were evenly matched in numbers, the advantage was Pengarron's . . . and he knew it.

Eyes narrowing, Pengarron studied his opponent. 'In deference to your age, Linsdale, you may nominate a man to fight in your stead.'

'I'm no greybeard yet!' Linsdale raged. 'When did I need a champion to teach a young bantam his place?' Drawing his sword, he charged forward, snarling, 'Stay where you are, men. Mine alone will be the pleasure of killing this upstart!'

An expectant hush fell upon the gathering as the two men circled each other. Morganna touched the cross at her throat, praying Pengarron would not die. Hate him she might, but in this he was her champion. She winced at the ferocity of ringing steel when the two men locked in attack. During her year at Court she had watched many tourneys, but they had been courtly masques compared with the primitive bloodlust aroused in these two combatants. Linsdale moved sluggishly, like a great bear, but the force of his strokes was lethal, his double-edged blade capable of cutting Pengarron in two with each pass.

Not that Linsdale's sword came near to Pengarron. To see her champion gracefully ducking, pivoting and weaving as he parried each stroke added to her confusion. Her hatred mingled with admiration for his skill. The years of infatuation had not been as easily crushed as she had believed. Why must this man, who was her enemy, be so devilishly handsome and possess a strength and a self-possession which were almost impossible to resist?

'You can't win, Pengarron,' the older man jeered, using both hands to give more weight to his blows. 'Daneton—the Lady Morganna—can never be yours.'

'A man shapes his own destiny!' Pengarron countered, his words rapped out with the same lightning speed as he pressed home his attack.

Despite her resolution to deny that she was bound to Pengarron, her heart traitorously leapt with pride at those bold words, and she willed him to win as she saw his arm judder from the impact of blocking a blow to his side. Within moments, it was obvious that he could not fail: Linsdale was tiring, his movements slow and haphazard. Yet Pengarron was making no attempt to move in for the kill; he was allowing Linsdale to retain what dignity he could in so unequal a match. It was an unexpected, puzzling and completely chivalrous gesture.

Convinced that Pengarron was in no danger, Morganna relaxed. She should be appalled that two men were fighting over her, but hearing Pengarron's deep laugh as he leapt aside to evade a thrust at his chest, a tangible excitement took hold of her, making her heart pound so loudly that it blotted out the clash of steel upon steel. There was a primeval beauty to Pengarron's skill at arms as he parried each blow and countered with a cool and deadly accuracy that had Linsdale's ruddy face gleaming with sweat.

A movement to her right distracted her, and, the blood freezing in her veins, she screamed out a warning. One of Pengarron's men grabbed the raised arm of Linsdale's captain, and the dagger aimed at the younger earl's unprotected back thudded harmlessly into a near by tree.

A cruel smile twisted Linsdale's lips, and Pengarron blenched at something the older man had said. Their speech was lost to Morganna, drowned by the blast of a hunting-horn disconcertingly close by, and her heart contracted. Giles was heading this way, and Pengarron would be captured!

'Flee, my lord, before it's too late!' she found herself screaming.

Whether Pengarron heard, she could not tell. His arm blurred as it circled and, catching Linsdale's sword just below the hilt, flicked it from his grasp. Now it was Linsdale's turn to grow pale, not from anger, as Pengarron had done, but from fear. He sank stiffly to his knees, the tip of Pengarron's sword pressed to his throat.

'Mercy,' he croaked.

Pengarron towered above the cringing figure, his rugged face taut and unrelenting. Morganna gasped when he drew her own dagger from his belt and held it, hilt upward, to form a cross before Linsdale's face. 'Swear on the cross that the Lady Morganna is legally bound to me and that you relinquish your suit.'

Linsdale hesitated, obviously loath to lose both Giles's influence at Court and the fortune her dowry would bring him.

'Swear it—or die!' Pengarron snapped, a trickle of blood appearing on the blade as he nicked the flesh.

'I swear. I swear!' Linsdale croaked. 'By Our Lady, I swear!'

A wave of relief flowed over Morganna. She was free! But when she saw Pengarron turn towards her, she knew she was far from being free. It was the devil himself who strode towards her. He had returned to England to reclaim his birthright, and her inheritence was part of that right.

Bowing, he held out her dagger. 'You're well versed in its use, my lady.'

'I am not *your lady*!' Morganna heatedly protested.

Insolently he raised a mocking brow. 'Are you not, *my lady*?'

She blushed. How dared he refer to her moment of weakness! The man was insufferable. Did he think she would forget her loyalty to her family, or that he was her enemy? She fixed him with a chilling glare, but at that moment the horn sounded ominously nearer. However exasperating he might be, she owed him her life. 'Go quickly, Lord Pengarron.'

Linsdale laughed harshly. 'If you are in England, Pengarron, then Bolingbroke means to return. That smacks of treason! There will be a King's warrant for your arrest, and I shall put up 500 gold pieces for your capture. Once you are dead, the Lady Morganna will be mine.'

At the sound of approaching hoofbeats, Morganna glanced anxiously at Pengarron. Why did he not go? Giles would be here at any moment.

With a smile, Pengarron plucked a bluebell from her hair and handed it to her. 'A keepsake, fair Morganna, until we meet again.'

Before she could reply, he signalled to his men, and they all ran off into the forest. By the time her brother's troop rode into the clearing, they had disappeared from sight.

'You missed a fine kill, Linsdale,' Giles proclaimed, his sweeping gesture indicating the huge boar swinging beneath a pole carried between two horses. Then his smile died as he noticed Morganna.

'Damn your hunt, Radford!' Linsdale blazed, swaggering forward. 'My life has been threatened! You duped me! Did you think to palm me off with a whore? Pengarron's been here. He and your sister are lovers.'

Torment wrenched at Morganna's breast as she saw Giles stiffen, his face hardening. She was innocent, but he chose to believe Linsdale's lies.

'Look at your sister,' Linsdale continued. 'Pengarron has been tumbling her on the ground like a common peasant!' An involuntary gasp escaped her at his coarseness, and Giles paled, his black eyes flashing murderously. Giving neither herself nor Giles time to speak, Linsdale added savagely, 'Pengarron swears their betrothal stands, and I'll have none of it, Radford. I leave Daneton within the hour.'

'He'll not escape justice this time.' Giles gathered up his reins. 'For this, he shall die!'

'No, Giles, don't let your hatred blind you to the truth!' Morganna shrieked. 'Pengarron saved me from Linsdale's lust.'

Giles rounded on her, his expression as forbidding as it was accusing. 'I'll deal with you later, sister! Mount up behind one of my men and return to Daneton. Once there, a guard will be placed outside your room.'

'You cannot do this, Giles,' Morganna implored. Arms outstretched, she stumbled towards him. 'Pengarron is . . .'

'Spare me your lies, sister. Your lover will die! Look at yourself . . . your hair loosed and tangled—your cloak soiled. Yes, I'll hear you out—after Pengarron has felt the wrath of my sword!'

Wheeling his horse, he dug in his spurs. 'I want Pengarron, dead or alive!' he shouted, leading his men in the direction Pengarron had taken.

Morganna raised a hand to touch her Saxon cross, and realised she was still holding the bluebell Pengarron had given her. Seeing its petals as crushed and bruised as her own heart, she slowly closed her hand over it, unable to throw it away.

She was numb, confused. Her head told her to condemn Pengarron to the devil, but an ache contracted her heart at the thought of him in danger. Dimly she heard Giles's troop crashing through the forest, while, close by, Linsdale ordered his men to round up their horses. Behind her, Jocelyn's sobs finally penetrated Morganna's torpor, and she turned to comfort her maid. Her way was barred by Lord Linsdale.

'You do not appear overjoyed that Pengarron claimed you as his bride!' He laughed cruelly. 'Is it you or your dowry he fought for? Pengarron has waited a long time to avenge Radford's insults. I shall enjoy learning that the three of you have destroyed each other by your greed and ambition.'

'You know little of the matter, sir,' Morganna

answered stiffly. She was shaking, though whether from the cold breeze that had sprung up or from dread of the outcome between Giles and Pengarron, she was unsure. 'There will be no marriage.'

'Oh, but there will!' Linsdale's pale eyes narrowed maliciously. 'You'll pay for having made a fool of me. When I return to Court, I shall reveal that you and Pengarron are lovers. Before witnesses he has declared his intention to wed you. Should the marriage not take place, you will both face ridicule and dishonour.'

Morganna shuddered, relieved that she had escaped his clutches. 'Giles will believe me. He'll have you dismissed from Court for spreading such lies!'

'He could try . . .' Linsdale sneered. 'If he has not already lost favour himself. The King will consider it treason for Radford to ally his house with one of Bolingbroke's followers.' With a short, angry laugh he swung on his heel and stamped off to where his horse had been led back to the clearing.

A pang of horror shot through Morganna. Linsdale was surely bluffing? Giles was high in the King's favour . . . but, then, so once had been Pengarron's father. Exile and ruin had followed his fall from grace. But was not Linsdale too craven to act against Giles? She could understand his anger, for he had lost much, not least the chance to climb high at Court. Would he dare to rise another way—by bringing about her brothers downfall? She wished she was more convinced he was just a braggart whose words were just empty bluster.

Worriedly, Morganna looked for Jocelyn, to find her already mounted. Upon seeing the hunched, trembling figure, clutching together the torn edges of her dress, she felt no remorse at the humiliation Linsdale had suffered at Pengarron's hands. Instead, her confusion deepened. Although Pengarron had used this day to gain his own ends, he had saved her from an unwanted marriage. How could she hate him when he had again played the knight-errant?

Conscious that Lord Linsdale was watching her, she lifted her head proudly as she walked to the horse held in readiness. She would not act as if she were being sent home in disgrace. This was but a nightmare from which she would wake to discover it had all never been.

But it was no dream. During the following days, when she remained a prisoner in her room, Giles refused to speak with her. She waited in dread to hear of Pengarron being taken or killed. Whatever else he had done, he did not deserve such a fate for having helped her. On the third day, Jocelyn brought her news that Pengarron had escaped, and strangely, she found she had not expected otherwise. This was Pengarron's domain: he would know every cave and hiding-place in the hills.

Some hours later, Giles finally summoned her to the solar. Now, hands clasped, she strove to remain calm as his wrath exploded over her. Within minutes, her control over her temper snapped at the injustice of each accusation he hurled at her.

'Betrayed!' Hands on hips, Giles paced the room. 'How could you so turn against me by taking Pengarron as your lover?'

Morganna drew a shaky breath. 'Pengarron is not my lover! I've told you that he challenged Linsdale to scare him off. And he succeeded! You have heard Jocelyn's story. What does it take to convince you that Pengarron saved us both from Linsdale's lust?'

'Do you deny you met Pengarron in the forest? That he made love to you?'

'It was not like that!' She cursed the blush which stung her cheeks. The memory of Pengarron's kiss was branded upon her mind.

From across the solar, he scowled at her. 'Your blush betrays you! Since the days of your betrothal to Ralph Warrender, he's intrigued you. For years you have imagined yourself in love with the knave. You're a woman governed by her passions, but he is not for you. I shall not permit your life to be ruined by Pengarron's shadow. Forget him!'

Morganna felt the colour drain from her face. Had her infatuation been so obvious? She thought she had hidden it well. Wide-eyed, she held her brother's glittering stare, and as though from a long way off she heard herself saying, 'That's over. Pengarron is our enemy. I know that now.'

'Swear on our mother's cross that Pengarron is not your lover,' Giles growled. 'Swear he means nothing to you.'

Her hand going to the chain at her neck, she stepped back from him. What he asked was simple enough, so why did it cause a pain to stab her heart? A lump formed in her throat, choking off her words.

'Your silence proclaims your guilt!'

Morganna recoiled from the fury of his tone. It was not because she cared for Pengarron that she could not speak. It was through anger at Giles's lack of trust. Swallowing hard, she finally found her voice. 'Very well, I swear that Pengarron is not my lover. I don't even like the arrogant knave!'

The effort it cost her left her shaken. Whatever she thought of Pengarron, she could not forget that twice he had saved her from dishonour. Now, as she denied him, she could almost hear his mocking laughter. Twice, he had claimed her as his own. Twice, time had stood still for her, her mind captivated by his will. She mentally shook herself, remembering other times, Twice he had used her; abused her trust. He had shattered her illusions. Never again would she fall prey to the spell of his husky voice, or respond to the seductive challenge of those fierce amber eyes.

Some of her anguish must have shown, for instantly Giles's manner changed, and he kicked at the rushes with the toe of his red shoe. Seeing his proud shoulders droop, her anger withered. He had never found it easy to admit when he was wrong.

He looked up, his eyes clouded. 'I want to believe you, Anna.'

His sincerity moved her. Having convinced herself she loathed Pengarron, she still could not explain the abandoned way she had responded to his kiss. But it was Giles to whom she owed love and fealty.

'Then let the matter end now,' she implored. 'Trust me?'

Giles studied her intently, the brightness of his smile easing her torment. 'Perhaps you're well rid of Linsdale,' he said lightly. 'I never realised, until his visit, what a cursed dull fellow the man was.'

Used to her brother's quick changes of moods, Morganna answered his smile. It was the closest Giles would come to an apology. Now was her chance to prove her loyalty to him.

There is unrest in the castle,' she said anxiously. 'Why have you not dismissed the bailiff? He's Pengarron's man, I am sure of it.'

'For the very reason I know he is Pengarron's spy. A watch has been placed on him, and he'll not be able to act the traitor.'

'But what will happen when you leave?' Morganna asked. 'Let me stay at Daneton. If Pengarron means to strike, he'll do so while you are away.'

Her heart thumped at the suspicion darkening his eyes. 'You will go to my wife, as planned. Or is it that you wish to remain near your lover?'

'Must you be so stubborn, Giles?' she flared back at him. 'I would help defend our home against our enemy. Once the Lady Elizabeth's couching is over, she can join me here.'

Giles slammed his fist into his open palm, his brows drawn down thunderously. 'What you say is impossible! It's unseemly.'

'Why?' she countered, desperate to make him see reason. 'Let me prove my loyalty. What do I care for proprieties when you could lose Daneton? It is my fault that Linsdale's men will not be here to defend it.'

'No, I said.' Giles's tone was final as he strode to the door. 'I'll not have you in danger. You go to Lady Elizabeth in two days.'

Morganna awoke from a troubled sleep. Throughout the night she had been haunted by dreams of fighting; at first reliving the outlaws' attack, and then they became wilder. There was shouting, anger—while over them all an eagle circled, ever watching, waiting to seize its prey.

Her eyes focused, and suddenly the dream became reality. Beyond the parted bed-hangings visible in the dawn light, a golden eagle loomed above her. With a cry she sat up, feeling foolish to discover it was only the eagle on the tapestry opposite her bed that had given her such a start. Or had it been only that? Her heart raced. Outside, there was shouting and the sound of running feet. The castle was in an uproar. Blessed Mary, were they indeed being attacked? The chapel tunnel had been sealed, but had Pengarron found another way in?

Throwing back the covers, Morganna scrambled from the bed, ran across the room and peered out of her window into the courtyard. She shivered in the chill air that penetrated her silk nightgown. A thick mist obscured the scene below her. Men-at-arms ran back and forth across the glowing light from the embers of the night watch-fires. Sharp, angry voices shouted commands. If they were being attacked, why was the alarm bell not being rung? Unable to calm her fears, she snatched up her robe and was halfway across the room when the door burst open and Giles marched in.

'What's happening?' she demanded. 'Are we besieged?'

'No.' His serious expression did little to soothe her

alarm. 'The King's messenger arrived after you retired last night. I leave to join his Majesty.'

Relieved, Morganna sank on to the coffer at the foot of her bed, but her frown remained as she regarded her brother. 'Take care! Lord Linsdale will lose no time in discrediting you.'

'That's why I must answer his Majesty's summons without delay.' Raising Morganna to her feet, he drew her close. 'Anna, I must know that you are safe. There is danger here, for I am sure Bolingbroke means to return from exile, and who knows where that may lead? Daneton guards this valley and, with it, the road to London from the North. Pengarron will try to take it, if he can, to open the way for Bolingbroke if there should be conflict with the King. I've sent word to Sir Percy Thornton at Evesham to garrison a troop of his men here; they should arrive in an hour or two. Promise me that you'll leave by midday. If you were taken hostage, I would be powerless to act.'

Gazing up into her brother's drawn face, Morganna knew the time for argument was past. How could she add to Giles's troubles? Instead, she asked, 'Will you visit Lady Elizabeth before you leave England?'

A smile transformed his bleak expression. 'Do you think I would leave these shores without first seeing my son?' As he spoke, his eyes sparkled with pride. 'The messenger arrived at dawn. A son, Anna! At last, a son! I cannot lose the King's favour now.'

Clearly impatient to leave, he bent and kissed her smiling lips. 'I would not have us part bad friends. I love you too well, Anna, to see you unhappy.'

She touched his cheek, but already he was moving away from her. 'Godspeed, Giles,' she called after his departing figure. But, once alone, even the joyous news of the birth of his heir could not banish the unease her dreams had left with her.

Five hours later, the packing almost done, Morganna

left the last of the supervising to Jocelyn. She was restless, unable to shake off the foreboding that had settled over her since Giles had ridden out. In less than an hour she, too, would leave Daneton. Brooding, she wandered through the corridors, deserted now save for a few passing servants. With most of Giles's retainers accompanying him, Daneton was eerily quiet. Why had Sir Percy not arrived? He owed fealty to the Marquess, and should have obeyed his summons two hours ago. The knowledge that she might have to leave Daneton inadequately protected worried her.

In her anxiety, she climbed the narrow stone steps to the battlements to scan the line of Cotswold hills for a sign of Sir Percy's approach. The road ahead was deserted, yet, apart from that, everything looked normal. Was she allowing her dreams to overrule her judgment?. Since Pengarron had challenged Linsdale, there had been no sign of his men on Daneton land.

Gradually the tranquillity of the countryside calmed her unease. A swineherd was leading his pigs to rummage in the forest. At the village forge, a lazy spiral of smoke rose skywards, and seeing the smaller children playing Hoodman Blind among the thatched cottages, she smiled. A loud trumpet-blast sounded from the Gatehouse Tower, and she looked eagerly towards the track. Had Sir Percy arrived?

Retracing her steps along the battlements, her glance fixed on the first horsemen appearing on the far side of the village, and shock checked her. The trumpet shrilled now in warning, sounding the call to arms. She leaned over the parapet, the rough stonework grazing her palm as she gripped the wall in disbelief. A black and gold standard streamed out menacingly from the front of the troop.

Morganna ran towards the Gatehouse, her voice echoing Sergeant Fletcher's commands. 'Raise the drawbridge! ' ,ower the portcullis!'

The creak of turning windlasses was deafening as she entered the tower to run up to its roof, from where she could overlook the slowly rising drawbridge. The peace of the village was devastated. Screaming mothers ran out to scoop up their children from the path of the horsemen. Pigs and swineherd scattered. In the fields, some men fled to the woods, while others, brandishing their hoes, ran back to defend their families. As the drawbridge shuddered, with a rattle of chains, against the tower wall, she let out a long-held breath. They were safe!

A glance along the curtain wall showed her the battlements already manned by archers, yet still her heart thudded as she turned her attention to the armed troop below her. Dressed in half-armour and mounted on a black horse, Pengarron rode forward to halt on the far bank of the moat. Insolently, he raised his sword in salute to her. As he did so, the pale gold pennant of her hair streamed out from its hilt.

Her cheeks flamed with humiliation. He wore the stolen favour as boldly as a lover. How dared he so mock her! Her hands gripping the wall, she waited for him to acknowledge defeat. For a long moment Pengarron remained silent, too assured of his victory for her peace of mind. The man was insufferable! As she watched, he was joined by two other riders, one powerfully built, the other obviously the herald, who raised his trumpet to his lips to sound out a fanfare.

'Lord Pengarron, master of Daneton, bids you grant him entrance,' the second man, presumably Pengarron's squire, proclaimed.

From the turret immediately below her, the steward answered. 'There is no lord of Daneton by that name.'

Pengarron held up his hand to silence his squire, and his husky voice resounded in the expectant stillness. 'I would speak with the Lady Morganna. Lower the drawbridge, and there will be no need for bloodshed.'

The audacity of the man! Morganna fumed. The black

and gold of Pengarron's emblazoned tunic blurred before her incensed gaze. Did he think her foolish enough to fall for his trickery a second time? Her anger drained the heat from her cheeks. It seemed that, even from this distance, those amber eyes pierced her soul. His spies had worked well, and he had known the precise moment to strike. Giles was already miles away, and there were no reinforcements. But she would outwit him. The drawbridge was still raised, and she would fight.

'If you are expecting aid from Sir Percy Thornton,' the taunting voice rang out, 'it's not forthcoming. At this moment he is riding North—answering a debt of honour.'

'Sir Percy swore fealty to Lord Radford,' Morganna burst out, the full impact of Pengarron's words leaving her cold with dread.

'As he also did to my father. Thornton has no quarrel with Radford, nor with myself. Lower the drawbridge now, my lady. I vow none within shall be harmed.'

Morganna ground her teeth with indignation. Deserted by Sir Percy, her plight was dire indeed, but not hopeless. For how long, with so few men, could she hold Daneton against so many? Long enough, she reasoned. Sir Percy might have found it impossible to take up arms against Pengarron, but he was a just man. If she judged him correctly, he was bound to send word to Giles that Daneton was under siege.

Confident of success, she looked down at Pengarron. 'The drawbridge remains as it is. It shall be lowered to none save its rightful lord, the Marquess of Radford!'

The black gelding tossed back its head, to be expertly brought under control as Pengarron rapped out, 'Tomorrow, we shall see who is lord of Daneton!'

As she watched him wheel his horse and canter back to his men, Morganna felt a surge of triumph. His bluster did not frighten her. His troop, now swollen to over a hundred, was still not enough to storm the walls. Daneton would not fall.

CHAPTER FIVE

NIGHT HAD FALLEN when Morganna again found herself
drawn to the battlements. Throughout the day, tension
within Daneton had grown as they waited for the attack
to begin. At first she was concerned for the safety of the
villagers, but so far they had been unmolested. Obviously Pengarron regarded them as his people. Though
she resented such arrogance, it meant he would not
harm them.

She looked towards the hills. There was no moon, and
the blackness of the countryside was forbidding. Her
glance returned to the village, and her fear intensified.
The mist that had settled over the valley floor at dusk
was steadily rising, and was now so dense that she was
unable to see the glow from the rushlights through the
window shutters. Soon the grey shroud would obscure
everything, giving Pengarron an advantage over them.

Sounds were distorted, and her ears and eyes strained
against the darkness. Was that a splash in the moat? She
leaned forward, suddenly tense, but only the muffled
tread of a nearby sentry broke the silence.

'My lady!' Jocelyn's voice called from the courtyard.
'Are you there? The castle officers await you in the
solar.'

Morganna turned to the page holding the lighted torch
for her, and followed him down the slippery steps as she
answered her maid. 'I had not realised the hour was so
late.'

'Oh, my lady, you should not be out there! On such a
night, the fairy-folk snatch away the unwary.'

Despite her anxiety, Morganna smiled at her maid's
fancies. 'It's not the fairy-folk I fear this night, Jocelyn.

Pray that Giles will learn of our plight and return to our aid.'

'Then we'll not be flogged and thrown in the dungeon, or murdered,' Jocelyn sobbed.

Morganna placed a comforting hand upon her shoulder. 'There are times when I despair of you! Lord Pengarron would not permit such atrocities, but the matter will not be put to the test. Daneton's defences cannot be breached.'

Walking on, Morganna set her lips in a determined line. The waiting was putting a strain on everyone's nerves, not least her own. Why had Pengarron not attacked immediately? If he waited, it was with good cause. Was there another secret entrance she knew nothing about? With so few men, she dared not risk bringing more from patrolling the battlements to search the castle precincts.

Taking care that none of her uncertainty showed, Morganna greeted the officers.

'We have food for only ten days,' Dick Crosfylde, the steward, announced, his bearded face creased with worry. 'The armourer travels with Lord Radford, and we have scarce enough arrows to repel a single attack, let alone a siege.'

'If we are short of arrows, we still have swords, halberds and burning oil to repel an assault,' Morganna encouraged him. 'Reinforcements will arrive, and someone will notify the Marquess of our plight.'

Sergeant Fletcher cleared his throat before speaking. 'With respect, my lady, apart from the oil, those weapons are effective only once the walls have been breached. Pengarron will not wait for us to get reinforcements.'

Father Matthew stepped forward. 'You speak bravely, my lady. What of your own safety? There is still time to surrender and ask safe passage for you to join the Lady Elizabeth.'

She shook her head. 'You mean well, Father, but it's Daneton I fear for, not myself.'

'Lord Pengarron will not give up without a fight,' Sergeant Fletcher said forcefully. 'No man would risk laying siege to another's property unless he had been so ordered by a higher authority.'

The bluntness of the Sergeant's words echoed Morganna's own fears. Henry Bolingbroke must have returned from exile, unknown to Giles or the King. In spite of her misgivings, Morganna savoured a glow of triumph. How Pengarron's pride must be smarting that he had been outwitted by a woman!

'All the more reason why we must fight,' she persisted. 'It is our duty to King Richard to defend this stronghold.'

'The Lady Morganna is right!' Sergeant Fletcher declared. 'Pengarron serves the traitor Bolingbroke. He's no more than an outlaw. Are we to be dictated to by such as he?'

A loud cheer accompanied the Sergeant's words, until Dick Crosfylde held up his hands for silence. 'I have no mind to fail Lord Radford. Or you, my lady. Are we agreed to hold Daneton, whatever the cost?'

Tears of pride stung Morganna's eyes at the fervour of their response. Seeing the resignation on Father Matthew's face, she moved to his side, raising her voice above the officers' loud discussion.

'Will you give us your blessing, Father?'

The priest nodded. 'Knowing the Marquess's orders, it was my duty to try and dissuade you. But your decision is the right one.'

'Is not our maxim "Stand Firm"?' Morganna smiled tiredly. 'Better to die upholding it, than surrender to Pengarron's mercenaries!'

A sardonic laugh greeted her remark and, the hackles rising upon her neck, she spun round. Sword poised ready to fight, Lord Pengarron strode into the solar.

Before her officers could draw their weapons, several men poured in behind him, crossbows aimed at the Radford men.

'A proud speech, my lady, but too late, I fear,' he taunted as he resheathed his sword.

They were betrayed! Hatred burned through her as she watched him remove his domed helmet and push back the hood of his chain mail. Had she not known him for a cold-hearted knave, she would have sworn she saw regret clouding his eyes.

The impression was fleeting, his expression uncompromising as he met her scathing glare. From across the room came a snarl of rage, and to her alarm she saw Sergeant Fletcher, sword drawn, bound towards Pengarron. His squire moved quickly. Lashing out with the hilt of his sword, he knocked the Sergeant to the ground.

'Order your men to stay where they are!' Pengarron commanded. 'Or they die.'

Ignoring him, she glanced at the Sergeant's prone figure and breathed easier when she saw him sway to his knees. Returning her gaze to Pengarron, she found to her annoyance that his thick lashes shadowed his thoughts from her. He had made a mockery of her defiance, and every particle of her rebelled against his high-handedness.

'Guards!' she shouted.

'Silence!' Pengarron moved closer, his face working with fury. 'Your guards below are tied up. Take care, my lady. So far, no blood has been lost. Would you have it otherwise? Another cry from you to summon those in the courtyard, and all these men die.'

Morganna's head shot up, her hatred smouldering. It was no idle threat. She threw the officers a beseeching look—warning them to make no further move. When next she looked at Pengarron, she did not trouble to hide her scorn. To her surprise, he had paled beneath his bronzed complexion. Had he really expected her to surrender without a fight? That a single kiss could change her loyalty? He would learn that a moment's weakness did not make her a slave to her emotions!

'Your treachery will serve you ill,' she flung at him. 'When his Majesty learns of this—this outrage, you'll pay with your life!'

'My lady, take care!' Father Matthew warned. 'If they kill us, then the castle is lost anyway.'

Her fury was so great that she forgot the respect due to the priest, and rounded on him. 'Are you asking me to surrender my brother's castle meekly?'

'We have lost the fight, my lady,' Father Matthew said quietly. 'Other lives will be needlessly sacrificed if you call out the guards. We cannot win.'

Conscious of the threatening stance of Pengarron's men around her, Morganna clenched her trembling hands, hiding them in the folds of her gown as she strove to remain claim.

'With respect, my lady,' interrupted Dick Crosfylde, keeping his head lowered as though ashamed to have to speak the words, 'they have us beaten.'

'Pay heed to your counsellors, Lady Morganna,' Pengarron said, thrusting his thumbs into his sword-belt, the lethal softness of his voice making her flinch. 'Your quick wits and courage saved Daneton earlier. Had it been anyone but myself laying siege, you would have sustained your victory. You were not to know of the hidden door by the moat.'

The atmosphere in the room crackled with tension. Sergeant Fletcher swayed to his feet and raised a fist, shaking it at Pengarron as he shouted, 'Trickery, that's what it was! What man of honour would . . .' His voice broke on a grunt of pain.

'When Lord Pengarron speaks, you listen!' The Welsh lilt in the voice of Pengarron's captain was roughened with anger, as he raised his sword to strike the Sergeant a second time.

'Stop!' Morganna screamed, as the old retainer doubled over and sank to his knees.

'Enough, Ifor,' Pengarron commanded, and nodded to another man to hold Sergeant Fletcher prisoner as he staggered to his feet. With a roar, the Sergeant shook off his hold and began lashing out with his fists.

Seeing the Welshman again start forward, Morganna cried out, 'Have done, Sergeant! I would not see you further hurt.'

'Wisely spoken,' Pengarron commented drily. 'Now order your steward to lower the drawbridge and allow my men to be admitted.'

For a long moment Morganna studied him in silence. The tight leash Pengarron was keeping upon his temper was obvious by the way his fingers drummed impatiently on his sword-hilt. Sick at heart, she knew she had failed Giles. She turned to Dick Crosfylde, saying wearily, 'Do as he bids. Have the drawbridge lowered.'

Pengarron nodded to three of his men to follow the steward, but his attention was held by the graceful figure of Morganna, who had turned away to speak to the old man who had been injured. She remained proud and dignified even though she had just acknowledged defeat. Or had she? he wondered. When she straightened to glare back at him, there was the light of combat in her violet eyes.

'What plans have you for your prisoners, my lord? It must be obvious to you that I cannot remain here.'

Her haughty tone stung him. 'How so? As my betrothed, your reputation will be safe under my protection.'

'I am not . . .'

He took a warning step towards her, and her protest died, although her eyes continued to flash. Would he have to kill one of her men before the stubborn jade admitted the castle was his, and all those in it at his mercy?

'Your ruse scared off Linsdale,' she continued in a harsh whisper that did not carry to the others present. 'You have Daneton. There is no need for it to continue further.'

Unaccountably, her resistance enraged him. He had used their betrothal to get rid of Linsdale, but hearing her so firmly repudiate it reminded him of the insults he had borne from her family. She would not escape so easily!

'It will continue for as long as I wish it,' he declared. 'The steward's wife is of gentle birth. She and your maid will sleep within your room. Does that satisfy you?' Their eyes gave battle, and he reluctantly found himself admiring her stubborn spirit.

Unblinking she held his stare, to reply scathingly, 'It will suffice for this night. Tomorrow may see Daneton released from your tyranny.'

'Your faith in Radford is misplaced,' he answered, enjoying the sparring between them. 'I yield nothing that is mine by right. I have never yet lost a fight.'

At the distant sound of the drawbridge being lowered, her heart-shaped face paled, then set rebelliously. She was looking at the crescent-shaped wound on his cheek, and her lips twitched. Her gaze moved to the Barnett coat of arms carved over the fireplace—three crescent moons.

'You carry my mark, sir,' she said with deceptive smoothness, her eyes dancing with fire. 'I, too, am used to gaining my own ends.'

The little minx flaunted her triumph over him. Was there any woman like her? She was at his mercy, yet refused to show fear. He respected that, but it was time she learnt who was master here.

Turning to his captain, his expression hardened. 'Take these prisoners to the keep and place them under guard. The Lady Morganna will be confined to her own chambers.'

He waited for the castle officers to be led from the solar. His mind already on strengthening Daneton's defences, he bowed to Morganna and followed them out.

Pengarron descended the stairs, but as he walked through the Great Hall, the familiar surroundings he had not seen for years provoked him to renewed anger against Radford. Ruthlessly he smothered the sudden rush of childhood memories as he gazed up at the wide span of timber roof. But as his spurs jangled over the flagstones, he found himself drawn to the apartments he had occupied in his youth. Flinging open the door, he glared at the startled serving-woman, dismissing her brusquely. Then his attention was caught by a tapestry he had once prized as his own, and the memories could no longer be suppressed.

Radford had owned all this, while his own father had died, broken in spirit—banished to the remoteness of Pengarron Castle in Wales. Daneton was only one of several castles lost at his father's fall from grace. It was not even the largest—Pengarron itself was the jewel of the Warrenders' fortune. But Daneton had become a symbol of the humiliation Radford had heaped upon him. It was a trophy his enemy valued highly—yet there was something Radford treasured more.

He smiled grimly to himself. With Daneton held by his men, he had other duties before he joined Bolingbroke when he landed. But Daneton must remain secure, and there was one way to ensure that Radford kept his distance.

Still fuming at the way Pengarron had tricked his way into Daneton, Morganna entered her chambers. There was no sign of Jocelyn. At the doorway to the inner room, she paused, the soft light from the oil-filled cressets throwing the object of her hatred into stark relief, clearly outlining his imperious profile. Unaware of her presence, he was staring at the tapestry which had given her such a fright that morning.

Over the years she had taken its presence in her chamber for granted. Now she recalled finding it there when Giles had taken possession of Daneton. Then it had been worn in places and had once obviously been part of a larger piece. Fond of animals, she had liked the image of the golden eagle and had insisted the tapestry be repaired. Only now did she realise that it was, of course, the Pengarron eagle, portrayed as the king of birds; the lesser species, even the peacock, over-shadowed by its magnificence. The irony of discovering its true meaning, and of finding Pengarron himself apparently at ease in her chamber, brought an indignant gasp to her lips.

He turned, clearly surprised to see her standing there.

'For what reason do you lurk in my chambers, sir?'

'So, these are your quarters now.' There was devil-ment in his eyes as his gaze held hers. 'These were once my rooms. The tapestry also . . . Clearly, a loving hand has restored it.'

Just what was he implying? 'The design was pretty,' she answered stiffly. 'I would not deprive you of it. The rest of my possessions will be removed without delay. I should have thought, however, that you would prefer the lord's chamber.'

He grinned, her sarcasm lost on him. 'It pleases you to cast me in the role of avenging outlaw, yet it was not always so. Have you forgotten our first meeting in the forest?'

Morganna's anger flared at the humiliating memories he stirred. 'I have not forgotten the way you used me to get back at my brother that same night in the chapel.'

'That was not what I referred to, and well you know it, my lady,' he said huskily.

She closed her mind against the images which still plagued her dreams—of golden eyes glowing with admiration, and forbidden delights. Her stare holding his, she answered coldly, 'Is it not, Lord Pengarron? I fear, then, you know more than I.'

His expression hardened. The light from the lamps hollowed his lean cheeks and threw the ridge of the crescent wound into relief. A nerve pulsated into life along his jaw when Morganna's stare lingered upon the cut she had inflicted, and she found herself thinking that the scar would add to his attractiveness.

'My work is done here,' he declared silkily. 'I shall leave a garrison to defend Daneton. You will accompany me to Pengarron Castle.'

'I shall do no such thing!'

'You'll do as you're bidden, lady. Have you forgotten that your officers are my prisoners?'

She felt trapped, but refused to admit she was beaten. 'I won't go with you! If you force me, I'll escape.'

Her body trembled with rage and frustration as he strode to the door, apparently unconcerned by her threat. Turning, he leant his shoulder against the stone arch, regarding her with an assurance that made her hand throb to lash out at him.

'Make any attempt to escape,' he said darkly, 'and your officers will die.'

Morganna coughed, almost choking on her fury. 'You are no more than a savage—a mercenary. Curse you! So, I am to be your hostage. Does the Lord of Pengarron need to hide behind a woman's skirts to protect his ill-gotten gains?'

Scowling, he thrust himself from the arch, and Morganna inwardly flinched at the anger blazing from his eyes. But, equally incensed, she stood her ground. He had made it impossible for her to escape without endangering the lives of her officers, but that did not mean she would meekly accept his tyranny.

His movement controlled, predatory, he flicked one of the bed-hangings with his fingers. 'What other reason would I possibly have, fair Morganna?'

At his velvety, enigmatic tone, her legs became suddenly unsteady but she held his stare. The lamplight reflected in his eyes set them aglow with a fire more pitiless than any striking hawk's. He did not trouble to hide his desire. Appalled, she backed away, but he was too quick for her, blocking her path to the door. As his hand reached out to grab her shoulder, she felt the high mattress of the bed press against her thigh. Trapped, she dared not move lest they both toppled backwards—that had proved disastrous once before!

'You are a beautiful woman. You would not be the first to use it for her own advantage!'

Morganna tensed when his fingers touched the skin above the scooped neckline of her kirtle. Had he raked her with talons, the pain would have been more bearable than the spirals of fire which leapt through her. Despising herself for the way her body responded to his touch, she declared icily, 'I would die before I dishonoured my family!'

Abruptly his hand fell to his side. 'Your reputation will not suffer. Once we are at Pengarron Castle, Lady Gwyneth, my brother's widow, will safeguard your honour.' The contempt in his eyes matched hers. 'I'm no Linsdale. I do not force myself upon unwilling women, though that's how you expect me to treat you, is it not? When I take a woman as my own, she will be as eager as I for the match.'

Did that mean he had dropped the pretence of being her suitor? There was something about the set of his jaw which stopped her asking. With a last stony glare in her direction, he marched from the room.

Morganna gripped the bedpost, her anger leaving her shaken. Each encounter with that inhuman devil left her less in control of her emotions than before. The bright eye of the eagle on the tapestry mocked her, and with an angry sob, she jerked it from the wall and flung it on the ground. She wanted no reminders of that arrogant knave near her!

Moments later, Jocelyn came into the room, and Morganna pointed to the offending tapestry. 'Have that taken to wherever Lord Pengarron has made his quarters. It's his property. And you can tell Edwina Crosfylde that I do not need her to sleep in my chamber. I am to be his lordship's hostage. He'll not risk losing his ransom money should his men dishonour me.'

'Ay, my lady.' Jocelyn's tone was unusually cynical. 'It is not for want of a ransom that that proud one will stop his men mistreating you.'

Choosing to ignore her maid's romantic notions, Morganna picked up her Book of Hours. She was uncomfortably aware that Pengarron desired her, but he certainly had no liking for her. Sitting by the fire, she tried to compose herself, but as the book fell open, a pressed bluebell-flower dropped into her lap. She flung it into the flames, wondering why she had been foolish enough to save it after Pengarron had championed her in the forest. The words on the pages ran together and the gold, red and blue of the illuminations became a jumbled blur until she found no comfort from the prayers.

She did not look up at hearing Jocelyn call a passing servant, or as they rolled up the tapestry and carried it from the chamber. When the room was quiet, she allowed the Book of Hours to fall shut, and stared unseeing into the fire.

The flames had burnt low when a slight rustling drew her attention to Helewise squatting on the floor opposite her. So deep were her thoughts that she had not heard the wise-woman enter.

'You have reason to be troubled,' my lady.' Helewise spoke softly. 'Beware Pengarron. 'Tis a dark place you go to.'

Morganna put up a hand to silence her, too tired to listen to her ramblings tonight.

'Let me speak, my lady. It's said that you travel to Wales. Heed me well. In my youth, I served on your grandmother's estate on the Welsh borders. My father was a wagoner and knew much of the land. He warned me about strange rituals. Many of the people resent their English overlords, and some villagers have returned to the old ways and customs.'

'That was a long time ago, Helewise,' Morganna said dismissively. 'The Earls of Pengarron would stamp out such rites, as we did on my grandmother's estate.'

'If they knew they existed?' the old woman persisted.

'Enough, Helewise! The Welsh are a proud race, and naturally some of their ways are different from ours. Superstition is always rife where customs are not understood.'

The old woman waggled the rune sticks at Morganna. 'These speak of danger. You mocked my prophecy before. But has not a change come to Daneton? Beware Pengarron!'

'I shall heed your words. I know to my cost that Lord Pengarron is a dangerous man to cross! I'll do nothing to endanger myself while I am his hostage.'

Apparently satisfied, Helewise shuffled out, but her words stayed with Morganna. Her infatuation with Ralph Warrender might be over, but the way her body responded to his touch bore out the danger she would be in at Pengarron.

CHAPTER SIX

MORGANNA LOOKED AT the stormclouds gathering over the Malvern Hills as Pengarron's troop steadily climbed the steep, bare slopes. They had been riding for two days, keeping to the lesser roads and avoiding villages. A rush of resentment filled her as she looked at the black-cloaked figure leading the column of men.

Several times since leaving Daneton she had been tempted to dig in her heels and try to escape, but always there was the threat hanging over her officers. And what would happen to Jocelyn? she wondered bitterly. Even if she managed to stay free, her maid could never hope to escape on the sluggish mare they had given her. Though any compliance with Pengarron's wishes goaded her, Morganna had finally accepted that to escape would only bring harm upon her servants, and she could not risk that.

Dejectedly, she stared down across the flat plain far below, her sharp eyes just discerning the dark outline of Worcester Cathedral in the distance. The forbidding clouds echoed the bleakness settling over her heart as each mile took her further from Giles. What would happen if they reached Pengarron Castle before her brother could rescue her? Pengarron's arrogant challenge set her blood tingling with renewed fury. Just what were his intentions?

Upon hearing Jocelyn muttering gloomy forebodings about Welsh outlaws attacking them or pagan Druids demanding human sacrifice, Morganna turned to rebuke her.

'Would you have Lord Pengarron think we're superstitious half-wits? You've listened to too many of

Helewise's tales. She's become muddled in her old age. The Welsh keep their own customs, but they're not devil-worshippers.'

'But Helewise says . . .'

'Jocelyn! I have no wish to hear what Helewise says. You pay too much heed to her ramblings,' Morganna said more sternly.

'I'm not the only one who agrees with her!' Jocelyn pouted. 'Some of Pengarron's men were speaking of curses and spells. I heard their Captain, Ifor, threaten to call down the wrath of Hecate upon them if they sat around gossiping like old women when on duty. Hecate is the moon-goddess. Does that not prove they're heathens?'

'It proves that Ifor is a man of little patience, who will not suffer fools readily.'

A jagged shaft of lightning flashed across the plain below, and Morganna started violently. The accompanying boom of thunder set the rocks vibrating around her, and Sweet Eglantine pranced nervously.

'There's a cave just ahead,' Pengarron said, his black gelding skidding to a halt beside her. 'We'll take shelter there.'

He scanned the track ahead at the sound of approaching hooves. Over the crest of the hill, a galloping rider bore down upon them. His face and clothing splattered in mud and his horse lathered from a long, hard ride, the stranger drew rein level with him. With a warning gesture telling the man to wait before speaking, Pengarron indicated he should ride on with him away from Morganna, as the troop quickened their pace.

Bowing her head against the increasing wind, Morganna gave no more thought to the newcomer as the first raindrops slashed down. Her cloak was drenched by the time they reached the cave. It was larger than she expected, its roof so high that it was hidden in blackness. While the horses were taken and tethered at the rear,

she shrugged off her dripping cloak and gave it to
Jocelyn to lay over a boulder to dry. She shook out the
heavy folds of her damp gown, and rubbed her arms with
her hands to revive some warmth.

'Start a fire!' Pengarron rapped out, obviously dis-
pleased by the delay. 'It's likely we'll be here for some
time.'

He withdrew to the far side of the cave with the
stranger, summoning Ifor and his squire, Emrys, to join
them, and the four men spoke for a long time. There was
something about the way he glanced across at her, as he
listened to the messenger, that alerted Morganna to
danger. Did the man bring news from Bolingbroke—or
of the King? Or was it to warn Pengarron that Giles was
following?

The questions raced through her mind. Drawn against
her will, she observed Pengarron as he stood, one leg
bent and resting on a small boulder, his profile hawk-like
and uncompromising. He straightened, easing back his
shoulders, and the firelight showed the lines of tiredness
and worry etched deeply at the side of his mouth and
eyes.

Catching her absorbed gaze on him, he looked ill at
ease. Could he regret that he was burdened by a hostage
who was slowing his pace? Whatever devils plagued him,
she reflected bitterly, they were of his own making! She
would not waste her sympathy on him.

The light was fading as she moved to the front of the
cave, where the rain fell like a waterfall over its entrance. The storm showed no sign of abating. Sitting on a
boulder, she lost track of time as she watched the
lightning snaking across the sky. Pengarron's mood
troubled her. Something had happened to disturb him.
And Giles? Where was her brother now? Had he even
learnt of her fate? Or, if Linsdale had carried out his
threats to discredit him, was he unable to leave the King
to come to her aid?

Deep in thought, Morganna started at Pengarron's voice. 'The hour is late, my lady. Should you not take some rest?'

The unexpected gentleness of his tone surprised her, catching her off guard, so that she responded without any thought of the hostility between them.

'My mind was occupied, and the storm echoed my mood.'

'You're not frightened by the storm?' He sounded amused. 'Your maid is whimpering and muttering ill omens.'

Morganna jumped to her feet. 'I'll go to her. She's terrified of storms.'

'A moment, my lady, if you please.' Taking her arm, he detained her, and the warmth of his fingers sent a shock of physical awareness through her body. Instantly his hand lifted, but he continued to stand close to her.

'Do you hate me so much that my touch is repulsive to you?' he demanded hoarsely.

His words puzzled her. What did he expect? His figure was a menacing black silhouette filling the entrance of the cave. 'How should I regard my abductor?'

The lightning flashed, and she saw he had exchanged his wet surcoat for a gold velvet short cloak. His shirt was open at the neck, partially baring his chest. A strange breathlessness overcame her at the sight of the dark curling hair against the sheen of his skin and the white-ness of his cambric shirt. Unconsciously, she shivered again.

'You're cold!'

His cloak, still warm from the heat of his body, was placed round her shoulders before she could protest. The fragrance of sandalwood and the musky scent of his maleness assaulted her senses. The firelight honeyed his complexion, the dark line of his unshaven beard, dis-turbingly masculine. His apparent unawareness of the effect his presence was having upon her made it harder to control the fluttering of her heartbeat. His proximity confused her. He seemed different from the antagonist of their earlier meetings, yet nothing had changed between them. Why, then, was she driven by the need to understand him?

'By taking Daneton you risk everything, and for a man who is traitor to our King!'

'Henry Bolingbroke is no traitor! He is Duke of Lancaster by right of birth. King Richard would steal that from him. Our Sovereign is a tyrant who must learn that even God's anointed is still subject to England's laws.'

'But he is the King!' She faced him, undeterred at the anger narrowing his eyes. 'You have suffered by his pettiness, yet by taking Daneton you committed treason. Do you not fear the King's wrath?'

'I acted before another could act in my place. Should the King not listen to reason, Daneton is important in our plans to reach London.'

'A victory at Daneton is not the same as success elsewhere. Your Henry Bolingbroke may find he aims too high,' she answered scornfully. He made it all sound so reasonable, but it was still treason. 'Are you so certain your cause will not fail, my lord?'

Pengarron eyed the woman's proud beauty coldly. Must she question everything he did? Still, she had a quick, enquiring mind and had shown an unusual grasp of the situation between Bolingbroke and the King. It was natural she would be biased in favour of her brother's beliefs. Unaccountably, her scorn pricked him.

'Time will tell, will it not, who is victor and who vanquished!' he taunted. 'The fight is not yet joined. It is our hope that, in this, our petty princeling will show wisdom and restore that which was unlawfully taken.'

'Will it come to a fight?' There was a catch in her voice that added to the unease he felt at having to break the messenger's news to her. His task was made harder, when she continued in all innocence, 'I cannot forget that our fathers were friends. Giles will listen to reason. It's not too late. If Daneton is safely held for King Richard, there can be no question of your loyalty, my brother will see to that.'

'With respect, my lady, what your brother sees or does not see matters not now.'

'Just what do you mean by that?'

All the hostility was back in her voice, making him regret the harshness of his words. If only there was some way he could break Barnaby's news to her without causing her pain!

'The King sailed for Ireland without his favourite.' He forced the words out. 'Radford is now a prisoner in the Tower of London. Linsdale wasted no time in spreading his lies.'

For a moment he thought Morganna about to swoon, so deathly pale had she become. Her large, expressive eyes pleaded with him to deny his words, causing an unpleasant pang of guilt to take hold of him. He should not have brought her from Daneton. It was Radford he had wanted to strike at—not her! Now he must be sure he protected her from the danger ahead. Radford's enemies would not hesitate to act against him while he was in prison, and Morganna could find herself at the mercy of men such as Linsdale. The thought of her in the arms of that lecher angered him. Had Linsdale been her lover, as he had boasted? She was long past marriageable age, and he had witnessed for himself the smouldering passion beneath her cool exterior—a fire he needed to set ablaze! Was her virtue lost, despite the angelic innocence of her beauty?

'I must go to Giles,' she said, breaking the spell, and clutched at his sleeve in distress.

Seeing her for once vulnerable instead of defiant, his anger and suspicion died. A strange possessiveness seized him. He wanted to protect her—to shield her from pain. Covering her hand with his own, he said gently, 'You have forgotten your place. You're my prisoner. You may speak with Barnaby before he rides on to announce our arrival at Pengarron. He will tell you all he knows.'

A shudder shook her slim frame, and her eyes closed as though unable to bear her agony. As she swayed, he caught her about the waist, steadying her. Instead of fighting him, she bowed her head, her defeat cutting him more sharply than a knife. No other woman had so bedevilled his senses. He could feel the scented softness of her body, and with difficulty he curbed his desire. While she was under his protection, honour decreed that she remain unmolested, even by himself. He raised her chin with his hand and brushed a tear from her cheek.

'Radford will be safe until the King returns and decides his fate,' he soothed her.

'Safe! Who is ever safe in the Tower?' she said, her eyes darkening with accusation. 'You have your triumph over my brother. I am no use to you now. He cannot pay your ransom, and neither can you let me go—I know too much.'

'You and Radford are two of a kind!' His temper rose at her continued defiance. Spirit he could admire, but her stubbornness was something he was not prepared to tolerate. 'You think only of gold and riches. You'll remain under my protection. But I warn you—just this once, my lady—that at Pengarron I am master. And you will do exactly as I command!'

When she tilted back her head, her eyes flashing rebelliously, a devilish fire raged through him as he fought against the urge to take her in his arms and kiss her into submission.

'You would defy me even now!' he said with deceptive quietness as he released her. 'At Pengarron, I shall tame you!'

As he strode back to his men, his thoughts were bitter. He approached Barnaby, whose guise as a troubadour had kept him informed of the latest news at Court, and told him to go to Morganna. Once at Pengarron, he was determined to teach that proud vixen who was master there—as he must show Gwyneth that her reign was at an end.

His brother's widow would not easily give up her hold on the estate. Pengarron had long been an obsession with her; it was as though it replaced the children she had never borne. He crushed the feeling of unease Gwyneth always roused in him. He had always found her possessiveness disquieting. Her Celtic beauty left him unmoved, and he had never fallen under her spell as Edmund had done. Somehow he sensed that she resented that, and his pleasure at returning to his castle dimmed. He could do without Gwyneth stirring up trouble at Pengarron just now!

During the next three days of travelling it became impossible for Morganna to banish Pengarron from her thoughts. She had been surprised when Barnaby, the messenger, had spoken with her, trying to assure her that her brother was in no immediate danger. Pengarron himself did not appear to be angry that she was now worthless to him as a hostage. Often he rode at her side, and his manner, although distant, was always courteous.

At first she had been wary, suspecting ridicule. He showed no pleasure in Giles's downfall and ignored her hostility, telling her about the places he had visited on the Continent. It seemed that he had been content enough with his life as a mercenary until it had been changed by his brother's sudden death.

On the occasions he spoke of Pengarron Castle, it was with pride and in a manner quite different from the way he referred to Daneton. Fascinated against her will at the passionate way he spoke of his home,

Morganna found herself asking,

'It must be some time since you were at Pengarron?'

'Two years. Not since my father died.' There was a sadness in his voice that made her look at him more closely.

He seemed not to notice as he stared into the distance, his eyes crinkled against the sunlight and his thoughts obviously upon Pengarron. Without anger hardening his bronzed face, he was too ruggedly handsome for her peace of mind. They rode in silence for some time, but strangely it caused no awkward tension between them.

Sometimes he was so like Giles, Morganna mused again, especially in the way he deliberately taunted her. Thinking about her brother reminded her that Pengarron was her enemy, and she looked away, feeling ashamed.

'Radford will come to no harm while King Richard is out of England.' He accurately guessed her thoughts, provoking her irritation.

'How can you be so unfeeling?' she responded heatedly. 'Because of you, he faces the King's displeasure.'

He frowned. 'Radford and I may have our differences, but it was never my intent to discredit him; merely to have Daneton undefended when he joined the King.'

Morganna stared at Sweet Eglantine's grey mane, trying to regain her composure. She had known she was no more than a pawn in Pengarron's plans. Why, then, did an inexplicable ache clutch at her heart?

Unwilling to dwell upon her own emotions, she turned her thoughts to more worrying matters. He had, so far, evaded her questions concerning Daneton. 'My lord . . .' she began hesitantly, unsure whether his unpredictable temper was about to break over her head. 'Provided I do not escape, what orders did you give concerning my officers?'

His full lips twitched with amusement. 'Still too stubborn to admit you're beaten!' His smile broadened.

'Your officers are unharmed. That is, except for Sergeant Fletcher. I had no choice but to confine him. He was caught trying to get word to the Lady Elizabeth. As to the others, your presence here ensures their loyalty.'

'Poor Fletcher,' she spoke more to herself than to Pengarron. 'The dungeon is poor reward for his faithful service.'

His smile vanished. 'He is merely confined to his quarters,' he snapped. 'That blow to his head did nothing to teach him caution! The priest is attending his wounds.'

Morganna's eyes widened in surprise . . . She had misjudged Pengarron. Most men in his position would have exacted a harsh revenge upon any who opposed them. Though she knew he would not hesitate to carry out his threat to kill them if she disobeyed him, he had shown unusual clemency. For that, she was prepared to drop some of her antagonism and give way to her growing curiosity.

'Are we close to Pengarron Castle, my lord?'

'In less than an hour we shall be there.'

'I confess I know little of the Lady Gwyneth, your brother's widow. From her name, I take it she is the daughter of a Welsh lord?'

'Not a Welsh lord, but a Welsh prince,' he corrected with a harsh laugh. 'An obscure one, but from the way she sometimes acts, you would think it was from Merlin himself.'

From the dryness of his tone, she guessed that Lady Gwyneth was an encumbrance Pengarron could well live without! Again she was prompted to ask more. 'How did your brother die?'

The pain that creased the fine lines at the corners of his eyes made her regret her inquisitiveness.

'Your pardon, my lord, my question was tactless,' she said hastily. 'Your brother's death must have been a shock, and very sudden. Giles knew nothing of it.'

'Edmund was struck down by a fever. An ill chance, when I had known him survive battle wounds to which other men would have succumbed. Lady Gwyneth is skilled with herbs and potions, but it proved beyond her power to save him.'

'You must miss him greatly. Your father spoke often of the closeness between you.'

Pengarron looked straight ahead, his profile coldly unnerving, and she thought for a moment that he would refuse to answer. Then, in a gruff voice, he said, 'As boys we were close, but in later years we led different lives. For a short time in France I thought us close again—until Edmund married. Lady Gwyneth is a beautiful and determined woman. She missed Wales, and so they returned to Pengarron. After my father died, I did not see Edmund again.'

He eased his weight forward in the saddle as though conscious that he had said more than he intended. 'I have missed Pengarron, though. It's strange how a place calls to you from distant lands.' He looked sideways at her, his voice taunting. 'It's not only the inviting smile of a woman that can lead a man astray! Wait until you see Pengarron. Perhaps then you will understand.'

'I doubt I shall see my future prison with the same enthusiasm as you do,' she answered tartly, feeling the need to armour herself against the passion glowing in his eyes as he spoke of his home.

Instantly his stare was guarded. 'I repeat, you're no prisoner! And you need not fear you will lack female company at the castle. Lady Gwyneth's ward, her cousin Bronwyn, will be there. She's little more than a child— a delightful creature, somewhat headstrong—like yourself.'

A smile touched his lips as he spoke, and Morganna experienced a sharp tug of pain in her breast. He was obviously fond of the young Welsh girl!

'Do not trouble yourself as to my welfare, my lord. I doubt my brother has so generous and considerate a gaoler.'

His eyes flashed dangerously. 'You must have considered your fate, lady, should your brother lose everything upon a whim of his Majesty. Perhaps, then, I will regard you as my captive. There's many a score unsettled between us. Does not a mercenary expect payment for his services?'

The insolence with which his glance appraised her figure made his meaning painfully clear.

'Your strength is greater than mine,' she replied coldly. 'You are no different from Linsdale if you take that which would never willingly be given.'

The bold assurance in his eyes did not waver. 'Are you certain you would be unwilling, Morganna?'

He rode off before she had recovered enough from his audacity to find her voice, and was still smarting when a distant fanfare came to her ears. Through the trees she could see castle battlements, and as she watched, the balck and gold Pengarron standard was unfurled upon the highest watch-tower, announcing their lord's arrival. The trees thinned. The castle, with its six great drumtowers, rose out of the granite rock as though it were a part of the great ravine over which it stood guard. Formidable, impressive, it dominated the cliff-top. Pengarron's eyrie was as prepossessing as its master!

Cheering villagers lined the roadway as they swept past, but once inside the castle, Morganna was struck by its stillness. The courtyard was remarkably uncluttered after the confusion she was used to at Daneton. Nothing was out of place; even the mounting-block by the timber-framed hall was freshly whitewashed.

Yet there was evidence of the ruin Giles had mentioned. Her sharp eyes noted repairs made during recent years: first to the battlements, which at one time must have sustained a prolonged attack, and then to the hall

itself, where glazed windows replaced the earlier
wooden shutters. But it was the central square tower, its
top storey roofless and crumbling, which reminded her
that this was to be her prison, and that England was
likely to be launched into an internal war.

They halted before the steps leading to the first-floor
entrance of the hall. A hush fell upon the villagers, who
had followed them into the courtyard, as a tall, slender
woman, wearing a black gown and plain, almost nun-
like veil and wimple, appeared. Lady Gwyneth moved
with the grace of a swan, and her pale complexion with
its dark-arched brows was a beautiful though impassive
mask. She paused, though not quite long enough for the
gesture to become insolent, before curtsying in homage
to Lord Pengarron.

'Well come, my lord!' Her voice was rich, like the
music of a harp. She showed no hint of the resentment
she must be feeling at this intrusion to what so long had
been her domain. 'Pengarron Castle has been too long
denied its master.'

'God's greeting, Gwyneth!' He dismounted, nodded
to Ifor to dismiss the men to their barracks, and walked
across to Morganna. 'I have not come alone. Let quarters be prepared for the Lady Morganna Barnett. She is
my . . . She is here under my protection,' he amended
quickly, and cast a significant look at Morganna as she
slid to the ground at his side. Taking her arm, he guided
her to the steps.

'Your protection?' The Lady Gwyneth's almond-
shaped eyes slanted with a flash of suspicion.

'Her brother, the Marquess of Radford, is suffering
the King's displeasure,' Pengarron declared ominously.
'The Lady Morganna is a guest here.'

'Radford!' Lady Gwyneth clearly recognised the
name.

They had reached the entrance porch, and Pengarron's fingers tightened upon Morganna's arm. 'I have

retaken Daneton. The Lady Morganna is to be treated at all times as befits her rank.'

Lady Gwyneth studied Morganna. From the coolness of the widow's gaze, she knew she was being assessed as to the exact degree of courtesy etiquette demanded. At that moment a feminine shriek of delight came from the entrance. There was a blur of pink silk and the overpowering scent of jasmine as a young woman threw herself into Pengarron's arms.

'Ralph! Oh, Ralph, you're home!' The longing was evident in the impassioned greeting.

Morganna stiffened with shock. This seductive, voluptuous creature, whose lips pressed so fervently against his neck, could surely not be little Bronwyn?

'By my oath, Bronwyn!' He disengaged the young girl's arms from about his neck and laughed with obvious pleasure. 'A woman grown! And a beauty at that.'

'Bronwyn!' Lady Gwyneth admonished. 'That's no way to greet your liege!'

'Most undignified!' he added, the laughter still evident in his voice.

Seeing the admiration with which Pengarron regarded the girl, an unpleasant burning sensation gripped Morganna's chest. When Bronwyn sank demurely into a curtsy, the discomfort grew to a searing pain. Even though the girl's eyes were modestly lowered, there was little innocence in the beautiful face. The coquettish smile would have done credit to an accomplished courtesan, and Morganna's instinctive reaction was strong dislike. The feeling intensified at Bronwyn's feigned humility after her obeisance to Lord Pengarron.

'My most noble lord, I crave pardon,' Bronwyn said sweetly, a dimple appearing at the corner of her mouth. 'You told me once you cared not for ceremony. You have been away a long time.'

'Two years, minx!' he answered, raising her up. 'Is this truly our little Bronwyn? Even the freckles have gone.

You must be all of fifteen summers now, far too old to hurl yourself at an aged cousin! What will the Lady Morganna think of your manners?'

'Oh, but we're not truly cousins,' Bronwyn began slyly, then, as she realised what Pengarron had said, the change in her was immediate. Her smile faded to a sullen grimace, her brown eyes blackening with hostility as they rested upon Morganna. The vehemence of Bronwyn's look so startled her that when her hand was taken by Lord Pengarron, she did not pull it free.

'Allow me to present the Lady Morganna Barnett —my future wife.'

Shock robbed Morganna of breath. Until now she had been convinced that he had forsaken his claim to her hand in marriage, but when she tried to jerk her fingers from his, they were gripped mercilessly.

'My lord, it was agreed that . . .'

'That we await your brother's release,' he brutally cut across her protest. 'So as to receive his blessing before the wedding takes place.'

His eyes warned her against denying his words. Aware of the stares of the two women upon her, she hesitated. Was this another of his tricks to humilate her? It had to be! He did not truly want her. There was no gentleness in his gaze, only the will to be obeyed. But to refute his words now would cause an undignified scene, and she had no intention of subjecting herself to that. Later, when they were alone, she would make him renounce them.

With a scathing glare at him, she masked her expression as she turned to face the women. In her travel-stained cloak and gown, she knew herself at a disadvantage. Bronwyn pouted, her glittering eyes unwelcoming. But it was the critical stare of Lady Gwyneth which made her more uncomfortable. Then, to her surprise, Lady Gwyneth smiled, and came forward to kiss her cheek.

'It's time Ralph took himself a bride! Well come, Lady Morganna,' she said warmly, and with a sweeping gesture of pride continued, 'Pengarron has need of an heir.'

That she referred to the estate and not to the man, Morganna found curious. Or had she misunderstood Lady Gwyneth?

There was no mistaking the sadness in her green eyes when the woman added, 'I was not blessed with children.'

For an instant Pengarron's hand tightened over Morganna's, before he released her. Glancing from him to Lady Gwyneth, Morganna sensed rather than saw the antagonism between them. Had the Lady Gwyneth's reference to her barrenness been deliberate, reminding him that he would still be a lowly knight had she borne a son? What had caused the rift between them?

Bronwyn suddenly claimed everyone's attention by a frustrated wail. 'With all this talk of brides and heirs,' she said spitefully, 'one would think it was a love-match! I don't doubt the Barnett dowry has something to do with it.'

Pengarron's hand rested protectively upon Morganna's shoulder. 'That's enough, Bronwyn!' he snapped. 'Go to your room until you've learned to treat the Lady Morganna with the respect her position demands.'

Bronwyn paled, tears filling her eyes. Then, whirling, she ran back into the hall and disappeared.

'The child needs disciplining, Gwyneth.' Pengarron frowned.

'She will apologise to the Lady Morganna.'

The mention of her dowry unexpectedly wounded Morganna, yet even so she understood the young girl's pain. Clearly, she was infatuated with Lord Pengarron. Whatever her own feelings towards Bronwyn or Pengarron, the girl was Lady Gwyneth's ward, and to repay the older woman's friendliness to her, Morganna resolved to ease the friction between her and her brother-in-law.

'My lord, I'm sure Bronwyn meant no offence,' Morganna told him. 'She's young, and the news of our betrothal was a shock to her.'

'She's old enough to know her place!' His eyes glittered. 'She insulted you. I'll not permit that.'

Following Lady Gwyneth into the hall, Morganna's heart felt as though it had been squeezed dry. He defended her only because he would see an insult to her, his betrothed, as a slur upon his own name. Too tired to try to understand his motives further, she said in an undertone that would not reach Lady Gwyneth,

'I don't know what trickery you have planned, Lord Pengarron, but I am no pawn to be used for your amusement! I shall fight you . . .'

She broke off as she noticed the splendour of her surroundings, and her step slowed in wonder. Giles had ridiculed Pengarron Castle as a ruin, but it was far from that. The hall was decorated with the richness of a royal palace, colourful tapestries decorated the walls, and on the polished oak tops of the long tables the pewter and silver gleamed. Obviously Lord Pengarron was not the impoverished mercenary she had at first assumed.

'We shall eat in an hour,' he declared.

An excited bark, followed by the sound of scraping claws against stone, made him swing round to the door, his eyes crinkling with pleasure. A grey wolfhound bounded into view, to halt by the entrance, his tail wagging furiously. Pengarron rubbed his hand across his stubbled chin, saying gruffly, 'So, Gwyneth, you still won't allow the dogs into your prized hall! Now I have returned, Wulfric will follow me where he pleases.'

He whistled the dog, who danced forward to circle his master, and Lady Gwyeth's thin mouth set with disgust.

'The orderliness of the castle is a tribute to the Earl and yourself, Lady Gwyneth,' Morganna said, trying to ease the tension, but received a cold piercing look from him for her trouble.

'As Ralph's dependant, I do my best to make his home presentable!' Lady Gwyneth continued to frown as she watched the wolfhound sitting obediently at Pengarron's feet. 'Though, as a soldier, he's more interested in the smooth running of the stables and armoury than in the disruption his men cause to the living-quarters.'

Pengarron straightened from ruffling the dog's ears, his glance as it flickered to Lady Gwyneth warning her that his conduct would not be questioned. 'And it's to those stables and armoury that I must now go. I shall leave you ladies to become further acquainted.'

The sardonic twist of his mouth cautioned Morganna against defying him as he slid his hand along her arm to take her fingers and press them to his lips. The warmth of their touch sent a flame of humiliation through her, and with an effort she controlled the urge to snatch her hand away, contenting herself by reproaching him with her eyes.

He grinned provocatively. 'In four days it will be the feast of St Swithun. A good time to present the future Countess to her people!'

Panic-stricken, Morganna stared after his departing figure. This, then, was no game. He was intent upon marrying her!

CHAPTER SEVEN

'MY DEAR, you're quite pale!' Lady Gwyneth said anxiously to Morganna. 'I'll show you to your chambers. Rest awhile, and I'll send you a reviving posset.'

By the time they reached the rooms set aside for her, Morganna began to feel calmer. It was impossible not to respond to the friendship Lady Gwyneth offered when she was feeling so isolated from her family and home. As she followed her hostess into a neat chamber, her eyes widened with delight. Though sparsely furnished, it was comfortable and luxurious. The tiled floor was patterned in ochre and black, and silk hangings painted with scenes from Arthurian legends decorated the walls. Through an inner door she saw a large bed hung with green velvet and tasselled with gold.

'These rooms are lovely, Lady Gwyneth!' she exclaimed.

'Please, let it be just Gwyneth? It's so long since I had a woman nearer my own age to talk to. Bronwyn is delightful, but so full of energy. I suppose now I must talk to Ralph of her marriage. Something must be arranged soon. In truth, I had hoped . . .' She fluttered her hands in a regretful gesture, and Morganna realised she had hoped he and Bronwyn would marry. Lady Gwyneth smiled as she continued sweetly, 'Of course, in the circumstances, it's only right that Ralph has chosen you for his bride. Pray, forgive Bronwyn? She is young and impressionable, and he has become her hero. I hope you understand?'

Morganna smothered a bitter laugh. 'Lord Pengarron is a handsome man and his feats of arms are legendary. I can imagine how a young girl could become infatuated by him!'

'I knew you would understand.' Lady Gwyneth's stare was searching.

For a moment Morganna had allowed her guard to slip. Had she revealed more to this woman than she had intended?

Just then, a tall figure appeared in the doorway, and, involuntarily, Morganna stepped back in alarm. A thick-set giant, with straight, dark hair falling past his shoulders stooped to enter, and touched Lady Gwyneth on the arm.

'Owain! You've given the Lady Morganna a fright!' She laughed softly as she looked at the man who, from the fine wool of his long russet gown, was obviously a servant of some standing. He made a movement indicating that Lady Gwyneth should follow him.

'Owain is my personal servant,' Lady Gwyneth explained. 'He's mute. His tongue was severed when he was a child. For many years he was slave to an Ottoman nobleman who visited the Burgundian Court, and Edmund brought him for me as a bodyguard when we were in France. Since then, Owain has proved an invaluable and faithful servant.'

'His name is Welsh, but surely he is not?' Morganna smiled tremulously, awed by the size of the black-haired servant.

'He answered only to "Slave",' replied Gwyneth. 'I named him Owain. I'll leave you now to prepare for the feast. If you desire, a tub and hot water could be sent up for you to bathe.'

An hour later, refreshed from her bath, Morganna entered the hall with Jocelyn a step behind her. The dazzling brightness from the burning cressets and torches showed the room already filled with retainers. As Jocelyn left her to sit with the other tiring-women,

Morganna was ushered to the dais. Pengarron was already seated at the centre of the high table with Lady Gwyneth on his left. Unaware of Morganna's approach, he leant sideways, his head bent, engrossed in conversation with Bronwyn on his right. The girl's rich auburn hair was unbound, and instead of a fillet, she wore a garland of gillyflowers.

Suddenly Pengarron threw back his head and laughed at something Bronwyn had said, startling Morganna by the change in the stern lines of his face: he looked carefree and much younger. She was so used to his cool reserve or sardonic mockery that she had come to think of him as older than Giles, instead of five years younger.

An unreasonable stab of resentment possessed her as she turned her attention towards the young girl, although girl was hardly the word to describe the voluptuous creature draping herself on Pengarron's arm. Bronwyn might be all of three years younger than herself, but she was no innocent maid; of that Morganna was certain. And Pengarron, devil take him, was enjoying every moment of the chit's seductive play of her wiles!

Belatedly, his glance fell upon Morganna, and the laughter died on his lips and his expression sobered. He spoke quickly to Bronwyn, who threw a hostile glare in her direction and with ill grace moved to seat herself on the far side of Gwyneth. Pengarron stood up and, to Morganna's surprise, came towards her as she approached the dais. It was a singular honour.

Used to seeing him in peasant's guise or half-armour, and to regarding him as a mere mercenary, Morganna was unprepared for the effect on her of his courtier's dress of rich velvet. The sweeping dagged sleeves of his surcoat were as fashionably elegant as any Giles possessed. Her throat seemed oddly dry, and her heart pounded unevenly at meeting his unswerving gaze. When he held out his hand to her, his long tapering fingers were cool against her overheated skin. He raised her hand to his lips, and a curious tingling reached her stomach.

'Your eyes sparkle like amethysts! I would have others see it as the light of excitement, and not the rebellion I know smoulders in your heart,' he warned softly. 'From the time you were eight years old, you have been mine, Morganna. Did not our fathers will it so?'

'My brother could not force me to marry the Earl of Linsdale,' she answered with barbed sweetness as he led her to the seat beside his chair. 'And I have no intention of marrying you!'

'There you are mistaken, my lady!' His full lips twisted into a sardonic grin. 'I have decreed you will be presented to my people on St Swithun's Day. After that, you will have one week to accept your destiny. Then we shall be married.'

Morganna's mind raced to overcome her growing panic. So little time. How could she escape? Once outside the castle walls, she would be hopelessly lost.

Something of her alarm must have shown on her face, because, unexpectedly, Pengarron frowned as he presented to her a slice of capon from the plate they shared. She took it from the flat of his knife, unsettled by his closeness. The spiced poultry could have been straw as she tried to swallow against the dryness of her throat. He passed her the large goblet, which again they must share. Accidentally their hands brushed, and Morganna's breath hung in her throat at the burning thrill palpitating through her arm.

'Why do you fight me?' His eyes sparkled like golden wine as his voice lowered to an intimate whisper. 'Whether we like it or not, we are trapped by the contract made by our fathers.'

Unsteadily she lifted the goblet to her lips, needing time to compose herself before answering. She was acutely aware that his lips had drunk from the same rim, and as she swallowed the sweet wine, it reminded her of the devastating potency of his kisses. Just what trickery was he planning?

If only he would not look at her in a way which promised her the world, and more, it would be easier to consign him to the devil. Why, oh why, did her pulses quicken towards him, of all men? She had given her word to Giles, and she must never respond to the fire now consuming her blood.

His smile was assured, no doubt mistaking her silence for agreement.

'Come, Morganna, the minstrels shall play while we dance.'

For a moment she looked at the lean brown hand held out to her, and was sorely tempted. Pride triumphed. It was her duty to defy him. It was torture enduring his closeness at the table. But to dance with him—when their hands would constantly touch—what if she were to forget he was her enemy? Her honour, her loyalty to Giles would be in jeopardy.

'I fear, my lord,' she evaded, 'I have not your stamina. The strain of the journey has tired me.'

She saw his eyes flash dangerously and could not resist adding, to test his reaction, 'I'm sure Bronwyn will be delighted to step a measure with you. She was entertaining you most capably before I arrived.'

'So, lady, you would have me slight my betrothed before all present, by dancing first with another!' His voice was low and lethal, sending an icy tremor through her. 'As you say, Bronwyn is most beguiling. She shall sing for us.'

He summoned a page and spoke to him. The boy scampered off to fetch a lute, which he presented to Bronwyn. Blushing prettily, Bronwyn looked at Pengarron and then at Morganna, a cunning smile touching her lips. Hips swaying provocatively, she sauntered to the front of the dais and seated herself in front of him.

With his reprimand still ringing in her ears, Morganna found her presence snubbed by Bronwyn as she began to sing a passionate love song, her eyes boldly inviting as she gazed up at her liege lord.

A hush fell upon the hall as Bronwyn sang. Pengarron sat forward, chin propped on his hand, listening intently.

'Is her voice not sweeter than a nightingale's?' he enthused when the last notes faded. 'The child is accomplished. She'll break many hearts once she goes to Court.'

'Bronwyn is no child,' Morganna replied sharply. 'She is young, beautiful, and therefore vulnerable. Before she attends Court, she would be advised to curb her boldness. There are many courtiers who would take advantage of such an open invitation.'

Pengarron looked sidelong at Morganna, his eyes eagle bright and penetrating. Disconcerted, she looked down at the platter and selected a portion of game pie. She could feel him gauging her thoughts; in future, she must guard herself against him. It was the casualness of his charm which disarmed her, often catching her unawares.

'Yes, very beautiful—and more vulnerable than she knows,' he repeated abstractedly. 'An enchantress.'

When Morganna looked up, he was again staring raptly at Bronwyn, who had begun another song. This time, she sang in her native language, and her languishing gaze fixed on Pengarron made Morganna's fingers clench round the stem of the goblet. A blind man could not mistake the longing in the passionate, throbbing voice, which seemed to be weaving a seductive web around him.

Were others aware of what was happening? Morganna scanned the hall. Many eyes were turned speculatively upon the singer who so intensely captured their lord's attention. Barnaby, the messenger who had brought the news of Giles, smiled encouragingly at her, so perhaps, after all, she was not entirely without friends in Wales.

But as her glance returned to Pengarron, who was still absorbed in watching Bronwyn, her stomach clenched again, making eating impossible. She dragged her eyes from the couple, to see Gwyneth raise an eyebrow knowingly at Owain, who was serving her wine. Clearly, the giant was no ordinary servant. Puzzled, she noticed Owain move among the pages. Was she imagining it, or did the young men keep their distance and avoid looking at him?

In an effort to shake off her unease and to ignore Bronwyn's rudeness, Morganna again scanned the hall. There was a definite tension in the atmosphere. From the way some of the servants glanced furtively towards the high table, she was convinced that all was not as it should be.

'The entertainment does not please you?' Pengarron regarded Morganna sternly, as her fingers thoughtfully rubbed the surface of her cross. 'My people would honour their future Countess.'

'My thoughts were elsewhere, Lord Pengarron,' she parried.

Bronwyn's song came to an end, and he beckoned to her to come forward. With a coquettish smile, she waited expectantly before him.

'Charming as your singing is,' he said quietly, 'in future you will not insult the Lady Morganna or exclude her from any gathering by speaking or singing in Welsh. You will now apologise to her for your ill manners.'

Bronwyn stiffened, her smile freezing to a grimace. For an instant Morganna thought she would defy Pengarron. Her flashing brown eyes slitting with hatred, Bronwyn bowed her head and made a semblance of a curtsy to Morganna, her voice grudging.

'Your pardon, Lady Morganna.'

Morganna nodded her acceptance, knowing she

had made an enemy.

The minstrels struck up a lively tune, but as Morganna watched the mummers capering in their huge animal heads, her mood remained heavy and the meal dragged. She was too aware of Pengarron's closeness, and that she was being feted tonight as his future bride. It all seemed unreal. Under lowered lashes she glanced sideways at him and noticed that, although he appeared relaxed, there was a sharpness to his gaze as it swept the hall.

Why did the slight frown drawing down his dark brows sadden her? He had spoken so proudly of Pengarron. After his long absence, did the castle no longer hold its former charm? Or did he, too, notice the tense atmosphere and that the sound of laughter was often strained?

By her second day at Pengarron Castle, Morganna felt as though she was wavering on the edge of a precipice. Surrounded by the preparation for St Swithun's feast and all it implied, she was beginning to see everything as bleak and sinister. The continued nearness of Pengarron himself threatened her peace of mind, and constantly she had to remind herself of her vow to Giles and remember that he was her enemy.

She left her rooms earlier than usual, determined to make Pengarron renounce their betrothal. Each time she had tried to raise the subject, Bronwyn, never far from his side, would appear, drawing his attention by flirting and laughing with him. As she descended the spiral steps from her turret chambers, Morganna's temper quickened at hearing the girl's voice from the corridor below.

'I tell you, Nesta, she'll not have him! I rode to the alder grove this morning and the omens were good. These will ensure that he's mine.'

Morganna stepped into the corridor as Bronwyn, carrying a posy of flowers and accompanied by Lady Gwyneth's maid, was about to enter her own chambers.

Nesta looked embarrassedly away on seeing her. Certain that Bronwyn had been talking about Pengarron, Morganna spoke coolly.

'You've risen early, Bronwyn. The dew is still upon your flowers.'

She suddenly noticed the sprigs of henbane and valerian among the gillyflowers, and lost patience with the girl's infatuation for the Earl. The two herbs were used for love-potions, but did the silly creature not know that henbane was poisonous?

'Is this how you would win a man's heart, by useless potions which could poison him?' Angrily she snatched the posy from Bronwyn's hand. 'If you stopped acting like a spoilt child for long enough, you would see that Lord Pengarron cares nothing for me. I have no intention of marrying him.'

Bronwyn paled, but her eyes remained bright with cunning. 'Do you think I'm blind? I have seen the way he watches you. You say you care nothing for him, but why then are you so angry? You're jealous of the attention he pays me.'

The sound of a firm assured tread halted Morganna's reply. From the way the girl provocatively smoothed her gown over her hips, she knew it was Lord Pengarron who approached.

'Do I hear quarrelling?' he said sternly. 'I came to invite you both to hunt before the feast. But if you intend to spend the morning bickering, I shall ride alone.'

'We were not quarrelling, my lord.' Bronwyn answered in honeyed tones, her eyes wide with innocence. 'I was just concerned for your safety. I noticed the Lady Morganna had picked some flowers, and among them herbs to soften a lover's heart. I was warning her that henbane is poisonous, but the Lady Morganna refused to listen to my advice.'

Bronwyn's lips thinned maliciously as she stared at Morganna, adding slyly, 'Perhaps the Lady Morganna fears that since your return to Pengarron, my lord, you have been distracted—that you have not been so attentive towards her as before.'

Morganna glared from Bronwyn to the posy she held in her hands and could cheerfully have throttled the scheming creature! There was no point in denying the lies. It would only make her look guilty.

'Have I been neglecting you, Morganna?' Pengarron said, apparently amused at the suggestion. 'What need has the Lady Morganna of love-philtres when her beauty enslaves me to her will?'

He took the flowers from her stiffened fingers and gave them to Nesta. Looking quizzically at Bronwyn, he laughed. 'The truth now, child! Is it not your heart which is set upon one of the pages? The hem of your gown is wet from walking through the dew, not the Lady Morganna's. Go and ready yourself if we are to ride.'

As Bronwyn disappeared into her room, he took Morganna's elbow and led her away from the open door, saying darkly, 'It would not be a love-philtre you made for me, would it? Somehow I don't think even you would resort to poison, for all it's a woman's way of ridding herself of an enemy. Or would you?'

Morganna moistened her lips, which had dried from shock. How could he think her capable of that? She stared up into his set, angry face, appalled he would believe such ill of her.

'I do not wish you harmed.'

From the half-smile tugging at his lips, she knew he had deliberately goaded her into revealing the emotions she guarded so closely.

'Accept your fate. Your attitude to Bronwyn is markedly cool, but you will find her a pleasant companion if you give her a chance. We leave at once to hunt.'

He rejoined Bronwyn, who had lost no time in collecting her riding-whip and gloves, and together they walked along the corridor. When the girl's seductive laughter drifted back to Morganna, renewed fury made her clench her fists with impotent rage. The dull ache about her heart could not possibly be jealousy . . . It was wounded pride! For a moment she was tempted to defy Pengarron's summons, but thought better of it. Besides, she enjoyed the hunt. Collecting her own gloves and whip, she arrived in the courtyard at the same time as Lady Gwyneth.

'Which way do we ride?' Lady Gwyneth asked as they mounted the waiting horses.

'I thought to the west,' Pengarron answered. 'There's always game aplenty by the waterfall.'

'Has the bailiff not told you of the landslides along the river bank?' Lady Gwyneth's voice was unusually shrill. 'The ground could be dangerous.'

'It was not reported to me.' He cast a sharp look at her. 'What other matters have I not been told about?'

'I did not see the need to burden you with little details,' Gwyneth replied haughtily. 'Since your arrival, you have been occupied with more important matters.'

'I regard everything that happens upon my land as important,' he said with unmistakable warning. 'I suppose, then, we had better hunt to the north.'

Lady Gwyneth smiled wanly at Morganna as they rode side by side. 'I seem to have angered Ralph. Was I wrong not to trouble him with such a small matter when his stay here is so brief?'

'You did what you thought best,' Morganna told her. 'It is natural for Lord Pengarron to be concerned for his estate. He takes the welfare of his people seriously.'

At the flicker of annoyance marring Lady Gwyneth's brow, Morganna wondered whether she had deliberately not mentioned the landslide to Pengarron. Something seemed to be troubling her. Was it Ralph's popularity with the villagers? It was clear that the people loved him, for they cheered and waved as he rode past. Yet as she and Lady Gwyneth approached, the cheering faded.

Lady Gwyneth seemed not to notice, however. Was it then herself the people disapproved of? Had they wanted their lord to marry his Welsh cousin instead of an Englishwoman?

Watching him and Bronwyn riding together, Morganna admitted they made a handsome couple, and the heaviness round her heart increased. He deserved better than a creature as shallow as Bronwyn! Morganna stared at the tasselled leather of Sweet Eglantine's harness, puzzled that she should be so disturbed at the thought of him marrying another. Surely she did not want him for herself . . . or did she?

'Why do you not ride with Ralph? Your place is at his side.' Lady Gwyneth broke across Morganna's thoughts. 'Take care lest you lose him to another woman!'

Morganna's head shot up. 'I told you how he abducted me. I am here against my will. He's my enemy—he has proved that!'

'But have you considered why he acted as he did? It is out of character. He should be with Bolingbroke now, not here at Pengarron. Why do you think he stays?'

'I would have thought Bronwyn provides the answer to that!' Morganna looked stonily in the direction of Pengarron, who was laughing as he rode at the girl's side.

Lady Gwyneth sighed. 'Bronwyn could never bring Pengarron the fortune you do, or hope to match your quick wits and courage. You'll bear worthy sons.

Embarrassed by her bluntness, Morganna became uneasy. Her pride and possessiveness in the castle and estate became more apparent with each passing day. All too often Lady Gwyneth spoke of the estate and not of the man, when she talked of Pengarron's future.

'Have you thought of your fate, Morganna, should Bolingbroke succeed?' she went on relentlessly. 'King Richard's power will be curbed—there are even some

who would see him deposed. Should that happen, the
Marquess of Radford will need the support of men such
as Ralph. Is that not good reason for you to marry him?'

Morganna's hands tightened over the reins, her uncertainty increasing. Was it possible that the Duke of
Lancaster could become so powerful? Or did Lady
Gwyneth fear it would be the Earl of Pengarron who
would need Giles's protection to safeguard what was left
of his estates? Why else should she be so eager for the
wedding, after which she would have to relinquish her
title of Countess to the new one?

Her thoughts broke off as Pengarron rode back to join
them, calling for the falconers to bring up the hawks.
With a peregrine settled on her wrist, Morganna looked
across at him as he removed the hood from his hawk and
with a smooth, decisive thrust of his arm, launched the
bird into flight. His face relaxed. Eyes shielded against
the sun's brightness, he watched the bird until it made its
strike at a fleeing hare.

He turned with a smile to Morganna as she prepared
her own bird, and her fingers trembled slightly on the
lacings of its hood as she felt his eyes burning into her.
Loosing the hawk, her heart raced as she watched it
swoop over the ground to strike cleanly at its prey.

'You handle the bird well and with confidence,
my lady,' Pengarron said admiringly. 'Not so poor
Bronwyn.'

He nodded with amusement at the girl, who was
flinching from her hawk's flapping wings. When the bird
soared upwards, it landed in the highest branches of the
nearest tree. From there, it would take some time for the
falconer to get it down.

'You should follow the Lady Morganna's example,'
Pengarron called out to Bronwyn with a laugh. 'Your
movements are too jerky. You upset the birds.'

Bronwyn's face twisted with fury. 'Must you always
compare me to her? First my hand is too heavy on the

reins—unlike the Lady Morganna. Then you say I slouch in the saddle. I am as good a horsewoman as she—just you watch!'

Cruelly pulling her horse round, Bronwyn brought her whip down across its back and set off at a gallop across the field.

'Go after her, Ralph!' Lady Gwyneth cried. 'She'll hurt herself.'

Pengarron had already started forward, and feeling partly to blame for Bronwyn's behaviour, Morganna suggested, 'I think we'd best follow, in case Bronwyn takes a tumble.'

At a more leisurely pace, they followed him, and as they entered a grove of trees, Morganna saw his horse cropping some grass. Lady Gwyneth's startled gasp drew her attention to the two figures on the ground. Bronwyn lay beneath Pengarron, her arms locked in a lovers' embrace as they kissed. Morganna turned away in disgust, heading back to the castle. Knowing Bronwyn, she suspected the baggage had feigned injury, and when he had bent over her, thrown her arms about his neck and kissed him. But, from what she had glimpsed, he had not been resisting!

She heard but was scarcely aware of the hunting party catching up with her. Lady Gwyneth rode in silence, and of Pengarron there was no sign. Not that she expected him to account to her for his actions. Did she not know to her cost the ease with which he succumbed to the temptation of a woman lying with him in a wooded glade?

Going straight to her rooms when they reached the castle, Morganna called out to Jocelyn to lay out her ceremonial mantle and finest gown. It was time she confronted Pengarron. And, when she did so, she would face him as the sister of one of England's most powerful magnates—a woman he could not browbeat or bully into submission.

CHAPTER EIGHT

RALPH STARED BLEAKLY out of his window in the bastion tower. As he heard the messenger from Daneton leave the room, he passed his hand tiredly across his chin. Everything was coming to a head faster than he had expected. He had come to Pengarron as a place of refuge from the troubles he must shortly face, but instead, from the moment of his arrival, he had felt a change there.

Distrust underlay the cheers from his people. When questioned, they were evasive, their eyes darkening with fear. In time he would win their confidence, as any new master must. He had lessened the number of days, imposed by Gwyneth, that they must toil upon his land. In her fervour to return Pengarron to its former glory, she had demanded too much from the people and lost their loyalty. Whereas he had expected trouble from her, he had found her strangely obedient to his wishes.

It was Bronwyn who was proving a complication he had not considered. The lecture he had given her after the hunt had sobered her, but it was obvious that a marriage would have to be arranged before her wildness led her into mischief.

A movement by the scaffolding that was being erected around the ruined King's Tower caught his eye. What was Owain doing, shaking his head at the masons? The workers had their instructions. Was this Gwyneth's doing, causing dissent because she had not been consulted on the rebuilding? Ralph frowned. That servant was a strange one. He could not help being mute, but he had an uncomfortable way of looking at people which upset the other servants. And where did he go early each morning when he rode out of the castle? Barnaby would have to keep a watch on Gwyneth's servant.

The men were still awaiting orders, and Ralph felt reassured as his glance rested upon Barnaby, brightly clad in green and gold parti-hose as befitted his guise as a troubadour. Any day now, he knew he himself would be summoned by Bolingbroke. With Barnaby as his eyes at Pengarron, his interests would be safeguarded.

'Summon the Lady Morganna to attend me,' he ordered Barnaby. When the troubadour left, he led his officers into an adjoining room to give them details of the changes needed to the festivities that afternoon.

Morganna adjusted the weight of her mantle upon her shoulders, satisfied she was dressed in a manner that would show Pengarron she was his adversary. Her scarlet and gold gown was bordered with a design of crescent moons—the Barnett colours and insignia. At her shoulder, holding the mantle in place, was a gold clasp. Her gaze lingered upon the brooch, where the maxim 'Stand Firm' set in emeralds shone brightly back at her, restoring her confidence.

Barnaby, having delivered Pengarron's summons, was pacing the outer chamber. With a smile Morganna noticed the way Jocelyn's eyes constantly strayed to the doorway—the maid seemed quite taken with the handsome troubadour! As Morganna approached, Barnaby paused in mid-stride, and the admiration in his gaze calmed her nervousness. Could she hope for the same effect upon Lord Pengarron? Somehow she knew that no woman, however beautiful or high ranking, could earn his favour by appearance alone.

In silence Morganna followed the troubadour as he led the way to Pengarron's chambers. Upon entering the bastion tower, she was immediately struck by the masculine atmosphere. Dogs sprawled on the rushes, and assorted weapons and pieces of armour were stacked against the walls; but it was the smells of which she was most aware: leather, old parchment, the dogs, and sunlight on warm metal. She was taken off guard, suddenly homesick for Daneton and Giles's room, which had smelt like this.

On the first floor she was led into a large room, and Barnaby bowed to her. 'If you will wait, my lady, I'll tell his lordship you're here.'

Her head crowded with the accusations she intended to level at Pengarron, Morganna looked critically about the room. In one corner his personal achievements—his shield painted with a striking eagle and the large tourney helm topped with the same device—were formidable reminders of the warrior who would break her to his will. On a wall hung the two-handed sword 'Fidélité', carried by all the Earls of Pengarron since the time of the Conqueror. She remembered the stories her father had told her as a child, and her heart fluttered alarmingly. The Warrenders were an ancient and noble family, while her own father had been little more than a country baron when he had arranged her marriage. Even Giles in his newly-won status could never truly match the honour that had been the Warrenders' for centuries. A reluctant, disloyal thought lodged in her mind. Was that why Giles resented Pengarron and all he stood for?

It was then, through a second doorway, that she saw him. His head was bent close to Ifor's as they studied a linen map spread across a table. Barnaby waited for him to finish speaking, and announced Morganna's presence.

As Pengarron turned towards her, a light flared briefly in his eyes, as evocative as it was challenging, and he dismissed his men. For a moment she forgot the arguments she intended to use against him as, handsome and commanding, he sauntered towards her. Outwardly, he was all she had dreamt her husband would be!

'If I did not know you so well, Morganna, I would think your finery was to do me honour.' He leaned back against a tall chest and folded his arms, regarding her mockingly. 'However, I suspect you wear it as armour. Is it against me or your own emotions that you would arm yourself? The time has come to accept what must be.'

'Like a sacrificial lamb!' Contemptuously she met the amusement shining in his eyes. 'I do not accept defeat so easily. I shall publicly denounce you, and declare to all that I am here against my will!'

Pengarron leaned forward, his eyes darkening to the colour of brandywine. 'It could take years to break the contract our fathers sealed,' he said measuredly. 'During which time, neither of us would be free to marry. Your name will never be free of scandal—Linsdale has seen to that. Is that what you want? By marrying you, Morganna, I would spare you dishonour.'

His nearness unnerved her, and she restrained her impulse to step back. It would seem like a retreat. The weight of the jewelled headdress made her neck ache as she was forced to tilt her head back to meet his stare. A full head taller than herself, his eyes burned into hers, until it seemed her very life-force throbbed in reluctant acknowledgment of his will. Then he lowered his lids, the thick dark lashes casting a shadow across his high cheeks and softening the hawk-like countenance.

'I would make amends for the wrong I did you,' he said simply.

'Amends!' she repeated, dazed by the change in his behaviour. Her breathing slowed. Pengarron dominated her vision, and for a moment she weakened. His argument was reasonable. There had been cases of disputed contracts that had continued for years.

With a conscious effort, she pulled herself back to reality. Why should he wish to save her reputation? He had made no excuses for the way he had abducted her from her home, or for what had passed between him and Bronwyn after the hunt.

'Why should I trust you?' she accused. 'Already you
have played me false with another.'

'How can I play you false, when you will have none of
me?' His eyes blazed amber shards. Then, as realisation
came to him, they shimmered with a light Morganna
could not fathom as he challenged her. 'Are you jealous
of Bronwyn?'

'Certainly I'm not jealous! Bronwyn makes no secret
of her infatuation for you, and I am disgusted that you
do nothing to stop her. Or do you encourage her
deliberately?'

'Take care of what you accuse me, lady,' he said
quietly. Then, as abruptly, his mood changed. 'Or would
you have me prove the nonsense of your words? Only a
fool hankers for the stars when the brightness of the
moon is his for the taking.'

Before she could guess his intent, his palms captured
her face, preventing her head from moving. Too late she
caught the golden warning lightening his eyes as his
mouth pressed down upon her own. Brusquely, her lips
were parted with expert insistence. As her hands came
up to push him away, he anticipated her movement, and
his fingers slid over her body. One arm rested across her
shoulders; the other, low in the hollow of her back,
pressed her hard against his taut, powerful frame. She
wriggled in his embrace, and to her shame, her breasts
and hips were crushed against his virile body. Without
warning, a scalding heat scoured through her, and her
senses ran riot. She was light-headed, floating on a crest
of awareness of this new and unimagined delight. And
still his kiss deepened. His tongue flickered over hers,
imposing his dominance upon her until a soft moan
welled in her throat.

Restraint was gone, banished by the fierce trembling
which possessed her body. Her hands clutched at his
shoulders for support, then, somehow, the silky softness
of his hair was cool upon her fevered fingers as they

roved through his locks, inexplicably binding him closer. Anger, hate and outrage were forgotten, her lips moving of their own volition beneath his. There was only hunger, and the need for this moment to last for eternity.

Finally he wrenched his mouth from hers. Half-swooning, her lids so heavy that they could not open, Morganna stood circled by his arms, his breath a caressing breeze across her heated skin when he spoke.

'That's how a man kisses a woman!' His voice was husky with emotion. 'I leave you to judge if that is what you saw.'

Her eyes flew open to encounter his golden gaze studying her with a fixedness that alerted her to impending danger, and her anger returned. He was amusing himself at her expense! Though his expression did not alter, he must have sensed her inward withdrawal from him. Abruptly he released her and she staggered, still uncertain of her balance. When he put out a hand to stay her, she shrugged it off with a gasp.

'You are despicable. I hate you!'

'If hatred stirs such fire in you, Morganna,' he said with a chuckle that showed he was unimpressed by her venom, 'how can I resist the challenge of winning your love?'

Still he mocked her! She wanted to hurt him as he had hurt her. 'That you'll never have! Should we have no choice but to marry, it will be a hollow victory for you, I promise. I thought you a man too worldly to mistake the success of your seduction for love. A woman must first respect a man before she gives her heart. Love is not won by brute force and tyranny.'

At last the mockery died from his eyes, and the look which replaced it sent a spasm of fear through her.

'Perhaps you were not so averse to Linsdale's advances, lady? The morals at Court are lax. I doubt you were ever short of admirers. Your response and your words betray you.'

He stepped back from her, and with a rough jerk straightened her headdress. 'In time, the good Lord willing, we may learn to tolerate each other. Go and splash your face with cold water. You look like a wanton who's just been tumbled by a man! I'll not present to the villagers my future wife looking like the whore she undoubtedly is.'

His tone cut her, and for a moment she was too shocked to answer. Curtly he indicated a bowl of water on a stand and turned his back on her, adding, 'I would have thought even a Barnett would be aware of her duty in such matters.'

Refusing to look at him, Morganna lifted a shaking hand to assure herself that her headdress was straight, and moved towards the bowl. The water was cold against her flaming cheeks. When she straightened, she felt calmer, but her hatred burned deeper than ever. She snatched the towel he held out for her and dried her face.

'My lady, our people await us.'

The sarcasm of his tone flicked her pride, and her temper exploded into white-hot fury. He could go to the devil before she proclaimed her innocence to him! 'Think of me what you will, sir. What do I care for the censure of an outlaw?'

His face grew pale, but his expression remained closed to her. 'But you care what Radford thinks of you. The Marquess is free, but . . .'

'Giles, free?' Morganna burst out. In her excitement to learn more, her resentment against Pengarron eased. 'Why did you not tell me at once?'

'He's free—but he refuses to pay your dowry or any sort of ransom for your return,' he declared coldly. 'He believes we are already lovers. Obviously he knows your scheming ways well, lady, to believe you capable of such infamy.'

'No! It's not true.' Morganna struck out at him with clenched fists, refusing to acknowledge his lies. Giles would never abandon her! It was another trick.

Beneath Pengarron's tanned complexion, there was a pinched whiteness about the lines of his mouth. He caught her wrists, holding them firmly but gently against his chest.

'None need know of your shame.' His voice was surprisingly mellow. 'As my wife, you'll be honoured here above all women.'

She stared at him blankly. Although she could feel the tension evident in the taut muscles of his chest, he appeared outwardly relaxed. Why was he so determined to marry her? When she tried to pull away, his grip tightened. Puzzled, she searched his face for some sign that he was provoking her because she had angered him. As usual his expression was guarded. What was he thinking? He despised her as much as she did him. Yet he remained adamant that they marry. There must be some reason for his ruse, but for the moment it escaped her.

'Your words are noble,' she challenged. 'Clearly my dowry is more important than your wife's honour, since you think such ill of me. How do I know this is not a trick?'

He raised an eyebrow sardonically. 'Perhaps you'll believe my messenger. Father Matthew is preparing the chapel for the wedding ceremony. He arrived a short while ago, and will marry us before the feast. I received word yesterday that the Duke of Lancaster has landed in Yorkshire. I await his orders, and must leave soon.'

Disbelievingly, Morganna shook her head. He could not mean to marry her today! At worst, she had thought he would formally announce their betrothal, and there would still be time for Giles to save her.

'I will give you some time alone with the priest,' Pengarron said, a shadow darkening his brow. 'When I present you to my people, you will appear a willing and devoted bride.'

Releasing her, he whistled to Wulfric, and with the wolfhound at his heels, he strode out. For several moments Morganna stood unmoving, lost in a confused jumble of thoughts.

'My lady!'

Morganna turned dazedly towards the familiar voice. Her eyes widened as she saw the priest, thin and small in his grey habit, move further into the room.

'Father Matthew!' She felt a rush of warmth at the sight of a friendly face. 'You are here!'

The priest's welcoming smile was sympathetic. 'I could have wished it were otherwise than as the bearer of such grave tidings for Lord Pengarron. But I am honoured at being chosen to join you both in marriage.'

'Honoured, Father?' Morganna's resentment returned. 'How so, when I am held here against my will?'

Father Matthew stared at her as if in amazement. 'You are angry with his lordship? But his action, though drastic—ruthless, even—was to protect you. It wounds me to say this, but it is my Lord Marquess who has wronged you, not the Earl of Pengarron.'

Seeking the comfort of its touch, Morganna clasped the cross at her throat, trying to steady the anger seething inside her. 'What lies has Pengarron told to have won you over? It's my dowry he covets.'

Father Matthew shook his head sadly. 'My child, you know little of the ways of men. It's not your fortune the Earl wants. Should his petition to the King succeed and more of his land is returned to him, he will be wealthier than Lord Radford. He has no need of your dowry.'

'And should my brother lose Daneton to Pengarron?' she persisted, undaunted in her loyalty to Giles. 'Will your allegiance be to the Earl then, not to the Marquess?'

'Has his lordship not told you?' Father Matthew looked taken aback. 'Daneton was part of the terms he offered Lord Radford to give his blessing to your marriage. Provided your dowry was no less than that agreed with Lord Linsdale, Pengarron agreed to relinquish his claim to Daneton.'

'Why should he give up so much?'

An indulgent smile softened the austere lines of the priest's face. 'He gains you, my lady.'

Seeing her eyes narrowing in scorn, Father Matthew sighed, and folded his hands beneath the full sleeves of his robe, his expression again serious. 'When you were a child, you created an image of Ralph Warrender in your dreams. A shining, glorious, courageous knight with no human frailties. Think back to the unknown knight who rescued you from the outlaws. The man that you dreamed of exists. He is also human.'

'He is a devil! Look how he has treated me . . . dragged me from my home!' Morganna bristled.

'With respect, my lady, I believe you have given the Earl little chance to prove his worth,' Father Matthew continued, undaunted by her outburst. 'He is no longer a lowly knight, but rich and powerful. While at Pengarron, have you not been treated with every honour? To me it is obvious why his lordship wishes to marry you.'

'Father Matthew!'

Morganna started as Pengarron's voice boomed from the doorway, cutting off any further remark from the priest.

'It's time we joined the others. Is all prepared in the chapel?' Pengarron's eyes hooded as they glanced swiftly from Morganna to the priest, who bent his head calmly.

'All is ready, my lord.'

Morganna looked coldly at Pengarron, as the priest bowed and left the room, but her heart contracted when he met her stare with equal hauteur. Father Matthew's wits must be addled to try to convince her that Pengarron cared for her! The dull throbbing of her bruised lips was a reminder of the authority of his kiss, and she rebelled against the memory of his mastery over her.

Yet there had been something else, almost imperceptible, through her anger. Surely there had been a moment, blissfully sweet, as she responded to the impulse of that kiss, when the dominance had changed, becoming a fusion of their two wills. Neither had been victor or vanquished. Both gave and received pleasure.

It irked her further to acknowledge that it had been he who had pulled away, putting a restraint on their desire. Thus she had been shamed by the abandon of her response. But she could not deny that moment of wanton yearning—that pleasure in the physical contact of their bodies and lips.

She looked at him from under lowered lashes, and her heartbeat slowed with expectancy. He watched her in silence—standing tall and assured, his golden gaze kindling—waiting. Her father had wanted this match. Had she the right to refuse to marry Pengarron? Compared to Linsdale and the dull foppishness of her other suitors, the thought of marriage to Pengarron was not so appalling. Nay—did it not even seem inviting, were she to acknowledge her feelings?

Pengarron held out a velvet-clad arm for her to take. Her glance, drawn to his bronzed face, saw his eyes glistening, silently commanding her to obey him.

'Morganna, I . . .' His deep voice checked. For once, he appeared hesitant as though he regretted his earlier harshness. 'Will you not accept what must be?' he continued, a touch of warm huskiness in his tone. 'I understand your distrust—we both have reasons for that. But . . .'

Again he paused, and some of her antagonism left her. Clearly he was unused to explaining himself to anyone. That he attempted to do so now caused a delicious thrill of pleasure to rise in her breast. His gaze, intense and questioning, transfixed her as he drew her arm through his. The muscular hardness of his arm beneath the soft fabric of his sleeve was no longer threatening, but reassuring.

'I have no wish for an unwilling bride, Morganna. I'll not hold you to honour your father's bond. If you believe Radford will stand by you—then I'll not keep you here.'

'You would release me!'

'The choice is yours, sweet Morganna.'

The endearment, spoken without mockery, flustered her, and she lowered her eyes from his questing stare. She should feel elated that he had given her back her freedom, certainly not this dawning desolation. She retreated behind her natural suspicion of him.

'I do not understand, my lord.'

The muscles of his arm corded beneath her fingers. 'Then, my dear, you are less perceptive than I give you credit for.'

Risking a tentative glance up at him, she saw the hollows in his strong throat and lean cheeks. They were the only sign of the tension with which he awaited her answer.

Disturbingly handsome, he would never plead or beg favours as others had done. Used to command, he had no need to coerce, but he had paid her the compliment of giving her a choice. He towered above those fawning suitors she had despised, not merely physically, but also by his strength and manliness.

What did she expect from marriage, anyway? At least, with Pengarron, no matter how he exasperated her, their life together would never be dull. It would be a tourney ground of opposing wills, their wits honed to needle-points, an equal and stimulating contest. And more—her body still simmered with warmth at the remembered pleasure of his slightest touch.

Realising she was weakening in her resolve, she fought against surrendering to his will. It still seemed like a betrayal of Giles, as her mind continued to wrestle with conflicting emotions. To whom was her duty? To Giles, or to her father?

'Morganna!' Pengarron's voice crackled with impatience. 'I must have your answer.'

Cornered, her stomach lurched in panic. Then his hand tilted her chin to face him. 'I am not your enemy, sweet Morganna. Let this be a new beginning.'

Her cool fingers were warmed by the pressure of his arm clamping them against his side, and under his compelling stare her limbs seemed to liquefy. Her resistance crumbled. Did not Father Matthew believe it right for them to marry?

Stifling her misgivings, she inclined her head graciously. 'Let the marriage take place, my lord.' Her voice quivered with the enormity of what she had done.

CHAPTER NINE

As THEY WALKED to the chapel, Morganna glanced
sidelong at Lord Pengarron, and catching her thoughtful
stare upon him, his lips parted in an enigmatic smile.
When his hand covered hers, she found the change
in him, since he had won her consent, disconcerting.
Though still imperious, there was a deeper reverence to
his gaze whenever their eyes met. His smile no longer
mocked but was tantalisingly provocative. Each time she
caught his look, the admiration in his eyes was clear,
making her decision easier to bear.

Still in a daze, she entered the chapel, where Father
Matthew stood intoning a prayer. His words drifted over
her until with a start she heard Pengarron's deep voice
making his responses. Her own in reply sounded little
more than a strangled whisper, and his comforting
squeeze on her hand gave her the strength to continue.

The ceremony was mercifully brief. Only as Lord Pengarron's lips brushed hers did she fully understand that
she was his wife. There was no time for thought or regret.
Lady Gwyneth, paler than usual, stepped forward stiffly
to hand over the castle keys attached to a long gold chain.

'These belong to you, now, Countess.'

Clipping the keys about her waist, Morganna felt
humbled by the responsibilities which were now hers.
'May I prove worthy of the trust placed in me.'

A light flared in the widow's green eyes, and her
answering smile was strained. 'It will cast its spell over
you, and I am sure you would give your life for it, as
would I. May you be blessed with strong sons to ensure
Pengarron's future.'

Used to Gwyneth's strange way of referring to the

castle, Morganna was not offended by her words. Already she felt a surge of pride towards the place which would in future be her home.

Even Bronwyn's sullen face could not spoil her pleasure. With a curtsy to Pengarron, her gaze was bold as ever. 'Congratulations, my lord. Now you are wed, the Duke may call you less often to his side. Pengarron is but a shell when its master is not here to give it life.'

Passing on to Morganna, the girl's eyes flashed. 'Be happy, Countess, while you can.'

Morganna felt Pengarron stiffen, his voice tinged with warning. 'It is the duty of all present to ensure that my lady wife finds happiness and contentment here.'

'But of course, my lord,' Bronwyn simpered. 'I meant only that the Countess must be saddened at your departure so soon after your wedding.'

With a stern look at Bronwyn, he turned to Morganna, his smile softening. 'As the thought of my leaving saddens me! Now I must present my wife to her people.'

Morganna's heart fluttered as he led her from the chapel. Bronwyn's sulky manner was forgotten as she walked at her husband's side. She knew he was playing the role of proud bridegroom before his people, but even so, his words held a promise of new discoveries and pleasures yet to come.

When they left the chapel arm in arm, the cheers from the castle servants almost drowned the sound of the watch-tower bell pealing out in celebration. Young children from the village and maidens in the best clothes strewed flowers in their path, and with her mind still in a whirl, Morganna was led outside to the inner bailey. The Earl, tall and proud, presented her to his people, his voice ringing out and echoing back from the walls.

'I give you the Lady Morganna, Countess of Pengarron! Serve her as you would serve me, and you will be loyally rewarded.'

'God bless our lady Countess!' The cries came from

a sea of upturned faces, some already ruddy from the ale Lord Pengarron had distributed among them. The cheers rose to a deafening pitch, resounding through the courtyard and startling the doves from the cote and from the roof-tops.

Morganna was surprised and overwhelmed by the fervour of their acceptance. It seemed disloyal, now that Lady Gwyneth was no longer mistress here. She dismissed the thought. Of course, the people were showing their pleasure that at last their lord was married, nothing more.

Smiling broadly, he guided her to the seats made ready for them under a pavilion erected on a raised platform. The shade protected them from the fierce heat of the sun while the villagers, now shy and curious, filed past to pay homage. Throughout the procession, Morganna was aware of Lord Pengarron watching her. He nodded his satisfaction as his men, resplendent in new black and gold livery, came forward to kneel and swear fealty to their new Countess.

Tears of pride stung her eyes . . . These were her people now. Dimly she noted the dancing bear, tumblers and a fire-eater providing an endless stream of entertainment for them, but all was little more than a blur, her every sense concentrated on the physical closeness of the man at her side.

She could scarcely swallow when he raised the loving-cup for them to share, but, slowly, normality returned. By the time the ring dances and games were over, and the pages were half drowned trying to capture bobbing apples in their mouths from water-barrels, she began to relax and enjoy herself.

The sun was still high when Emrys bowed to her. The squire spoke softly to the Earl, and gestured to a travel-stained soldier waiting by the edge of the platform. Pengarron frowned, his eyes guarded as he excused himself to Morganna and joined the soldier.

Puzzled, she looked for reassurance from Lady Gwyneth, but instead discovered Bronwyn standing at her side. Eyes narrowed with spite, the girl was staring at the embroidered hem of Morganna's gown.

'So, you think you've won!' Bronwyn's hand trembled as she pointed to the Barnett insignia. 'Do you think yourself protected by Hecate's sign? There are others who are stronger than your moon-goddess. Nothing, and no one, will stop me having Ralph! You are not his true wife yet, and from the look of that messenger, you won't be for some time.'

'Go to your room, Bronwyn!' Lady Gwyneth's cold voice commanded sharply from close by.

Wild-eyed, the girl swung round and backed away, her auburn hair whipping about her like writhing snakes in the stiffening wind.

'You promised him to me!' she spat at Lady Gwyneth, and then turned and ran, disappearing into the dancing crowd.

'Pay no heed to the child!' Lady Gwyneth dismissed Bronwyn's strange behaviour. 'She is overwrought and doesn't know what she is saying.'

The summer's heat seemed to have died from the sunny courtyard, and Morganna shivered. 'Her words were so strange! She spoke of a moon-goddess.

Lady Gwyneth laughed, a thin, forced sound. 'Oh, she refers to some Celtic myth. Her old nurse used to fill her head with such nonsense . . . Think no more of it. Look, here comes Ralph, and looking dour for one who has just wed! Cheer him. A smile from you, and he'll cast aside all cares in anticipation of bedding you this night.'

Morganna blushed, knowing Pengarron must have overheard these remarks as he returned to the platform. Most of her own preoccupation during the celebrations had been due to the expectancy of what awaited her once they were alone. Now, as she looked into his impassive face, she felt the first stab of apprehension.

'I have been summoned by the Duke of Lancaster,' he said resignedly. 'I must leave as soon as my horse is saddled.'

Lady Gwyneth's outraged gasp gave Morganna a moment to calm her thudding heart. Pengarron leaving! There would be no wedding night! Momentary relief was followed by a stab of disappointment.

'Ralph—you cannot leave your wife!' Lady Gwyneth admonished. 'You have your duty to her.'

'My first duty is to my lord Duke,' he snapped. Then, seeing the effort Morganna was making to hide her confusion, he took her hand, his voice gentling. 'For myself, I would wish it otherwise.'

Was it regret that drew down his arched brows as he regarded her? Or merely worry about the summons? But his hands were tender as he raised her to her feet, and his hard glare across at Gwyneth caused her to step back, allowing them a measure of privacy as they stood alone on the platform.

'I must go,' he said hoarsely. 'Pengarron is now your home. I had hoped time would allow me to show more of it to you and tell you of its legends. Especially the waterfall.'

His sincerity moved her. Until now, everything had happened so quickly. Having accepted the idea of her marriage and all it implied, it was cruel she should be robbed of his company. His eyes darkened, and a shaft of longing and regret shot through her. Proudly she fought to hide it from him.

'I understand, my lord.' She wanted to touch him to ease the tension between them, but was beset by uncertainty, not knowing whether he would resent such a gesture. 'When you return it will be, as you say, a new beginning for us.'

A light, as fleeting and bright as a shooting star, flashed in his eyes. Or had it? For, as quickly, his emotions were again guarded and she was unsure whether she had not after all imagined it.

'Ralph?' It was the first time she had used his name, and he looked at her inscrutably. Suddenly she could not bear the thought of his leaving with so much unsettled between them, and picking up the goblet they had been sharing, she passed it to him. 'A stirrup-cup, my lord, to drink to your safe return.'

He drank sparingly and placed the goblet on the table. His expression taut, he drew her behind the silk hanging of the pavilion, away from prying eyes. Her breath hung suspended as he brushed aside her veil, which had blown across her cheek. The fleeting touch of his fingers upon her skin set her pulse clamouring, then his arms were hard about her, pulling her to him. The restrained passion in his kiss was bitter-sweet, yet even so he had the power to leave her trembling in his arms. Raising his lips from hers, he smiled wickedly.

'Duty or no, my fair Morganna, I'll find a way to return quickly and make you truly my wife.' A fervour lit his eyes, and she steadily met his challenge as he declared, 'Use my absence well, sweet wife, to accept what must be.'

Blushing furiously, she managed to answer without too much of a quaver in her voice, 'I have accepted it already.'

His mouth touched her eyes and cheeks, and with a swift hard kiss upon her lips he wrenched himself away. Morganna followed him back to the platform, where Emrys was waiting. The squire handed him his sword-belt, and after Ralph had buckled it, he returned to Morganna.

'Never was duty so cruel as to take me from you this day,' he said. 'You are the Countess now, and rule here in my stead. The people have taken you to their hearts. I would have Pengarron return to the happy place it used to be when I was a boy. I shall leave Barnaby here. His music will lighten your hours, and you will find him a worthy counsellor, should you need him.'

Moved by his thoughtfulness when so much must occupy his mind, Morganna smiled, and held out her hand. It was firmly grasped and raised to his lips, the pressure of his mouth lingering for a long moment before he released her. At his reluctance to leave, her anger and resentment vanished. No matter how she fought against it, she could not deny the bond of attraction which sparked between them.

'Godspeed, my husband,' she said shakily, controlling the urge to bid him to stay.

Through a blur of unexpected tears, she watched him mount up and ride out through the Gatehouse at the head of his men. The courtyard had become expectantly quiet, and she realised that all faces were turned towards her.

Gwyneth nudged her elbow, and murmured, 'They await word from their Countess for the ox to be carved.'

Morganna signalled for them to continue, although all pleasure in the entertainment was gone for her now. Beckoning to Jocelyn, she mumbled an excuse to Gwyneth and hurriedly sought the sanctuary of her rooms.

She paused in the entrance, surprised and delighted to see the tapestry with the Pengarron eagle hanging in her chamber. It was a subtle reminder from him of the bonds between them, before the mistrust and suspicion had begun. Then the peace of the chamber was shattered by the piercing scream from one of her tiring-women working in the bedchamber. Fearing the woman had been hurt, she ran into the room.

Jocelyn stood by the bed, her eyes bulging with terror as she stared down at a blackthorn branch laid on the covers.

''Tis a bad omen, my lady,' wailed the maid. 'It foretells a death. It's evil, this place, evil! I can feel it!'

'It's a prank, and one in poor taste. That is all,

Jocelyn. The blackthorn is not even in bloom. It was just
meant to warn—by Bronwyn, I suspect—that I am not
wanted here. When she realises I am not frightened by
silly superstitious threats, she'll soon stop this nonsense!'

'That's as may be, my lady, but you'll sleep in no bed
unless it has a sprig of rosemary and wild garlic under it
to ward off evil spirits! Or eat from any spoon unless it is
made of rosemary to protect you against poisoning.'

'I'll not have my chamber reeking of garlic, Jocelyn!
Now leave me. I would be alone.'

'Morganna, my dear, do stop that pacing,' Gwyneth
chided from the seat set into the surrounding wall of the
rose garden. 'Ralph will soon return.'

Sighing, Morganna paused at the end of the path. She
clasped her hands and stared up at the cloudless sky,
watching a flock of doves circle in a wide arc before returning to the dovecote built into the rafters of a store-
house. Gwyneth meant well by her kindly words, but
how could she know the turmoil they created within her?

It was almost a month since Ralph had ridden out.
Morganna caught her thoughts, realising with a start that
she rarely thought of her husband now as Pengarron, but
as Ralph. Although, as yet, he was her husband in name
only. The nervous anticipation that kept her sleepless at
nights again beset her. She both longed for and dreaded
his return.

Irrationally, she felt cheated. From the start, Ralph
had ruthlessly played upon the physical attraction which
had sparked between them. How expertly he had overcome her reluctance, astounding her by the hunger of
her response to his kisses. But he had never wooed her,
as she had always dreamed a knight would win his lady.
Instead, he turned her reasoning around, his presence
bedevilling her judgment. It rankled to recall that he had
always declared he would have her, and had achieved his
aim with seemingly little effort. What had happened to

her during their month apart? Having accepted her marriage, it seemed that his absence had been as devastating to her senses as his presence. Daily she anticipated his return, until she was as nervous as a love-lorn maid.

Collecting her wayward thoughts, she returned to Gwyneth's side. How could she explain that she felt more like a victory trophy than a bride? She wanted to be wooed and won, to be an important part of her husband's life, not just a piece of property, another chattel to be manipulated.

'It's no good pining for your husband,' Gwyneth reasoned. 'You're drawn and pale. Do you want Ralph to return and find you looking like a wilted flower?'

Morganna paced restlessly in front of her, her glance shy as she confided, 'I almost dread his return!'

'A woman of your spirit!' Gwyneth laughed. 'I know Ralph can be difficult at times. It's no secret that he and I have not always agreed as one would wish.'

Gwyneth shrugged, clearly unwilling to talk of the differences which had come between herself and Ralph. 'But pay no mind to me,' she continued. 'Ralph and I have always had our differences. It's obvious he cares for you. No matter how difficult a man may be, a wise woman can charm her husband to do anything she pleases.'

'I cannot see myself hooding the Pengarron eagle,' Morganna returned with an amused chuckle, and knew with certainty that she would not wish to do so. She did not know whether Ralph cared for her or saw her as a means to strike at Giles, but he had always treated her with respect. Somehow, his unpredictability set her husband apart from other men, and was what intrigued her most.

Gwyneth peered closely at Morganna, her green eyes calculating. 'Give Pengarron an heir, and you'll find the eagle all too easy to handle, I promise you.'

Embarrassed by her outspokenness, Morganna

walked to the far end of the garden. Almost daily she
made some reference to a child. It was easy to understand Gwyneth's distress that she had been barren, but
she seemed to be becoming obsessed with the thought of
an heir.

Stooping to pick a rose, Morganna smelt its fragrant
scent, and struggled to maintain her composure. She was
nervous enough at the thought of Pengarron's return. It
did not ease her disquiet to know the duty which was
expected of her. Of course she wanted children, but she
sometimes thought Gwyneth regarded her as little more
than a brood mare for the further glory of Pengarron.

Through the open archway leading to the inner bailey,
Morganna saw Bronwyn accompanied by Owain returning from a ride. The girl dismounted and, seeing
Morganna watching her, came towards her, a secretive
smile making her pointed, impish face glow.

'Old Emma, the wise-woman, came to the castle
today,' she announced, throwing a malicious glance at
Morganna as she swept past to sit beside Gwyneth.
'Emma told me my fortune. She said I shall have all I
desire—that no man can gainsay me.'

'The old woman is wise enough to foretell just what
you want to hear,' Gwyneth said firmly. 'I thought you
knew better than to fill your head with such nonsense!'

'It's true,' Bronwyn cried. 'I shall have all I desire.'

Weary of Bronwyn's sly hints, Morganna said darkly,
'If you desire that which is beyond you, only disappointment will follow. When Lord Pengarron returns, a
marriage will be arranged for you.'

Brownyn scowled. 'But I want . . .'

'Remember to whom you are speaking, Bronwyn,'
Gwyneth snapped.

A torrent of Welsh sprang from the girl's lips. When
Gwyneth reprimanded her in the same language,
Morganna's temper rose. Aware that both women had
deliberately snubbed her, Morganna walked away,

declaring. 'I think it time you taught Bronwyn her manners, Gwyneth. In the meantime, I shall leave you both while I ride out to inspect the south pasture, where several sheep were killed by foxes in the night.'

'Take care you do not ride too close to the river valley,' Gwyneth called after her.

Morganna swung round. Gwyneth's words had been tantamount to an order. Framed by the white wimple, her dark features remained haughty as she added less harshly, 'I am concerned for your safety. The ground, after the landslides, is not safe. You take your role of Countess seriously. Surely Ralph does not expect so much of you?'

'Would you not act as I, were you still mistress here? It's time something was done about that land. One of the men from the village was found dead there this morning.'

Morganna looked pointedly at Bronwyn. 'It is only assumed that the villager fell to his death. He could have been set upon and murdered. You ride daily with only Owain as escort, and in future you should take more men with you. There is much unrest since Bolingbroke raised his army. Outlaws and deserters grow more daring at such times.'

'I need no one else,' Bronwyn scoffed. 'All hereabouts think Owain possessed of some demon because he's mute. And he has the strength of ten men.'

'Bronwyn!' Gwyneth said sharply. 'I won't have you repeating such tales. Owain is a proud and loyal servant. If the villagers are wary of him, it's because they know little better.'

Bronwyn's eyes flashed and her beautiful face screwed up with fury. 'Sometimes I think you care more for your precious servant than you do for me! Before the Lady Morganna came, everything was perfect here. Now you take her side all the time, just so that your precious Pengarron can have its son! What I want doesn't matter any more.' Glaring at Morganna, Bronwyn jumped to her feet and ran from the walled garden.

'I must apologise for my ward's manners!' Gwyneth
said stiffly, red spots of anger rising to her ashen cheeks.
'I have indulged Bronwyn's whims for too long.'

Feeling uncomfortable after the scene between the
two women, Morganna excused herself and made her
way back to her chambers. There had been more than
malice in the girl's outburst, Morganna thought un-
easily. Or was it just her imagination? Bronwyn had
never troubled to hide her hatred since Ralph had ridden
away.

Growing impatient with her fancies that something
was wrong in Pengarron, Morganna crossed the inner
bailey, and was about to call a passing page when she saw
a movement from the open door of the bastion tower.
Wulfric, Ralph's favourite wolfhound, walked out and
flopped down in the sun.

Cautiously she approached the dog, whose temper
was at times uncertain. Pink tongue lolling from the side
of his mouth and dark eyes regarding her warily, Wulfric
wagged his tail in a conciliatory manner and permitted
her to rub his ears. She had been drawn to the dog many
times over the past weeks. The wolfhound looked just as
lost as she felt without his master, and it had been a
shock to discover that she actually missed Ralph and the
conflict between them.

Straightening from patting Wulfric, Morganna
shielded her eyes from the sun and looked across at the
masons at work on the ruined tower. 'The heart of
Pengarron', Gwyneth had called the King's Tower. It
was the only surviving part of the original castle, and had
once been the living quarters of the first Earl, who had
been granted permission to fortify and crenellate it by
Edward I. When the work was completed it would be a
grand and imposing structure. Even now, its vast ex-
panse of mottled grey, green and brown granite walls
was formidable and daunting. Once whitewashed the
same as the other buildings, it would be majestic.

Behind her, over the sound of chisels and hammers, she heard a steady clop of hooves on the sunbaked ground. Turning, she saw Father Matthew, his face drawn and serious, dismounting from his donkey. He looked across at her, hesitated, and then, handing the donkey's reins to a servant, hurried across the courtyard. Sensing that something was wrong, Morganna met him halfway. Before she could ask what made him look so troubled, a page emerged from the armoury and, seeing Morganna, ran forward and bowed to her.

'My lady, I saw your tiring-woman a short while ago. She was searching for you, and seemed upset. I'll go and fetch her.'

'There's no need.' She smiled at the fresh-faced youth. 'I'll find her in my rooms. Please summon Barnaby to me there, and ask the Captain of the Guard to have an escort of six men ready in half an hour.'

The page scampered off, and she turned to the priest. 'Father, will you attend me? You seem worried. Is something troubling you?'

The priest glanced furtively over his shoulder to where Gwyneth was talking to Owain by the archway. When Owain walked off, Gwyneth looked across at Morganna and the priest, staring at them for several moments before she climbed the steps to the hall.

'Ay, my lady,' the priest muttered crossly. 'There's much amiss. I need to talk to you, but this is not the place to speak of such matters.'

She had never seen Father Matthew so agitated, and it was a strain to keep their conversation upon trivial matters as they passed the servants busy about their tasks. Once inside her chambers, with the door closed, Morganna called out to Jocelyn. The maid, her eyes huge and stricken in her pale face, hastened from the inner chamber.

'Oh, my lady—Father Matthew—we must leave this place before something terrible happens. Helewise said there would be danger here, and she was right!'

CHAPTER TEN

'WHAT HAS UPSET you so, my child?' Father Matthew asked gravely.

Jocelyn looked frantically from the priest to Morganna, her voice breaking. 'The Lady Bronwyn—she's a witch!'

Father Matthew led the now sobbing maid to a stool, gently patting her hand as he soothed her. 'That's a serious allegation! Calm down, and tell us why you think that.'

Puzzled, Morganna frowned as she watched the priest. Did he believe Jocelyn's outlandish tale? Surely not! Knowing her maid so well, she suspected Jocelyn had seen something to set herself in such a taking, but had imagined most of it. She remained silent. There was no point in upsetting Jocelyn further, now that the priest had succeeded in calming her a little.

'I know you think I'm foolish, my lady.' Jocelyn wrung her hands in distress as she looked up at Morganna. 'But I swear, by all that's holy, I saw Bronwyn casting spells!'

The fear in her eyes was too real for Morganna lightly to sweep aside her statement.

'Tell us what you saw, Jocelyn,' she commanded, adding firmly, 'But only what you saw. Not what you think the Lady Bronwyn was doing.'

Jocelyn wiped her eyes on her sleeve. 'I'd gone to the herb garden to pick some fresh rosemary, but I found it all dead. Someone had uprooted it. I was frightened, then. I know you laugh at my fancies, my lady, but I've always felt danger here. I wanted to protect you in the only way I could. I went outside the castle to see if I could find some rosemary growing wild. I hadn't gone far when I heard horses approaching. I was scared, and hid in the long grass until they passed.'

The maid broke off with a sniff, and Morganna smiled encouragingly at her to go on.

'It was Bronwyn and Owain heading for that alder grove to the west of here,' Jocelyn said in a rush. 'Barnaby told me it's supposed to be haunted.'

'Barnaby, like all troubadours, has an ear for the mysterious,' Morganna said soothingly. 'He was probably teasing you.'

The maid shivered. 'It's a bad place! I've never been so frightened, but I had to find out if the Lady Bronwyn meant you harm. I'm sure she put that blackthorn branch in your room, my lady.'

Jocelyn drew an uneven breath, but neither Morganna nor Father Matthew spoke, waiting for her to go on.

'I crept closer . . . It was only a short distance. I saw the giant keeping watch. He had his back to me.' The fear returned to Jocelyn's eyes. 'There was a pool beneath an old oak. The Lady Bronwyn was scratching writing on to a piece of slate. Then she threw it into the water and chanted some words—devil's words, I couldn't understand them. I expected at any moment that the horned one himself would appear and carry me off! I dared not look any more. I stayed hidden in the grass, too frightened to move, until I heard them ride off.'

As Jocelyn's voice broke and she buried her head in her hands, Morganna put a comforting arm around the maid's shoulders. Uncertain what to make of Jocelyn's story, she looked askance at the priest.

Father Matthew bowed his head, his hands hidden by the deep sleeves of his gown while he considered the matter, before replying.

'It's likely that the strange words the Lady Bronwyn was speaking were Welsh. It's her native language, after all,' he reasoned. 'I've heard of a ritual performed by young maids to win their lovers. They write his name on a piece of slate and toss it into a sacred pool. Usually its done on St Agnes's or Midsummer's eve.'

'But today's not such a day, Father!' Jocelyn sobbed. 'And Barnaby said to write a name on a piece of slate is to curse that person. The Lady Bronwyn resents the Lady Morganna.'

The priest frowned. 'The Lady Bronwyn is young and rather undisciplined, but she would not harm the Countess. A maid in love will not always consider it necessary to await a favourable date to perform such a rite.'

With his back to Jocelyn, he gave Morganna a meaningful look, and she added her own comfort, saying, 'My dear, did you not tell me that Bronwyn has been flirting with one of the pages? The handsome blond one, related to the Percys. Why, she even flirted with Barnaby until the Lady Gwyneth rebuked her for such unseemly conduct! You were frightened. Bronwyn may resent my marriage to Lord Pengarron, but, at her age, a maid's fancies will change with the moon.'

At her maid's despairing look, Morganna added, 'I left my Book of Hours in the rose garden. Go and fetch it, and think no more of what you saw . . . I'm sure it was all perfectly harmless.'

As Jocelyn hurried out, Morganna turned to Father Matthew. 'Her fears for the moment are quieted, but what she said has disturbed you, Father.'

He nodded. 'I often go among the villagers. They say nothing, but I feel something is not right. They're scared of the mute man. Since Lord Pengarron left, they have become sullen and distrustful. Their ways are strange —secretive. Outwardly, they live Christian lives, attending church every Sunday, but . . .'

The priest's eyes shadowed with concern as he looked forthrightly at Morganna. 'Places as remote as these often retain traces of the old religion,' he added heavily. 'That doesn't mean they practise the black arts—devil-worship—but the old ways and beliefs still exist.'

She sighed. 'I understand, Father. These are simple people with their own language and culture. They are Celts, justly proud of their heritage. They venerate our Lord Jesus, but old superstitions die hard. Even at Daneton, Helewise consulted the runes.'

'I fear it's more than that. It could be that a Druid is hiding in the hills and has some hold over them.'

A sickly sensation bubbled in her stomach. It seemed incredible that such could happen at Pengarron. Remembering the strange words Bronwyn had said to her on her wedding day, Morganna said, reluctantly, 'Bronwyn was upset when she saw the crescent moons of the Barnetts on my gown, and muttered something about the moon-goddess being unable to protect me . . . That there was another, more powerful. Oh, Father, you don't think she's got herself mixed up with the old religion? She is of an age to think all problems can be solved by magic.'

'Has anything happened to make you suspect that the Lady Bronwyn wishes you harm?'

'Not really.' Morganna shrugged off her unease. 'But she does not trouble to hide her infatuation for Lord Pengarron. There was a childish prank played on my wedding day. I suppose it was meant as a warning that I was not welcome here. I'll talk to the Lady Gwyneth. I fear the silly child will bring harm to herself if she continues in this wickedness! And I must also talk with the Lady Gwyneth about this other matter.'

To her surprise, the priest said flatly, 'We had best not meddle. I'm certain her ladyship knows something of this—perhaps she finds it best to turn a blind eye to it. The English are still only tolerated here. Wait until Lord Pengarron returns. He will know how best to deal with this matter.'

'But the Lady Gwyneth is Welsh, like Bronwyn!' Morganna, more troubled than before, sensed that the priest was concealing something.

'My child, I do not like what's happening here,' he said, guessing her doubts. 'Until Lord Pengarron returns, I shall keep a close watch on his people. Should anything wrong come to light, I shall let you know.'

'These are my people, too,' Morganna said firmly. 'Tomorrow, I sit at my first Manor Court to hear their grievances. I wish there was more I could do to win their trust.'

'Then insist that the Lady Gwyneth is not also present,' the priest counselled. 'Or there will be a pull between her old authority and your own, my lady.'

There was a note of warning in his words, but he gave no sign of saying more, and Morganna allowed him to leave. Afterwards, she fretted over the strange tale Jocelyn had related. What was it about Pengarron Castle that made her tiring-woman so edgy?

When Jocelyn entered the room, accompanied by Barnaby, Morganna had made up her mind to do more than investigate the killed sheep in the south pasture. She would go among the villagers and try harder to win their trust.

For a moment she watched the glow of pleasure lighting her maid's face as Jocelyn laughed at something the troubadour said. How easily he had made her forget her fears! It seemed that he often sought the maid's company, and the thought of a romance blossoming between the two servants took the sting from Father Matthew's warning. Not everything was sinister about the people of Pengarron. Unfortunately, no matter how tempted she was to encourage the young couple's affection, there were weightier matters which must be dealt with first.

'I would ride to the south pasture,' she declared. 'Send a page to order the horses saddled, Jocelyn.'

As the maid left them, Barnaby bowed to Morganna, the tiny bells jangling from the silk baldric draped across his chest. For an instant there was a sharp, questioning look in his vivid blue eyes.

'Has something happened which troubles you, my lady?'

Not sure how much she should tell the troubadour, Morganna answered cautiously, 'Sometimes I feel all is not as it should be here. The people seem unusually wary. Did Lord Pengarron mention anything to you?'

'I'm just a humble troubadour, my lady,' Barnaby hedged.

'Are you, Barnaby? I think you're more than that. You must have been at King Richard's Court to have learnt of my brother's fate. A troubadour can visit many places and, in his role as an entertainer, remain invisible. Lord Pengarron told me you would prove a wise counsellor, should I need one.'

'I am at your service whenever you command, my lady.'

'Then await me in the courtyard. I would value your advice during our ride. But first I must speak with the Lady Gwyneth.'

As Morganna made her way to Gwyneth's chambers, she felt her confidence slipping. During the past weeks the widow seemed to have accepted the change in her status, but how would she take the news that a pagan priest could be hiding in the hills? Since nothing had been mentioned to Pengarron, Morganna feared Gwyneth would see it as criticism of her management of the estate.

After knocking on Gwyneth's door, Morganna's patience frayed at the length of time she was kept waiting. There were definite sounds of movement within, yet her second knock was again ignored.

Was this another snub by Gwyneth? Her patience snapped. What right had anyone to deny her entrance, now that she was the Countess? She lifted the latch and, smothering a twinge of guilt, entered.

The outer room was deserted. Morganna paused, struck by the magnificence of the gold velvet hangings and carved furnishings. Even the wooden loom by the window was painted with red and blue flowers. Uncomfortable at being uninvited in someone's rooms, she called Gwyneth's name, but there was no answer. As she looked around, her attention was caught by a large polished crystal on a table, at the same time noticing the strange smell—almost like burning incense, but not so pleasant—which lingered in the room.

Suddenly there was an unearthly screech behind her, and her blood ran cold. The hair prickling on her scalp, she whirled round, and froze. Perched on a golden stand, its black wings flapping menacingly, was the largest raven she had ever seen. The bird continued its raucous squawking as it flew about the room, swooping low each time it passed Morganna's head. Throwing up her arms to protect her face, she felt a sharp stab as it gave her a vicious peck on her finger. Backing away, her only thought was on escaping from the room and its vengeful guardian, when her heart jolted as a hand clamped on her shoulder.

'Countess, take care!' Nesta spoke from behind her. 'The bird doesn't like strangers. He once had a maid's eye out.'

Morganna watched Nesta as she picked up a piece of fruit and coaxed the raven back on to its perch.

'That's a strange pet,' Morganna said shakily, as Nesta stroked the glassy black feathers and spoke softly in Welsh to calm the bird.

'Owain found it last summer with its wing broken,' she answered defensively. 'The Lady Gwyneth has a way with herbs . . . she can heal anything. The bird is so tame that he'll not leave the castle. The Lady Gwyneth says he brings good luck to Pengarron.'

'Where is your mistress?' Morganna asked, feeling safer now the bird was back on his perch.

'The Lady Gwyneth went to inspect the work on the King's Tower, my lady. Shall I summon her to attend you?'

'No. I shall speak with her when I return from my ride.'

The unexpected encounter with the raven had shaken Morganna more than she cared to admit. She cast another look at the strange pet, who stretched himself up on his legs, his wings beating furiously. Not until the chamber door was firmly shut behind her did her pounding heart return to normal. She shivered as she walked the narrow corridors. A strange pet indeed, she reflected. Especially since Gwyneth had shown a marked dislike for the cats and hunting-dogs roaming about the castle. Having grown up with several birds of her own, Morganna felt no attraction for the evil-eyed raven, and was relieved to walk out into the bright sunshine in the courtyard. Even so, she could not easily shake the image of the cruel beak and malignant glinting eyes from her mind. It certainly was a powerful and forbidding guard to keep intruders from Gwyneth's chambers.

Barnaby and her escort were awaiting her outside. By the time they had ridden across the drawbridge, she had pushed the frightening incident from her mind. What had Gwyneth been doing in the King's Tower? she wondered. Recalling how cross she had been at the slowness of the work being done, Morganna hoped she was not upsetting the master mason.

They took the fork at the far end of the village, which followed the path along the top of the ravine over which Pengarron Castle stood guard. As she looked down at the tumbling, white-flecked water far below, she relaxed, soothed by the playful sound.

When they approached the south pasture, a harassed-looking shepherd came out of his dwelling. The man gabbled away in Welsh for several moments, and Morganna looked askance at Barnaby, who was frowning.

'I've learnt so few words of their language. What does he say?'

'He no longer thinks it was foxes who killed the sheep. Several are missing. It could have been outlaws.'

'Then a patrol must be sent out at once.' Morganna sighed. 'If only we had more men!' She broke off, as a column of black smoke rose above the trees some distance away. 'There's a village in that direction, isn't there?'

'Ay, my lady,' Barnaby answered. 'You had best return to the castle with the escort. With the King's and Bolingbroke's armies gathering, it could be deserters or outlaws attacking the village. I'll go and see what's happened.'

'No, Barnaby, if my people are in danger, I would help them—not take what few men we have. It could just be a fire.'

The smoke was thicker as they approached, and the cries and screams from the villagers filled her with dread at what they would find.

It was worse than anything she could have imagined. Four of the eight thatched dwellings were on fire. Those villagers capable of standing had formed a human chain to drag water up from the nearby stream in buckets and cooking-pots. Others, less fortunate, nursed split heads as they lay propped against the upturned carts. Everywhere was in turmoil. The livestock pens were empty of animals, but only a few goats and chickens ran freely about. Arrows stuck out of timbers and doors. The hard ground, covered with scattered utensils and spilt provisions, showed that this had been a cold-blooded raid upon the village. Praise God no one had been killed! Morganna thought, as she stared at the havoc around her. Dismounting, she moved among the wounded, while her escort shouted orders as they tried to save the remaining cottages.

An hour later the fire was out, but five of the dwellings had been destroyed. Looking up from bathing a wound of a crying child, Morganna saw the smoke-blackened faces of the villagers about her. She stood up, feeling helpless as she clasped the child against her. Why had the warning beacons not been lit? Who had dared to strike so boldly on Pengarron land?

'What happened?' she asked Barnaby, as he came forward to make his report.

He pushed a dirty hand through his dark, sweat-streaked hair, shaking his head tiredly.

'They won't say. They're frightened the men might attack again.'

'Was it outlaws—deserters?' Morganna persisted. 'Which way did they ride off? A patrol must be sent after them.'

Barnaby took the child from her and gave it to its waiting mother. 'I think it best we leave, my lady. Whoever raided here spoke English, but the hayward believes he recognised their leader. Although the man's features were hidden by a hood, there are few men in these parts with Owain's height or build.'

'He must be mistaken!' Morganna gasped. 'Why should Owain lead a raid against our people? He's one of us.'

'It probably wasn't him. Owain is feared, and the people would discredit him if they could, but strange things have been reported here. This village is furthest from the protection of the castle. And it's not the first raid here. On other occasions, women and children have been carried off.'

Morganna stared incredulously at the troubadour. 'This must be reported to Lord Pengarron. I know his duty prevents him from returning, but he must learn what is happening here.'

She glanced anxiously over the dejected peasants. 'Tell them that blankets and provisions will be sent from the castle. Men from other villages will come to help them to rebuild their homes.'

As Barnaby repeated her words, Morganna saw the expressions on some of the women's faces brighten, but most of the men remained surly and suspicious.

'Find out what they need, Barnaby, and have it brought from the castle. Tell them that Lord Pengarron will return soon. That he cares what happens to his people, even though duty keeps him away from them.'

Morganna walked tiredly towards her palfrey, and when Barnaby cupped his hands to help her to mount, she put a hand on his shoulder. 'Will you teach me Welsh, Barnaby? I shall be an outcast here until I can speak with my people in their own language.'

'I would be honoured, my lady.' A gleam of pride replaced the worry in his eyes. 'Lord Pengarron will approve of your taking the interests of his people so quickly to heart.'

Swinging into the saddle, Morganna adjusted her long skirts and looked sadly back at the village. 'My interest came too late to save them today.'

The ride back was one of silent recrimination for Morganna. No matter how Barnaby tried to reassure her, she felt she should have sent out more patrols to safeguard the villagers. Other things also disturbed her. There were few villeins at work on their own strips of land, while on the lord's demesne, a score of men toiled. Who had countermanded Pengarron's order that the work days on his land were to cease for a time? It seemed that Gwyneth had not relinquished her role as completely as she had believed.

When they returned to the castle, Morganna stifled her longing to bathe the stench of smoke from her body; there was still a duty to perform before she could seek the seclusion of her chambers. Wearily climbing the steps to the hall, she ordered a page to summon the Lady Gwyneth to her in the solar.

She pressed her hot brow against the cool glass of the traceried window and stared at the mass of people below. Soldiers, masons, servants and villagers were all busy about their duties. A hundred or more must be working and living in the castle, but she had never felt so alone.

A soft footfall warned her that Gwyneth approached, and she gestured to her to be seated. Joining her, they spoke briefly of the raid, but at last Morganna said heavily, 'It's not about the raid I would speak with you. It's Bronwyn.'

As Morganna feared, Gwyneth stiffened, her face set and haughty. 'What has she done?'

'She was seen at the alder grove, and appeared to be performing a ritual which would win her a lover—or bring down a curse upon someone's head.'

Gwyneth's eyes were veiled, but as Morganna spoke, she had become very pale, so that Morganna added sympathetically, 'We both know this nonsense is just superstition! There are no such things as spells and the like, but I believe it could all have a harmful effect upon Bronwyn.'

For several moments Gwyneth remained silent, her fingers twisting the rings upon her hands. 'I'm shocked, Countess,' she said in a brittle voice. 'Deeply shocked that Bronwyn should dabble in magic. It's not all nonsense. Who knows what evil she could conjure forth in her ignorance? Leave the matter with me. I shall speak with her.'

Her manner was still reserved as she stood up. 'Was there anything else, Countess?'

'I'm afraid there is. It concerns the villeins at work on the Earl's demesne. Lord Pengarron ordered that no more work was to be done until the villeins' own land was cleared.'

'The peasants are so lazy that they'll do nothing if they're not forced to!' Gwyneth's eyes narrowed. 'As the weather has been dry for so long, it's best to get the winter crop sown. Ralph would order the work done if he were here.'

'He would not permit the villagers' work days to be miscounted,' Morganna corrected, aware of Gwyneth's growing antagonism. 'I am always ready to listen to your advice, but it is no longer your place to overrule the Earl's orders.'

Fleetingly, Gwyneth's eyes flashed with a cold green light before her expression was again veiled. 'Your pardon, Countess. It was not my intention to interfere,' she answered frigidly. 'I merely tried to lighten the burden of your new duties. If that's all, Countess, I shall return to my weaving.'

'You have proved a good friend, Gwyneth,' Morganna hastened to reassure her, knowing that her knowledge of the people and the estate would prove invaluable in the future. 'I do need your counsel, but I cannot permit either Lord Pengarron's or my own authority to be questioned.'

'We are both shaken by the raid upon the village,' Gwyneth said with a smile that did not reach her eyes. 'And also this incident with Bronwyn has upset me. We both have our roles here, and while you are Countess, I would serve you in any way I can to restore Pengarron to its former glory.'

Retiring early, Morganna dismissed Jocelyn. The night was humid and airless, and as she restlessly tossed and turned, the silk sheet slipped until it covered little of her naked limbs. Even so, its lightness was a smothering irritation against her overheated skin. For hours, it seemed, she drifted in and out of sleep, coming awake suddenly, with a heart-thudding start. She lay still, listening. Close by was the unmistakable sound of breathing and the smell of candle-smoke, though she had snuffed all the lights when she climbed into bed.

Clasping the sheet to her breasts, she sat up. 'Who is there? Answer, or I shall scream for the guards. Is that you, Jocelyn?'

'Nay, my lady Countess, it's not Jocelyn!' The deep, languid voice stopped her breath. From behind the opened bed-hangings stepped her husband.

Instinctively Morganna clutched the sheet closer to her body and drew her legs, which had been exposed to the thigh, under the cover. Dry-throated, she watched him place a candle on top of a coffer by the bed, its light hollowing his lean cheeks and revealing lines of tiredness about his eyes.

Although he made no further movement towards her, his gaze slowly explored the partially-hidden curves of her body until her nerves coiled like a whip ready to spring free at the slightest change in his position. The moonlight streaming through the mullioned window illuminated the bed in a silver glow and his long black velvet robe belted at the waist.

'When did you arrive? I heard nothing—no call from the Gatehouse,' she blurted out inanely, trying to draw herself up as small as possible so that the sheet covered her more modestly. 'Have you eaten, my lord? Shall I summon a servant?'

His low chuckle stopped her foolish gabbling. 'I arrived a short time ago, ahead of my main party.' Laughter, and something far more devastating to her senses, sparkled from his eyes as he added huskily, 'Pengarron, too, has its secret passages. I wanted no fanfare to announce my arrival—my stay is brief. And, in answer to your question, no, my lady wife, I'm not hungry—not for food, anyway.'

The bed moved as he sat on its edge. Morganna cursed the blush stealing over her body, and consciously slowed her breathing to stave off the light-headedness his nearness was causing. He made no secret of his desire for her as he leant forward to place a light kiss on her exposed shoulder.

As he moved, the neck of his robe gaped open. Her breath caught in her throat upon seeing the strong line of his neck and the tantalising play of muscles beneath the dark curling hair of his chest. With a start, she saw he was as naked as she, under his robe. The realisation sent a spiralling quiver of expectancy through her. When he fingered the thick coil of her loosely plaited hair, her heartbeat slowed to a painful thud. Slowly he untied the ribbon and ran his fingers through the pale brightness of her hair.

'You're more beautiful than I remember!'

He smiled provocatively. Winding the tresses of her hair about his wrist, he drew her closer, and she gasped when his hand brushed the nape of her neck, a shock of pleasure bathing her flesh.

Their glances fused. The admiration and tenderness she discovered in his eyes was more heady than the strongest wine. Breathlessly, she waited for his kiss, but his lips remained teasingly poised above her own until her nerves strained in an exquisite torture of longing for their touch. A month spent anticipating his homecoming had dulled the antagonism and resentment of the weeks before their marriage. He was so handsome, so strikingly manly but at the same time so considerate of her vulnerability, that she found her body responding to his will.

'Fair Morganna,' he said huskily. 'The troubadours belittle your charms! You're a siren luring me from my duty.'

His hands stroked her hair, his attention absorbed as he spread it over the pillow. 'Your hair's the colour of moonbeams. Were you sent by some pagan goddess, I wonder, to bedevil my life?'

Easing his weight forward, he hovered above her. He

had bathed, and his body smelt of soap and sandalwood.

'I'm just a woman, like any other,' she answered softly.

His tender smile destroyed the last of her calm. 'You're too modest, my sweet.'

As he spoke, he traced the outline of her lips with his finger until they tingled and quivered from the delight of his touch. Her gaze clung to his, suddenly fearing the unknown. Then his lips were fierce and demanding upon hers, chasing all thoughts of resistance from her mind. Music sweeter than the strumming of harps rang in her ears as his lips played expertly over her mouth. She had never imagined that a single kiss could so devastate her senses. Momentarily she hesitated before entwining her fingers through his longish hair, which was still damp and curling from his bath. Every particle of her body and being was dissolving into molten fire as her lips responded to his ardour. Her arms tightened, feeling the hard suppleness of his body as they bound him closer to her.

Impatient at the touch of velvet, she slid her hands beneath his robe. At the sound of his indrawn breath, she marvelled that she could rouse him as easily as he awoke her dormant passion. Their legs entwined, he lay across her, and as his mouth moved over hers, his hands moved slowly, sensuously, across her fevered skin. Somehow the sheet was no longer protection between them, and every pore of her body cried out for his caresses. When he eased back, his breathing hard and unsteady, she could not contain a gasp of dismay.

Then, as she saw his face in the moonlight, his expression no longer gently but dark and tense with desire, she relaxed. Shrugging off his robe, Ralph lowered himself close to her again. As he leant over her, the control he was exercising became a tangible barrier between them. Sweeping aside the Saxon cross resting on her throat, he kissed the throbbing pulse beneath.

'Ralph!' She breathed his name softly, her body trembling from the unbelievable pleasure his touch could bring her.

He raised his head. A spasm almost of pain crossed his face. Then his lips again plundered hers, his hands bold and insistent, drawing a sigh from her as they caressed her breasts. Trails of fire ran through her body as his hands travelled over her stomach and hips. With a moan, she spread her fingers over the smooth muscles across his back, surrendering to his mastery. Nothing existed but the demanding ecstasy of his body covering hers and the need for surcease from the tumult building within her. She was carried away on an upsurge of passion which seemed to begin at her toes and gradually consume her entire being, leaving her floating, disembodied with fulfilment.

'Morganna!' His voice was hoarse against her ear. 'Why did you go on letting me believe the worst of you? You and Linsdale were never lovers. No man has known you before me.'

Still drowsy from his lovemaking, she looked at him in puzzlement. 'Would you have believed me, my lord?'

Feeling his muscles flex along his back, she knew that the truth of her words pained him. Relenting, she smiled. 'Even though you believed the worst of me, you still married me,' she said lightly. 'It is time to forget our differences. I vowed on our wedding day that our reunion was to be a new beginning.'

'It was more than that, my sweet.' He rolled her on to her back, his lips again demanding as they moulded upon her own in a long breath-searing kiss. Finally he drew back, looking down at her intently. 'It makes it harder still for me to leave on the morrow.'

'So soon!'

Ralph laughed softly, clearly delighted at her obvious disappointment. 'This night was stolen! I must ride to Flint. King Richard has returned from Ireland, and at present he's at Conwy, but his army is deserting.' He looked at her steadily, adding, 'Giles is with the King.'

Morganna closed her eyes to hide her pain. Tonight had made her irrevocably Pengarron's wife. She was not so naïve as to believe that the attraction between them, even this new tenderness, was anything approaching love. But it was to him now that she owed her first allegiance. He had shown her a respect and consideration she had not expected. If only there was not this dissension between the King and the Duke of Lancaster, which set her husband and her brother on opposing sides! Dear God, how could she bear it, if it came to a battle between the two armies?

She opened her eyes and was heartened by the remorse she saw tensing her husband's expression. 'If we have only tonight, my lord, then let us not speak of the differences that are still between us. I can never entirely forsake Giles.'

'He's not worthy of your devotion. He washed his hands of you when he learned of our marriage! Radford shamed you by refusing to pay your dowry.'

'Then it is I who am not worthy of you, my lord.' Morganna turned her head away, unable to face him.

His fingers gripped her chin, gently turning her head back towards him, his expression stern. 'You still care for him, no matter what he's done to you!'

'Giles is my brother, and I've hurt him deeply. He thinks I betrayed him. God willing, in time he will forgive me.'

'Then Radford's a fool to risk losing the treasure you offer him.'

The throaty whisper was barely audible as his lips nuzzled her ear, and as they travelled along her cheek to reclaim her mouth, she wondered whether she had imagined it.

Hurt by her brother's rejection, she clung to Ralph. The consideration he had shown her was a balm upon her wounded pride. Desperately she sought reassurance —wanting to be needed for herself, not for money or power.

In a fever of longing, her hands slid down Ralph's back, silently dwelling on a few rigid scars from some unknown combat. She gave herself up to the pleasure of the feel of the cording and uncording muscles beneath her fingers. Her body glowed warmly, pulsating in answering delight as he drew her again into forgetfulness, into a world of raptuous harmony where only they existed.

CHAPTER ELEVEN

RALPH STARED DOWN at Morganna, who lay sleeping in the circle of his arms. The pre-dawn stirrings both inside and outside the castle warned him it was almost time to leave, but still he lingered. After long hours spent in the saddle during the past weeks and the constant arguing among the Duke's followers, he was reluctant to leave Pengarron. No woman had so tempted him from duty as this one.

As dawn brightened the room, the pale sleekness of his wife's body was revealed to him in all its perfection. A treasure, he mused, beautiful, brave, quick-witted and at last his wife as had been ordained. Soon all his birthright would be restored to him. Marrying Morganna was just the beginning.

She stirred in his arms. When she opened her eyes, their violet depths were heavy-lidded and still drowsy from her night of passion. Raising himself on his elbow, Ralph stroked the curve of her back, his throat oddly tight as he smiled down at her.

'Would that duty did not take me from you, sweet wife.'

'Must you go so soon?'

From the castle grounds a cock crowed, and his regret deepened. 'I must leave within the hour.'

To his astonishment, a tear glistened on the corner of her thick lashes. 'Then I must not detain you.' Her voice sounded strained. 'Though our people will think I'm a poor wife, who cannot keep her lord at her side!'

He frowned. 'Have the villagers been disrespectful? Is Gwyneth causing trouble?'

'Oh, no, my lord,' she replied quickly. 'But it will take

time for the people to accept a new Countess. Barnaby is teaching me Welsh to help me to win their trust.'

Would she never cease to surprise him? he wondered. He had expected a token show of rebellion from her at the way he had rushed their marriage. Not only had she accepted it, however, but her interest in the people was genuine. He felt a stab of pride, and could not resist teasing her.

'It pleases me that you take your duties seriously, my dearest. The people have been long neglected, and my absence does not help. Yet, until last night, I thought you would have preferred it thus.' She looked away, clearly flustered, and when she tried to rise from the bed, he pulled her back against him, smiling. 'It seems I was wrong!'

'I am aware of my duty, my lord,' she said stiffly. 'I would not fail you.'

Unaccountably, his anger flared. She had become rigid in his arms like a clay doll. What had she hoped to entice from him by her display of affection the previous night?

'Duty!' he said coldly. 'Is that all that passed between us last night? I thought I had brought you pleasure.'

A becoming pinkness tinged her cheeks, and her voice was indignant. 'You did, my lord. Great pleasure.'

At her unexpected honesty, his anger faded. He had misjudged her. 'Then may the King and the Duke of Lancaster speedily resolve their differences, that I may return once more to your side!'

Sensing from the stubborn light in her eyes that she was about to question him, he snatched the sheet from her hands, refusing to be denied. As she moved away from him, he kissed her into submission until she responded with an ardour that surpassed anything he had experienced before.

When finally and with great reluctance he turned away from her and drew on his robe, she put out a hand to detain him. Apparently unaware of the torment she created within him, with her silvery-gold hair ruffled in seductive abandon and her lips swollen from his kisses, Morganna asked sweetly, 'Will you not stay and break your fast with me, my lord?'

To his surprise, Ralph found that he had no desire to go straight to his room; satiated from their passionate lovemaking, he wanted to spend more time with her. He rang the hand-bell, and when the servant entered, ordered food and ale to be brought. When, some time later, the Angelus bell sounded, they looked guiltily at each other, and Ralph leapt from the bed where they had taken their meal.

'Now we must hurry if we are not to keep Father Matthew waiting at morning prayers!' he said with a rueful grin.

Leaving his wife, he returned to his chamber, dressed quickly and made his way to the chapel. But when he knelt at Morganna's side in prayer, the familiar words failed to bring him peace. His troubled glance roved over the chapel, and he was shocked to discover how neglected it appeared. He knew there had been no resident priest at Pengarron since the death of Father Gregory, who had died of the same fever that had killed Edmund, but until now he had not given it much thought, assuming that Gwyneth relied on passing friars to perform the services.

The prayers at an end, he drew Morganna to one side. 'I am withdrawing some of the masons from their work on the King's Tower to restore the stonework here. I had not realised how badly some of the figures had become defaced over the years. It is not fitting that we neglect God's house.'

'I, too, had noticed the decay,' Morganna replied. 'I have begun a new altar cloth, but the hangings are also rotting where the roof has at one time leaked.'

'Then they must be replaced.' He laughed, amused at

the expression of uncertainty on her lovely face. 'Until my estates are restored, I may not as yet be as wealthy as Radford or Linsdale, but I'm no pauper. Pengarron is your home. When we journey to London, you must buy whatever you consider necessary.'

When Ralph took Morganna's arm to escort her from the chapel, she looked up at him, her face drawn with worry. Raising a questioning brow, he waited for her to speak.

'What of your differences with the King, my lord? I fear that his Majesty will show little clemency to any man who has stood against him.'

Ralph was moved by the anguish of her tone. The few hours at Pengarron had brought him unexpected plea-sure—and more, a contentment of a kind he had not thought possible. His wife's understanding of politics pleased him. Besides, there was that stubborn light in her eyes, which warned him she expected her words to be taken seriously.

'If King Richard is reconciled to his grace of Lancaster, he must also be to his followers,' he confi-dently answered her fears. 'I lost Daneton on the King's whim. Would you have me skulk in France until he decides to rob me of Pengarron also?'

Noticing the gold and enamel cross she always wore, he flicked it with his finger. 'You wear this always, and with pride. I remember seeing your mother wear it . . . It's part of your heritage. Would you have me give up without a fight the land my family has governed for two centuries? I have tried sending petitions to the King —each one was ignored. Believe me, if there was any other way to regain what is mine by right, I would so.'

'That could take months!' She still looked anxious. 'You have so many burdens that I don't like to worry you about estate matters.'

'I do not expect you to cope alone,' he replied, delighted that she had taken the welfare of Pengarron so much to heart. 'You have done more than you know, by your presence here.'

He looked cheerfully down into her frowning eyes, but as he listened to her account of the raid on the village and of Father Matthew's suspicion that a pagan priest might be hiding in the hills, his smile faded.

'I am sure there's no possibility of a Druid practising hereabouts. My grandfather stamped out the last of their kind,' he reassured her. His anger mounted at his present inability to act against the raiders. 'But you are right to be concerned about that attack . . . Something must be done. Unfortunately I've already earned the Duke's displeasure by coming here last night. I cannot delay in rejoining him, and it could take days to track down the raiders. We must hope they are by now far from here. All I can do is to leave a dozen men to help patrol the estate.'

He drew her back into his arms. 'Stay close to the castle. I would not have you in danger.'

Morganna shook her head. 'I will not hide myself away while our people face peril. If I ride out as normal, it will give them confidence that we are safe.'

Struck again by her courage, he kissed her brow and released her, his voice roughened by the emotion she stirred in him.

They walked together to the courtyard, where his men were already mounted and awaiting him. He settled himself in the saddle, and Morganna reached up to offer him the stirrup-cup. At seeing the regret at his leaving glistening in her eyes, Ralph had never found it so hard to ride out from Pengarron.

Morganna sat at her needlework, her hand poised over the gold thread of the scarlet altar cloth as she listened to Barnaby singing a love song. The afternoon light was still bright in the solar, but already she was restless from concentrating on so passive an occupation. With a

twinge of guilt she saw Gwyneth's fingers moving rapidly
in and out, bright thread colouring the stiff material of a
stool-cover. She schooled herself to patience and applied herself to her task, only to find within moments
that her stitches again slowed. Barnaby's rich voice
throbbed with emotion, and she looked up. Upon discovering the troubadour's adoring gaze upon Jocelyn,
she inwardly smiled.

A spasm squeezed her heart. From her maid's dreamy
expression, it was obvious that she loved the troubadour. When Ralph returned, Morganna resolved to
speak to him about the couple. There seemed no reason
why Barnaby and Jocelyn should not marry, since they
both served the same household.

Thoughts of romance took her mind back to her last
meeting with Ralph. The two weeks that had passed
since their single night together seemed to have spanned
an eternity. Yet, whenever she recalled it, a warm glow
spread through her veins and sent shivers of delight
down her spine. Certainly, marriage to Ralph was not
the trial she had imagined. It was disturbing to acknowledge that she actually missed her husband, and time
and time again she found she was listening for the
sound of a herald's trumpet that would announce his
return.

After the tenderness of their night together, it was no
longer possible to think of him as her enemy. The King
had wronged his family, and Ralph's cause was just. He
wished the King no harm. If only Giles would reconcile
himself to her marriage, she knew she could find contentment in her new life. One single night of passion
could not allay the distrust that still festered between
Ralph and herself, but it was a beginning.

Barnaby stopped singing as a page announced a messenger from the Earl. A travel-stained figure entered,
and bent his knee wearily to Morganna. Seeing him near
to exhaustion, she suppressed her curiosity and gestured

to a page to bring him some wine. The man gulped down the contents of the goblet, and wiped his sweating face with his sleeve.

Morganna demanded, 'My husband—you have news of Lord Pengarron?'

The stocky man nodded, and drew a long breath. 'His lordship is in good health and bids me tell you that King Richard is now a prisoner at Flint. His Majesty will shortly be escorted to London.'

For a moment Morganna looked blankly at the messenger, unable to believe the implication of his words. He shifted uncomfortably on his knees, continuing more gently, 'Lord Pengarron also bade me tell you that the Marquess of Radford was not among the prisoners taken by our troops.'

She sank back in her chair, absently gesturing to the messenger to rise. She was stunned, but gradually one thought emerged uppermost in her mind. Thank God, Giles was safe! Or was he? Panic churned her stomach. Had he been wounded? Killed? She raised a shaking hand to her throat, the touch of the cross bringing her no comfort.

Conscious that the messenger was looking at her thoughtfully, she recovered her wits to ask, 'Does Lord Pengarron now travel to London?'

'Yes, Countess, he rides with the Duke of Lancaster. The King's procession will travel slowly. His lordship says that when they rest for the night at a nearby castle, he will come to you.'

'Oh, are we to be denied seeing the King?' Bronwyn broke in impertinently.

'Pengarron is too far out of the way,' Gwyneth told her with obvious relief.

Morganna shrugged both remarks aside, more concerned at the seriousness of the news than at the extra work involved in a royal visit.

'What happened?' She addressed the messenger. 'I

thought the Duke of Lancaster came to parley with the King.'

He fidgeted with the buckle of his sword-belt. 'Ay, Countess, that was so. The King was making his way to Flint, but by then, most of his followers and army had deserted him. His party was ambushed, and the King taken under guard. For his Majesty's own protection, his Grace of Lancaster escorts the King to London.'

'But as a prisoner!' Morganna exclaimed, aghast. 'What is to happen to him?'

'Some of the nobles are urging the Duke to take the crown,' the man answered cautiously. 'His Grace has refused, but I doubt he will hold out against his nobles for long.'

'My husband . . . Is he among those who would make Bolingbroke king?'

Morganna waited, her throat drying with fear.

'Nay, Countess. His lordship counsels restraint, but his voice is one of few.'

'Then Ralph must agree,' Bronwyn interrupted excitedly. 'It's the only way Pengarron can rise to the greatness you foretold, Gwyneth.'

'Bronwyn!' Gwyneth cut in, startling Morganna by the shrillness of her tone. 'Such an outburst is unseemly! Naturally Pengarron will prosper if the Earl stays in the Duke of Lancaster's favour. But King Richard is still our anointed sovereign.'

The withering, almost warning glare she gave her ward disturbed Morganna. Troubled, she stood up and walked to the window, unable to rid herself of the notion that it was the estate that obsessed Gwyneth, not the Earl or his future.

She leaned forward against the leaded window, the gold circlet across her temple pressing unnoticed into her brow. If the Duke of Lancaster was crowned King, Giles would be in danger. If Richard Plantagenet remained on the throne, he would never forgive this insult.

Ralph could be attainted with treason! Her head spun at the very horror of the thought.

A cough behind her drew her attention to the messenger. She looked over her shoulder, and saw he had followed her and was holding out a leather pouch.

'His lordship commanded me to give you this as a token of his esteem, Countess.'

A rush of emotion overwhelmed Morganna, leaving her breathless as she took the pouch, like a child receiving its first gift. Her hand trembled with excitement as she untied the leather binding. A diamond- and pearl-studded brooch, as long as her finger and shaped like a crescent moon, fell into her palm. A lump formed in her throat as she gazed at the delicate workmanship, deeply touched that Ralph should choose her insignia for such a gift. Desolate that he was not here in person so that she could thank him, her eyes misted with longing. She was so absorbed by her thoughts that she scarcely heard the messenger leave or the sound of a soft step rustling the rushes at her side.

'So, my proud Countess, should the Duke of Lancaster be crowned King, your brother will lose everything!' Bronwyn laughed cruelly. 'Without your dowry, what use are you to Ralph? In nearly two months of marriage, your lord has visited you but once. What a disappointment you must be for him!'

Her sarcasm tore into Morganna. Her head jerked up as she closed her hand over the brooch, while the girl continued spitefully, 'Ralph will soon tire of you, and I shall be waiting for him! He will love me.'

Sudden rage blasted Morganna's composure, and she rounded on her, her voice harsh. 'You dare to threaten me!' The clasp of the brooch bit into her palm as she clenched her fist to stop herself striking the insolent smile from the girl's face. 'Remember your place here, Bronwyn! You are the Lady Gwyneth's ward—a penniless orphan. Do not be so foolish as to mistake my husband's fondness for you for something which can never be. If you continue to act in this spoilt way, you'll lose even that affection from him.'

'Shall I?' Bronwyn crowed triumphantly. 'I know how to pleasure a man and keep him at my side.'

Trembling with fury, Morganna drew herself up, and though she was a handspan shorter than the younger girl, her rage remained undiminished. 'Your childish spells are useless! A man such as Ralph needs a woman, not a spoilt superstitious brat! I have no intention of sharing my husband with anyone.' The truth of her words added to her determination to put an end to Bronwyn's mischief.

'We'll see about that!' The girl's face screwed up like that of a spitting wildcat. 'Ralph will be mine, and you'll pay for every glance he gave you instead of me! He only married you out of duty.'

Morganna opened her hand, holding out the brooch for Bronwyn to see. It took all her will-power to keep her voice low and smooth. 'I am not frightened by your silly threats! Why do you think my husband sent me this? Not from a sense of duty, I assure you.'

Had she thrown icy water in Bronwyn's face, the change in her could not have been more marked. She turned grey, her dark eyes rounding with fear. She staggered backward, staring at the brooch, and Morganna heard her gasp 'Hecate!'

There was a movement behind the girl, and Gwyneth rose to her feet, also deathly pale.

'Bronwyn!' she cried sharply. 'Have you taken leave of your senses? You will ask the Countess's forgiveness.'

Bronwyn put out a hand as though to ward off evil, and backed away from Morganna, her voice like crushed grit. 'Never! I hate her!'

'You'll do as I say, *'demoiselle*,' Gwyneth demanded, 'or you'll find yourself banished from this castle! I'll send you to my sister in Ireland. That should keep you out of mischief!'

Fresh horror contorted Bronwyn's ashen face as she stared at Gwyneth. 'But you promised me . . ' Her voice broke in a hoarse sob. 'Oh, I hate you. I hate you both.' Stamping her foot, she swung round. 'I won't go to Ireland!'

Watching the girl run from the solar, Morganna drew a long breath and tried to calm herself, wondering why the girl's spite should have shaken her so . . . She was only a spoilt, wilful child. Tired of her constant tantrums and even finding Gwyneth's friendship wearying by its smothering possessiveness, Morganna longed for the quiet life she had led at Daneton. How she missed Giles's love and understanding! Her heart ached at the impossibility that he would now forgive her. If the King was a prisoner, the rift between her brother and herself would widen.

Frowning, Morganna racked her brains for any answer to the problem. The gold brooch was warm against her skin, and again her heart lightened as she looked down at it. Did this gift mean that Ralph cared . . . just a little? The thought made her pulse race. Despite the seriousness of the events surrounding him, he had taken the time and trouble to choose a very personal gift for her. Did he think of her often? she wondered hopefully, and a shaft of longing drove through her. Were his nights plagued, as were hers, with memories of their lovemaking?

A shadow passed across the window, and she looked up to see Gwyneth regarding her steadily.

'In all my years in France, I never knew Ralph present a woman with a favour.' Her voice was strained as though it hurt her to speak. 'Yet, if a man in his troop proved his valour in battle or acted courageously, he never failed to show his approval by bestowing a gift. It is plain that you have succeeded in hooding the eagle! I congratulate you, my dear.'

'I have pleased him. That's enough.'

'Spoken like a dutiful wife!' Gwyneth's green eyes slanted venomously. 'How delighted Ralph would be to hear such words! He said he would tame you, and clearly he has succeeded. Such is his way. Always he must be the victor: when the sword fails, he resorts to charm. He'll never take second place to any man. He sees your brother as a rival to your affections, and his pride will demand that he wins first place in his wife's heart.'

Morganna tensed at Gwyneth's bitterness. She would not let her words poison her pleasure in Ralph's gift, but, even so, her doubts returned, showing her how fragile was her happiness.

Too often she had compared Ralph to Giles. Her brother, too, must always be first in everything: countless times she had seen the potency of his charm when it was used to bring an adversary to submission. Was Ralph's solicitude no more than that?

Aware of Gwyneth watching her, Morganna hid her disquiet. 'You see too much in Lord Pengarron's gift.'

'I have hurt you by my words!' Gwyneth was instantly contrite. 'My dear, I meant only to warn you. Accept Ralph for what he is.' Her eyes glowed with a passionate light. 'Give Ralph an heir, and you will have his undying gratitude.'

'How can you speak like that?' she replied, stung. 'Edmund loved you!' She turned away and walked to the window, knowing that she did not want Ralph's gratitude. What did she want, then? Respect? Love!

'Your pardon, Countess,' Gwyneth said with unusual humility. 'Bronwyn's behaviour has upset me. The child is dear to me—like a daughter. Will you reconsider, Countess, and not have Bronwyn sent away?'

'I will say nothing to Lord Pengarron of her conduct —this time,' Morganna said pointedly. 'He has troubles enough without being burdened by women's bickering. But Bronwyn must either mend her manners or stay away from my presence.'

Gwyneth curtly nodded her acceptance, and as she picked up her sewing, Morganna was puzzled that she had not answered her comment about Edmund. In all the weeks she had been at Pengarron, she could not remember Gwyneth ever speaking of her husband. Perhaps grief affected people in that way . . . Gwyneth was certainly not a woman to wear her emotions on her sleeve.

There seemed so many questions without answers. Ralph—Giles? The two people she cared for most deeply. She pulled herself up with a start. Was that why Bronwyn's words had cut so deep? Was she beginning to fall in love with Ralph?

The atmosphere in the solar was stifling—she had been cooped up too long. Summoning Barnaby to attend her, she declared impulsively as she left the room, 'I shall go hawking.'

Descending the steps from the solar into the hall, Morganna saw the steward talking to one of the masons. When the steward noticed her presence, he bowed to her, saying, 'My lady, the master mason would speak with you.'

Morganna nodded, ordering Barnaby to arrange an escort for the hunt as the harassed-looking mason bowed to her.

'My lady, now that some of my men are working on the chapel, the tower will not be finished by Michaelmas.'

'Did Lord Pengarron set such a date?' she asked.

'He did not, Countess. His lordship is always most understanding of the problems in rebuilding. It is the Lady Gwyneth who insists the works must be finished by then. Her ladyship has now brought in some masons from another lodge—men whose ways are not as mine. They speak only Welsh. It makes it very difficult, my lady.'

'Why did you not come to me sooner?'

The mason looked embarrassed. 'I was told by the Lady Gwyneth not to trouble you. To get on with my work without complaining. With respect, Countess, Lord Pengarron would not expect us to work under such conditions. And as to working by torchlight once it's dark—I cannot be responsible for the accidents that will happen.'

'There'll be no work done at night; it is far too dangerous. As to the other masons who have been brought in, since they have arrived, it would not be right to send them away,' she said evenly, though her resentment flared at Gwyneth's interference. 'However, in future I shall deal with any problems you may have, unless his lordship is in residence.'

Looking happier, the mason left her, but as Morganna rode out of the castle surrounded by her escort, she was troubled at Gwyneth's attitude. As they rode through the village, her spirits lifted at the welcoming cheers from the people coming out of church after the Sunday service. She waved to Father Matthew, and calling her party to a halt, she spoke a few halting words in Welsh.

The babbling, excited chatter which greeted her attempt was beyond her understanding, and she looked blankly at Barnaby.

'You've pleased them, Countess,' Barnaby said, smiling. 'It's because they speak so fast that you cannot understand them. They're thanking you for bringing Father Matthew here, and for allowing them to spend more time on their own land.'

'It was Lord Pengarron who gave those orders, not I. Tell them that. But I am pleased they seem happier.'

At the sound of approaching horses, the villagers' expressions changed.

'Countess, the weather is so fine that I hope you don't mind my joining you,' Gwyneth called from behind Morganna.

Although she resented the deliberate intrusion, Morganna smiled comfortingly at the peasants, whose change of attitude told her all too clearly that Gwyneth was unpopular with them. Only when she had hidden her annoyance did she turn.

Gwyneth was seated on a bay mare a few yards away, staring straight at Morganna, her expression cold and haughty, a hawk perched on her gauntleted hand.

'You are welcome, of course, Gwyneth.'

The widow looked at the villagers standing around Father Matthew. 'Your priest has brought comfort to our people. It was regrettable that my cousin, who was to replace Father Gregory, broke his hip. The bone is slow to heal, and it will be some weeks yet before the poor man is fit enough to join us here.'

'Let us hope your cousin recovers soon,' Morganna said, wondering why Gwyneth had not explained the absence of the priest before.

They rode for a while in silence, passing the alder grove and up on to the sloping hills behind the castle. Drawing rein, Morganna removed the hood from the merlin on her wrist, lifted her hand high and propelled the bird into flight.

She watched the hawk, the bells on its trailing jesses tinkling as it flew low across the ground. Then it soared gracefully to hover in search of prey. When it swooped, like an arrow straight and true, talons outstretched, to pounce on an unsuspecting hare, Morganna was reminded of the last time she had hunted with Ralph and the events that had led to their marriage. How she longed to be once more in the haven of his strong arms and be able to forget the nagging worries over the estate!

With her merlin again settled on her wrist, and hooded, Morganna waited for Gwyneth to loose her hawk. When she gave no sign of doing so, Morganna suggested they ride to the waterfall.

For an instant Gwyneth looked taken aback. 'Oh no,

my dear, we don't want to ride that way! I fear the
waterfall will disappoint you. It's not rained in weeks.
Wait until the rivers are in full flood for your first sight of
it; then it will be worth visiting.'

She wheeled her mare in the opposite direction and,
urging the animal into a trot, called back over her
shoulder, 'Come! We will ride to the next hill—the view
from there of Pengarron cannot be equalled.'

Morganna was tempted not to follow, but she had
made one stand with Gwyneth that day, and for the sake
of peace, the visit to the waterfall could wait. It was
strange, though; that was the second time Gwyneth had
made an excuse not to visit the waterfall.

As they crested the hill, the view of the castle below
them was remarkable. The sunlight turned the white-
painted walls a rich gold, while the steep cliff-face of the
ravine set it on a platform so that it looked like one of the
huge sugared confections served at Court. Morganna
sighed, regretting that inside those majestic walls there
was little sweetness. Bronwyn's and Gwyneth's bitterness robbed her of much of the pleasure of her new
home.

During the ride back, Morganna slowed her pace and
drew level with Barnaby. Gwyneth, apparently eager to
return, rode ahead. As they rode, Morganna studied the
swarthy countenance of the dark-eyed troubadour.
When not performing, he was quiet and gently spoken,
and over the past weeks his advice had proved invaluable. Rather guiltily, she wondered whether the young
man did not miss his former active life.

'Have you served Lord Pengarron long, Barnaby? I
notice that your dialect is not the same as that of those
native to this valley. Where was your home originally?'

'I come from south of here, from one of the estates
taken by the King. His lordship liked my singing, and
I was taught by Father Gregory to read and write—
when I first came to Pengarron. Now I serve Lord

Pengarron in any way I can.'

Morganna stared thoughtfully at the gold-embossed leather of her reins, suspecting that there was more behind his words. Had Ralph suspected that all was not well at Pengarron, and left Barnaby to keep him informed of what went on?

Barnaby was about to speak, but at that moment Gwyneth slowed her pace, frowning back at Morganna.

'You spend much time in your minstrel's company!' She cast an accusing glare at the handsome singer. 'Is it wise? After all, with your husband away, gossip soon spreads.'

Morganna controlled her burst of temper. Always, it seemed, Gwyneth must spoil her slightest pleasure. 'The Earl left his troubadour for my entertainment, knowing how much it pleased me to listen to his music.'

Looking across at Barnaby, she added mischievously, 'Anyone with an ear for gossip would know that Barnaby has shown preference to my tiring-woman. I would say he was quite smitten by her.'

Seeing the troubadour flush beneath his dark skin, she went on, pointedly touching the crescent brooch pinned to her gown, 'My lord husband is an exceptional man. He has no fear of rivals to my heart!'

'I wonder!' Gwyneth said with unaccustomed harshness. 'You never did tell the full story of your courtship. During his years in France, Ralph never mentioned your name. Nor did he ever lack solace in the arms of willing admirers! When you first came, you made no secret that Ralph had abducted you. Strange how one thinks one knows a man so well, and yet really he is quite different.'

Morganna let her hand linger upon the brooch, painfully aware that she knew so little of the man she had married. An unpleasant tightness settled over her chest. She had no wish to learn of the many women Ralph had paid court to, and suddenly she realised that she wanted more from her marriage than for it to be one of convenience—or, worse, complacency. Pengarron was the most fascinating man she had ever met. Would not the lady who won his heart be the most fortunate in all England?

The afternoon was still warm when they arrived back at the castle. Seeing Jocelyn come out of the laundry outbuilding and cast a languishing glance at Barnaby, Morganna dismissed him, saying, 'I would be alone for a while. I've no need of you or Jocelyn for the next hour.'

As she handed her merlin back to the falconer, she watched the couple. Joy shone from the faces of the two lovers as they clasped hands and ran back over the drawbridge towards the river. They made love appear so simple, yet reality was seldom so uncomplicated. A troubadour and a superstitious tiring-women—both dreamers in their way. Perhaps that was the secret of true romance. During the following days, it was obvious that Barnaby and Jocelyn were in love, and each time Morganna saw them together, she became more aware of how much she missed Ralph.

One afternoon, too restless to settle, Morganna sought the seclusion of the rose garden to enjoy a rare moment's solitude. The wolfhound followed at her heels as she hummed a song, revelling in the peace and beauty of her surroundings. Even the noise of the masons at work on the last stages of the King's Tower was muffled on this side of the castle. Overhead, the cooing of doves added to the languor spreading over her while she idly watched a peacock strut along the top of the high wall.

Abruptly the calm was shattered by a long blast from a trumpet. The doves' wings flapped alarmingly, and the peacock emitted a sharp cry, several of his long tail-feathers dislodging as he fluttered to the grass. Morganna whirled, her glance darting to the roof of the watch-tower. To her delight, the black and gold of her husband's standard was slowly being raised. Ralph had returned.

CHAPTER TWELVE

TAKING A MOMENT to calm her flustered nerves, Morganna straightened her gold coronet and smoothed the veil draped over a gold wire caul. As she walked towards the main courtyard, the clatter of hooves told her the riders were already in the outer bailey.

Ahead of her, framed by the open archway, Ralph dismounted. He was dressed in green, his short gold-lined cloak, its edges fashioned into leaf shapes, thrown casually back over his shoulder.

She saw his powerful elegant figure, and her body trembled with longing. How she wished for Wulfric's freedom, as the dog gambolled forward to caper around his master's feet. Ralph stooped to pat the dog and, straightening his gaze, met Morganna's eyes. He smiled, dispelling the sombre set of his rugged, bronzed face.

Sweeping the long peaked hat from his dark hair, he tossed it to a page and strode towards her. The impatient way he stripped off his gauntlets and tucked them into his belt, before clasping her hands, took her breath away.

The warmth of his touch coursed through her whole being. Belatedly, recalling the honour due him, she made to curtsy, but his hard grip upon her hands stayed her. With a glance over his shoulder, he ordered his retainers to stay back, and pulled her through the arch into the privacy of the garden.

Momentarily his eyes clouded as he looked down at her, then, with a laugh which seemed rather strained to her taut nerves, he said softly, 'I'll not greet my wife with a score of eyes watching.'

'For shame, my lord, what will your men think of us?'

Secretly overjoyed at his action, her rebuke ended in a throaty giggle. She had not dreamed he could be so impetuous.

'Let them think what they will,' he replied, enfolding her in his arms so that she could not escape, even had she wanted to. 'I did not ride a dozen miles to see the Lady Gwyneth!'

Seeing his eyes darken to the colour of brandywine, Morganna marvelled at the change in him. She smiled tremulously, unsure whether she had heard him aright. Could it be that he had missed her? Or was he taunting her?

Did it matter? He was here, and apparently pleased to see her. His mood was infectious, and she was caught up by the irresistible role of her husband playing the ardent lover.

'An enchantress could not tempt a man more sorely to ride to her side,' he said, raising her hand to his lips.

'You're too bold, my lord,' she gently reproved, while her eyes encouraged him not to end this glorious madness.

Smiling provocatively, he flicked the crescent-shaped brooch at her shoulder. 'Only moonstruck, sweet wife.'

Then she was crushed in his arms, his kiss hungry and demanding, as though he was indeed the lover she had always dreamed would make her his own. Her response was instant. She clung to him, her fingers winding about his thick hair. As his kiss deepened, her senses whirled in tumult and her head fell back. The touch of his lips upon the feverish skin at the hollow of her neck roused tingling, pulsating sensations which exploded through her body.

She moved her hand to secure her headdress, while the insistence of his lips made her forget all decorum —or that they could be overlooked from the castle. After the weeks of separation, she was conscious only that nothing had tempered the magic of his touch, or her body's craving for him. The air was filled with the scent of the roses as they fused, heart against heart. When a low ecstatic moan escaped her, her eyes flew open with shock, suspecting ridicule at his answering chuckle.

The desire she saw smouldering in his eyes sent twirls of excitement through her limbs. Their gazes fixed upon each other, Morganna was aware of the imperceptible sharpening of his features, his brows drawing together as though something troubled him.

Did he doubt her pleasure at his return? The thought appalled her. Her heart too full to speak, she caressed his warm cheek, and her finger followed the line of the small crescent scar. Overcome with emotion, she rose on her toes to kiss the white ridge. Ralph's expression was impassive. Yet, as though drawn by a force outside his will, his lips pressed against her palm moving down along his jaw.

A shocked gasp from behind drew them apart. Scowling, Ralph looked over his shoulder, and Morganna saw Bronwyn gaping at them. The girl's lovely face contorted in a spasm of jealousy, and for an instant her dark eyes flashed venomously before she flounced back through the arch.

'What's the matter with the minx?' Ralph asked, clearly puzzled. 'She did not look very pleased to see me.'

'The look you gave her probably terrified the poor girl,' Morganna teased, refusing to let Bronwyn's attitude destroy the pleasure of her reunion with her husband. 'Obviously, Bronwyn was disappointed that you were not alone, my lord.'

He looked searchingly at Morganna. 'Bronwyn is headstrong—she's always been difficult.' His frown deepened. 'Has she caused you trouble? If so . . .'

'I can handle Bronwyn's moods,' she assured him.

At a further disturbance from the far side of the archway, Ralph gave her a rueful smile, and pulled her arm through his. 'I suppose I must show myself to my household. We'll dine alone tonight in your chamber. Alas, I must rejoin the Duke by dusk tomorrow.'

In vain did Morganna try to hide her distress, and a devilish gleam danced into Ralph's eyes.

'The household can wait, and so can the Lady Gwyneth! I don't doubt that that Welsh dragon has been breathing fire because I spend so little time with my Countess.'

She could not contain a laugh at his allusion to Gwyneth, but hastened to correct him. 'Gwyneth does not find it easy to accept that she is no longer mistress here, but her advice has been a great help.'

'It sounds as though she is mellowing. Pengarron has always been an obsession with her.' His frown returned. 'Somehow the place has never seemed the same since Edmund brought her here. She tried to turn it into a showpiece, not a home.'

'Perhaps you have spent too long away?' Morganna suggested, comfortingly. 'Places are not always as we remember them.'

'Daneton was!' He pulled himself up, his expression guarded. When Morganna said nothing, he added ruefully, 'The atmosphere at Daneton was carefree. It was not easy to find discontent even from the older tenants. The people respected Radford. They spoke with great affection of you, dear wife.'

The endearment upon his lips made her heart sing. 'Once this conflict between the King and the Duke is over, Pengarron will be as you remember it,' she said. 'The people will be more settled once their lord returns to govern them.'

'And, once I am home, we'll have new lodgings in the King's Tower,' he said, leading her into the courtyard. 'It's time I told you of my plans.'

His step was quick and firm as he guided her towards the imposing tower. When they made to enter the lower floor, there was a whimper behind them. Ralph turned to look at Wulfric, who hung back uncertainly by the doorway. He paused as he seemed about to call the dog to follow, and looked searchingly at Morganna.

'Here, Wulfric,' she called, having no intention of barring the dogs from their apartments, especially as Ralph enjoyed their presence.

The approving grin she won from him heartened her, and as they entered each room, he spoke of its function. The enthusiasm was obvious in his voice as he spoke of his plans for their future. When they reached the large room on the second floor, Ralph dismissed the dusty masons at work on the carving over the fireplace, and with a proud sweep of his arm, declared.

'This will be our private chamber. It will be quieter than the solar, which has all the noise of the hall.'

Discovering the almost completed crest above the fireplace, Morganna moved towards it, delighted to see it was of the impaled coat of arms of Warrender and Barnett. But when she looked up at Ralph, she was startled by the grimness of his expression. Clearly, something was troubling him.

In her new-found happiness she had forgotten the precarious foundations upon which their relationship was formed. It was unlikely he would speak of his worries, and that saddened her. As she watched the lines at his mouth whiten with tension, her heart went to him.

'Come, there's more to see.' Ralph appeared to push whatever was troubling him from his mind as he led her back down the stairs. When they reached the ground floor, he moved to where a door led to an underground chamber. Morganna pulled back.

'Must we go down there?'

He looked at her questioningly, and taunted, 'It's to be the strong-room. What are you afraid of? Rats? As Countess, you must know all the castle's secrets. I must show you the niches where a secret hoard of money will be sealed in case the castle is stormed and its defences breached.'

Still she hesitated, unwilling to enter such a dark, confined space. Ralph called for a torch. Taking it from a servant, he squeezed her hand as he drew her towards the stairs, and with an effort she conquered her fear. At that moment she would have followed her husband into the bowels of hell itself, rather than have him think her a faint-heart.

Ill at ease, Morganna stumbled as she followed him down into the vault. Already the hair on her neck and arms prickled, a stinging sweat heating her spine. Her heart thudded alarmingly as it had in the tunnel at Daneton. Inhaling deeply, she controlled an involuntary shudder. Instantly Ralph was at her side, his arm circling her waist as he helped her down the last of the narrow steps. Even the nearness of his commanding presence could not banish the panic building within her. She wished the shadows were not so deep, or that the walls did not seem to close in on her.

When Ralph held the flambeau higher, she was surprised at the amount of work that had gone into the design of the underground chamber. Eight arched alcoves rose from around its sides, turning the square structure into an octagon. Within some of these were deep niches, obviously where he intended the gold and important documents to be safely hidden. The black holes of the niches were a sinister reminder that there was one treasure which should take its rightful place there.

'Gwyneth has been urging the masons to finish the work by the summer's end.' Guilt and shame made her voice unnaturally high. 'Perhaps, by then, Giles will see reason and my dowry will be paid.'

'You torture yourself needlessly,' Ralph said, pulling her round to face him. 'Your dowry is the least of my worries.'

'It's your right!' she continued stubbornly. 'Is that not what you have spent all summer fighting for—for what is yours by right?

'I can see that the confined space down here upsets you.' His voice was curt. 'Now that you have mentioned Gwyneth, it is time I presented myself to her.' Then, as though regretting his sternness, he kissed her brow, saying lightly, 'Though, dear wife, I could think of more pleasant ways to spend my time.'

She was glad that the gloom hid her blushes, and as they ascended the stairs, the panic fell away from her. When Ralph paused outside her chamber, desire blazed in his eyes. Her body glowed with anticipation of the evening ahead. He kissed her hungrily, and when he wrenched his lips from hers she knew that Gwyneth would not be able to detain him.

Seated on a stool an hour later, Morganna fretted with impatience whilst Jocelyn combed her unbound hair. Suddenly, the chamber door was flung open.

'Leave us!' Ralph rapped out to Jocelyn in a tone which made her drop the ivory comb and run from the room.

Shocked by the change in her husband, Morganna rose to face him. The glittering hardness in his eyes warned her of the control he was keeping upon his temper.

'What's amiss, my lord?'

Scowling, he strode to a coffer where a flagon and goblets were set, and poured himself some wine. He drank it down before answering in a scathing voice, 'Women! That's what's amiss! I return here for a measure of peace, and am bombarded by complaints and sly hints.'

'Does that include all the women at Pengarron?'

His glance whiplashed over her—he was furious. Her heart fluttered. 'My lord, if I have done aught to displease you . . .'

In three strides he was at her side, his hands resting on her shoulders.

'Not you, my sweet. It's that Welsh dragon!' he confessed heavily. 'I've had an hour of her shrewish rantings . . . She forgets her place. She made Edmund's life a misery with her constant demands and interference. I walked out when she began insinuating that you spend a great deal of time closeted with Barnaby.'

She looked askance at him, worried at the haunted look that clouded his eyes. Surely he had not believed Gwyneth's lies? No—something had been on his mind when he arrived at Pengarron. She had sensed his unease from the beginning, although he had been at pains to hide it.

He lifted a sardonic brow, and she gasped as his hands slid over her shoulders to fondle her neck, his fingers entwining through her hair, easing her head backwards. Assured that, whatever devil rode him, he was not angry at her, Morganna relaxed. It was her duty to give him peace. The conflict between the King and the Duke must be a constant strain upon his sense of loyalty, and the position between him and Giles remained unresolved.

Heavy-lidded, Ralph's gaze strayed to where her robe had parted. Her breathing grew uneven, conscious that her shift clung revealingly to the full curves of her rising and falling breasts. She swayed against him as his hands caressed her shoulders and moved lower, his thumbs stroking the sensitive skin along the side of her firm breasts. When his gaze lifted to hold hers, he said hoarsely,

'How enticing those violet eyes can be—so expressive —so fiery! Lost in their bewitching invitation, a man could lose all honour.'

When he did not kiss her, she knew something serious was nagging at him. It had nothing to do with Gwyneth's spite, of that she was certain. Now might not be the best time to ask him for a favour, but it might take his mind off his worries.

'My lord, there's a matter I wish to discuss. Barnaby and Jocelyn love each other and wish to marry. Surely there can be no reason why they should not do so?'

'Morganna, I did not come here to talk of servants or lovers,' he answered with a wicked grin as his arms encircled her body. 'Do with Barnaby and your maid as you will.'

Her body curved into the fold of his arms as he stooped over her. The rays of the sunset through the window deepened the gold of his eyes, reflecting his desire. Yet, even so, she could not rid herself of the feeling he was keeping something from her.

But as his mouth sought her breasts, it was no longer possible to examine her thoughts. A fire coursed through her, leaving her questions unspoken. She was aware only of the hard-muscled thighs against hers, of her bare breasts, pulsing, beneath the heat of his lips . . . of the male scent of him and of his restrained desire as he lifted her in his arms to carry her to the bed. Her body cried out for him with an abandonment which surpassed reason. Passionately she yielded, her caresses boldly answering his, until she was drawn into an ecstatic world of oblivion.

The shadows had lengthened considerably when they drew apart. Morganna lay contented in her husband's arms. She nestled against his chest as Ralph rolled on to his back, but gradually his stillness made her uneasy. Looking up at him, her throat constricted with alarm. The bleakness about his eyes and the rigidity of his jaw frightened her.

'My lord, can you not tell me what troubles you?'

She had sensed his withdrawal moments before he moved away from her. He got up from the bed and paced across the room, drawing on his robe as he did so. As she waited for him to speak, it seemed her heart had been squeezed dry, her whole body a tearing ache, sensing his inner anguish.

Wrapping a sheet around her, Morganna stood up. 'My lord, sometimes just to talk can ease a burden.' She crossed the room to him and flattened her palms against his chest in a tender gesture, questioning him with her eyes.

Abstractedly, Ralph touched the silvery tresses of hair curling over her breast. 'I've been trying to tell you all day. But when I saw you, framed in the archway, you looked so beautiful—so pleased at my homecoming —that I could not destroy the harmony of that moment.'

At the haunted look again shadowing his eyes, fear plunged through her breast. 'It's Giles!' she blurted out. 'Something has happened to him!'

He nodded. 'He was taken prisoner yesterday. There was an attempt to rescue the King, and your brother was wounded, though not seriously. He's being taken to London.'

'Then I must see him.' She made towards the hand-bell on the coffer to summon Jocelyn. Ralph's hand clamped over hers, preventing her from lifting it.

'No, Morganna. Your place is at Pengarron.'

She struggled to ring the bell, her efforts helpless against his iron strength. Refusing to back down, she glared at him, her voice strained by fear.

'I must go to Giles. He's hurt. He needs me!'

'I should not have to command you a second time, wife!' An unreasonable fury swept through Ralph. Radford had made it plain he had washed his hands of her, yet still she put Radford before him. He had thought for a short while it had been different: that she had truly accepted her role at Pengarron. He had been pleased at the subtle changes he had noticed on his arrival. The peasants seemed more at ease. Every night since he had left the castle, he had been bedevilled by memories of this woman. The lure of what awaited him had given him no peace. Did she care so little for Pengarron that she would destroy the hard-won trust of the people by leaving Gwyneth in charge here? His anger rose. 'Your duty is here, Countess.'

'My duty is by my husband's side! Take me to London with you, Ralph? You'll be away for weeks.'

The temptation of her softly yielding body almost swayed him, but he steeled himself against her charms. Lifting his hand from the bell, he said cuttingly, 'It's not my companionship you seek, is it? Radford has disowned you, and I'll not have you risking your life because of him. The journey is too hazardous. Who knows what mood the London mob will be in? There could be riots—fighting.'

'I'm no craven!' Her eyes continued to flash their defiance, their brilliance reflected in the fading light. 'I'll make Giles see reason. I could plead his cause before the King—or Bolingbroke.'

'A doltish notion!' he snapped, angered by her lack of faith in him. 'Leave Giles to me. I'll do what I can for him. You'll harm your brother's cause, not help it, in London.'

Morganna backed away from the coldness in his stare, her blood turning to ice. Ralph was no longer the considerate lover. He was looking at her in that cold, implacable way she remembered so well from their time at Daneton. With the recollection, the old enmity returned and, with it, self-loathing at her naïvety. She had believed that the tenderness of his lovemaking meant he cared for her. How could she have been so wrong? He was using her for his pleasure as he had used her at Daneton to gain his own ends.

'Are you afraid, my lord husband?' she scoffed. 'Would not my presence at Court remind the Crown-seeking Bolingbroke of your disastrous marriage to the sister of the King's favourite?'

Her shoulders were gripped in iron talons, the amber

brightness of the Earl's stare emphasising the cold-blooded rage that possessed him.

'Always it's to Radford you give your loyalty! I am master here, and I command your obedience.'

She knew now what what it felt like to be the hawk's prey, as it lay trapped, staring up into the eyes of the bird about to deliver the death-blow. But even as her skin grew clammy she tossed her head, boldly outfacing his rage.

'Only a slave obeys without question! You made a poor choice of wife if you expect that from me. You cannot command me to stop loving Giles. I would give my life for him.'

The evening dusk cast saturnine shadows across his features, and their eyes locked in a silent contest of wills, from which she refused to back down. She felt a shudder go through him as he mastered his temper. His hands dropped from her shoulders. Striding across the room, he jerked his belt tight, as though it were her neck he was wringing.

At the door he paused, spun round, and folded his arms across his chest. 'It is the custom for wives to obey their husbands. Defy me at your peril, my lady Countess! Give me your word that you will not leave Pengarron.'

She continued to eye him defiantly. Her breathing shallow and painful, she clutched the sheet against her body. Giles needed her . . . clearly, the Earl did not. Not in a way that mattered—as a helpmeet and companion. He wanted to dominate her, to rule her life without thought of her feelings. He had spoken no word of consideration for the misery she was feeling.

Dumbly she shook her head.

'Then you will remain at Pengarron under guard.' The words sounded hoarse, as though they had been forced out of him. 'You will be given no opportunity to escape, as you did from Daneton when you defied your brother's orders.'

With a last withering glare, he wrenched open the door. Again he hesitated, and wearily pushed the door to as he proclaimed, 'Your loyalty to your brother is misguided. I saw Radford when they first took him prisoner. He told me that while King Richard lives he will have no traffic with anyone, especially you, who sides with the traitor Lancaster.'

Morganna closed her eyes against an onrush of pain, though she had to admit that, to his credit, Ralph dragged the words out reluctantly.

'My words have hurt you, but they are the truth. I'll trouble you no further this night. I shall be with my steward for some hours, and shall be gone from the castle before dawn.'

Morganna's eyes flew open. From the shadows, she could feel the power of Ralph's stare upon her as he added,

'You're a resourceful and intelligent woman. Should you find a way of leaving Pengarron, I shall find you, wherever you go. Many a disobedient wife has spent her life shut in a convent.'

She looked steadily at him, taunting him for the agony he had caused her. 'And if I'm guarded so well that I cannot escape, you will never know whether I wished to leave, and failed, or chose to stay of my free will. That knowledge will haunt you for the rest of our days together. You will never know whether my loyalty was to you or to Giles.'

Even as she flung her scorn at him she was aware that he looked taller and more handsome than ever. The robe open at his broad chest and the commanding tilt of his head emphasised the rugged manliness of this dangerous and exciting knight who had been so determined she become his bride. But now the glitter in his eyes was cold and merciless, like a sword-thrust through her heart.

'Wise words, my lady Countess.' The velvet smoothness of his tone was more threatening that his anger. 'Very well, no guards. But I shall take your maid and Barnaby with me. You will find it more difficult to conspire against me without their help. They shall leave Pengarron with my party tomorrow and shall be wed in Barnaby's village. We pass close to it on the road to London. They shall stay there until I bid them return.' Ralph, looking angrier than ever, opened the door. 'As I said, wife, the choice is yours. I would have you at my side willingly, or not at all.'

The controlled quietness of the latch clicking shut sounded like a battering from a siege-ram to her ragged nerves, and for several moments she stared at the closed door. Sweet Jesu, what had she done! Desolation swept over her. Did she really want to throw away all chance of happiness with Ralph?

Tripping over the folds of the sheet, she stumbled to the door and pulled it open.

'Ralph!'

The corridor was empty. Her heart plummeted, and conscious of her nakedness beneath the sheet, she moved cautiously along the passage to the stairwell. Far below, she heard Ralph shouting orders to his squire and captains. It was too late to call him back . . . already he would be surrounded by his men. She could not run through the castle dressed only in a sheet! Sighing, she turned back along the corridor and in the flickering torchlight saw a pale frightened face peering out of the shadows.

It was Nesta. Morganna clenched her hands in growing frustration and rage. Had Gwyneth sent her maid to spy on Ralph and herself? She turned away from the cowering figure. What was the point of putting the poor creature to the question? All Gwyneth's servants were frightened of their mistress.

Too disturbed by Ralph's changing moods, she dis-

missed Gwyneth's prying as unimportant. It was Ralph
who concerned her. He had made his position clear: he
would tolerate no defiance or disobedience. If she went
to him now, would he, in his fury, even see her? His
moods were unpredictable, and he was capable of being
as obstinate as Giles when he chose. If she did not want
to destroy forever the fragile bond which had begun to
grow between them, she would need all her patience to
deal with her husband. In her distraught state, patience
was the one thing she was sadly lacking.

Entering her room, she leaned tiredly against the
doorway. Delusion was stripped from her. Ralph had
paid court to her to soften the blow of the news about
Giles. The pain spreading out from her chest made her
clutch at her breast in agony. How skilfully he had
imposed his will upon her! Yet she had been a willing
victim; she had welcomed his passion.

Slowly her head came up. Her own stubbornness
had made her blind to the truth. She loved Ralph
Warrender!

So, he wanted her to prove her loyalty. She could not
go to him and declare her love tonight. He would think
her words a trick to get him to take her to London. In her
heart, she knew Ralph would do all he could to help
Giles, because of his promise. It would not be long
before he returned to Pengarron. And then?

A smile formed on her lips. Then she would prove her
love. She would learn more of the fears she sensed still
troubled the people of Pengarron. When Ralph returned, he would find her not only willing, but determined to win his love.

CHAPTER THIRTEEN

AFTER LEAVING Morganna, Ralph stormed towards the bastion tower. 'Summon the steward and the bailiff to my chamber, Barnaby!' he snapped. 'Immediately!'

By the time he had dressed and was ready to meet his officers, his anger roused by Morganna had lost its edge. He listened gravely to the reports, relieved there had been no further evidence of outlaws on his land, and was surprised to learn how involved in estate affairs his wife had become. But his disquiet returned when the bailiff reported a young woman missing from her village after she had gone to gather berries from the river valley. There had been several strange incidents in the waterfall area of late.

'I want a full report on the landslides in that area,' he commanded the bailiff.

Dismissing his officers, he called Barnaby aside. 'The Countess tells me you wish to marry Jocelyn, and I can see no reason why you should not. The ceremony will take place in your village.' Seeing his astonishment, he added, confidentially, 'It's unlikely that the new owner of my manor will be in residence, and I need someone I can trust to be at hand in the village. When my messenger arrives to announce that the estate is restored to me, you will be my agent until I can visit the estate personally.'

'I'm honoured, my lord. But the Countess—she has need of Jocelyn?' The troubadour looked concerned.

In no mood to explain his actions to a servant, however trusting, Ralph answered sharply, 'Your marriage was the Lady Morganna's suggestion. She is content to manage without her maid for a few weeks.

There are other tiring-women to serve her needs. You do wish to marry the wench, don't you?'

'Yes, my lord, but . . .'

'Then tell Jocelyn to pack what she needs,' he cut in. 'We leave at first light.'

Ralph glowered at the troubadour, who appeared about to speak, and the man remained silent, although his bow on leaving was stiff with affronted pride. Left on his own, he resisted the temptation to return to Morganna's room. Why did his wife goad him so? Although he had come to Pengarron with every intent of taking her to London; she had defied him as no man had ever dared to. Yet was it not natural that she would defend her brother, even now? He had even admired her loyalty. Why, then, had he been so angry when she challenged him? Because her loyalty was for another?

On reflection, he knew it was safer for her to remain at Pengarron with the country so unsettled, and he did not want Gwyneth interfering with the estate. Without being able to establish what it was, he could not rid himself of the feeling that something was wrong here. If only he had more time to stay and make his own investigations! The people were different from how he remembered—they seemed secretive. But he had angered the Duke already by insisting on returning to Pengarron today. No matter how strong his ties of friendship with the Duke, he would never forget he was but a vassal.

And Morganna? Ralph rubbed his chin thoughtfully. When would she remember that, as his wife, her first duty was to him? Why must she challenge him on every issue?

Lord Pengarron had been gone from the castle over two hours when a page announced Father Matthew to Morganna's presence.

'My lady, I must speak with you.'

Morganna dismissed Nesta as the priest came forward. 'What troubles you, Father?'

The priest waited until Nesta left the room before saying, 'It concerns Owain. Something I heard during confession from one of the villagers has disturbed me. The woman was too frightened to say much. She said he was a devil . . . that he had the evil eye. As you know, it has been forbidden for anyone to go near the river valley because of the danger from landslides. Why, then, does Owain ride that way each day?'

'Do you think the missing girl could be something to do with him?'

'I don't know, my lady. But I'm concerned for the villagers. Superstition can easily get a dangerous hold on people's minds. The matter must be resolved and a stop put to it. As it is, I saw Owain heading towards the valley when I left the village church this morning.'

Morganna frowned and rubbed her temple, which ached dully. Father Matthew was clearly upset and angry, most unlike his usual manner. 'To put your mind at rest, Father, and to clear Owain's name if need be, we shall ride to the valley. I have long been curious about the waterfall. We'll go this morning,' she said decisively. 'Order an escort—just four men. We do not want it to be too obvious that we are spying on the Lady Gwyneth's servant.'

'But the bailiff has already ridden that way, my lady. Would it not be better to await his report?'

'Lord Pengarron is still only a day's ride away. I think we should act now,' Morganna said, touching the cross as she tried to shake off the foreboding which beset her. 'Let the escort await me in the outer bailey. I would have our outing escape the Lady Gwyneth's attention, or she will find an excuse to join us.'

Because of the need for secrecy, Morganna followed Father Matthew from her rooms, parting company with him as they approached the courtyard. To her irritation, she saw Gwyneth coming out of the King's Tower. Had she not told her to cease overseeing and annoying the masons? On meeting Gwyneth's flustered stare, she saw her control her features into a serene mask as she drew nearer.

'Countess, the masons have nearly finished the work,' Gwyneth said with a tight-lipped smile. 'Have you come to inspect it?'

Morganna looked up to where the workmen were removing the scaffolding and pulleys around the tower. 'Ralph showed it to me yesterday,' she said, noting her agitation. 'Once the work inside is finished, I shall have the upper rooms furnished as the Earl instructed.'

A strange light flared in Gwyneth's eyes as she raised them towards the freshly whitewashed stonework, her voice taut. 'Pengarron is whole again, its heart is restored. It is a day for celebration! Our past and our future are again one.'

Impatient to join Father Matthew, Morganna took little notice of Gwyneth's odd ramblings and replied absently, 'When the Earl returns, the tower will be blessed by Father Matthew. Now I have duties to attend to, Gwyneth.'

The older woman's face hardened. Was it disappointment that she must wait until Ralph returned before the tower would come into use? Morganna wondered. Or was it the dislike she suspected Gwyneth felt for Father Matthew? She seemed to resent the priest taking the place of her cousin.

'You look pale, Countess,' Gwyneth said, her eyes narrowing. 'Was it wise to anger Ralph as you did? It could be months before he returns from London.'

'I have a headache,' Morganna replied curtly. She was too concerned about the strange happenings in the valley to confront Gwyneth about either the tower or her relationship with Ralph.

Some of the tension eased from Morganna when she

joined her escort. It was better to solve the mystery
surrounding the valley than to sit worrying about Giles
and the uncertainty of her future with Lord Pengarron.

They rode along the top of the ravine to where the two
rivers met and turned up the valley. A short distance
further on, the green slopes of the valley were scarred by
the fallen brown earth, some of which was already
covered with wildflower seedlings. As they rode on,
there were no other signs that the land was unsafe. It had
been months since the first landfall, Morganna
reasoned, so why had Gwyneth insisted that the valley
was dangerous?

But something was not right. There was a stillness
about the valley which was unnerving. As they passed a
grove of rowan and hazel trees, the sound of gushing
water was carried to them. It must be the waterfall. They
came to an overgrown pathway leading into the grove,
where they were forced to dismount, for the trees were
so closely packed that their mounts could not push their
way through. Leaving a guard to watch the horses,
Morganna found herself holding her breath as they
entered the wood.

After the bright sunlight, the grove was dark and
gloomy, the smell of rotting vegetation unpleasant after
the freshness of the open valley. She shivered. The
headache which had begun when she was dressing grew
worse as she peered into the eerie shadows. The waterfall must be close by, but the noise of cascading water
sounded oddly sinister in the otherwise silent grove.
Lifting her trailing skirts out of the oozing moisture
covering the ground, Morganna smothered her disquiet.

Accompanied by her escort, she followed Father
Matthew as they descended a steep slope. When, after
some distance, the trees thinned, they came out on
the edge of a sloping rock-face. Looking over Father
Matthew's shoulder, she bit back a gasp, and unwittingly
crossed herself against the apparition of a towering

white maiden. Once her eyes grew accustomed to the sun's brightness the illusion vanished, and she gave a shaky laugh at her foolishness.

Opposite them was the waterfall. The narrow band of foaming water plunged into a shallow rock pool. Twice the height of a tall man, it was not impressive, but after the darkness of the grove it rose before them like a giant water-goddess.

Suddenly Father Matthew reached out and snatched something from a hazel tree.

'Pagans!' he raged, holding out a clay figure to show Morganna. Placing it on a small boulder, he chanted several words in Latin and ground it to dust with his sandalled foot. His thin face deathly pale, he said worriedly, 'Perhaps you should wait here, my lady. This place is cursed.'

Morganna shook her head. 'I would know what evil has come to this land,' she said, but her knees shook as they began to climb down the narrow pathway leading to the pool.

The captain of the escort halted, signalling to them to draw back behind a jutting boulder and remain silent. Bewildered, Morganna did as she was bidden, but could not resist leaning forward to follow the soldier's frowning stare.

The hair at the nape of her neck prickled. On the far side of the pool was the black-clad figure of Owain, who had come out of a cave partially hidden by the undergrowth. As she watched, Morganna saw him raise a round object in his hands and hold it towards the waterfall. Then he tossed it into the water as though offering a sacrifice. For several moments he stood with arms raised high, looking up at the waterfall, before hurrying to walk along the river's edge and climb out of the grove from the opposite side of the bank.

Morganna put out a hand to prevent Father Matthew rushing forward.

'Did you see what that heathen did, my lady!' the priest seethed. 'Devil's spawn! He made a sacrifice to the Earth Mother.'

'I know, Father,' Morganna said sadly. 'Who knows what god his heathen heart serves? The Lady Gwyneth must be told of this. But first I think we should find out more; we need proof to show Lord Pengarron.'

As they made their way cautiously down the steep slope, her worry increased as she noticed several pieces of rag tied to the hazels near the water.

'The villagers must have put these here.' She looked at the priest for confirmation. 'Do they then regard this place as a healing pool?'

'I fear it's more than that, my lady!' Father Matthew flung out an accusing arm towards the falling water. There, quite clearly revealed behind the drought-affected cascade, was a primitive stone figure set on a rock ledge.

The priest moved in front of Morganna, deliberately blocking her view of the image, but not before she had seen the huge phallus and jutting breasts symbolising the figure as some ancient fertility goddess.

Turning her back on the image, she stared down into the clear pool. Was that why Gwyneth had tried to stop her coming here? To preserve her modesty? Or was it to stop her seeing that the villagers still used the pool in some healing or other ritual? And what strange ceremony had Owain been performing?

'My lady, I think we should leave this place,' Father Matthew prompted. 'There is evil here.'

Morganna frowned, wishing her headache did not make it so difficult to think. 'But the Earl told me of the waterfall. Surely he would have mentioned so sinister an effigy—if he knew of its existence?'

The priest glanced back at the waterfall, his brow creasing. 'There's been little rain for weeks. If the river was at its normal level, the image would not be visible.

But there's no moss upon the idol . . . it has not been here long. Although for centuries the villagers may, as you say, have retained some of their old beliefs and looked on this as a healing pool.'

Morganna followed the priest's stare. Again, the waterfall appeared like a tall white lady rising from the pool. The white lady! Was that name not given to a pagan goddess? She touched the crescent brooch at her shoulder. Ralph had called her his moon-goddess. Dear God, surely her husband could not be connected with pagan rites!

She stared hard at a whitish object that caught her attention in the pool, but could not make it out. There was another, similar, shape further along among the shimmering rocks. Morganna shivered. How disquietingly they looked like skulls! Peering closer, she rubbed her eyes in disbelief, and her stomach cramped. There was no mistaking the fleshless grin from a yellowing jawbone. Her eyes dilating with horror, she staggered away from the pool and retched on the grass.

'My lady, what ails you?' Father Matthew said worriedly.

'The pool . . .' she gasped, 'I saw . . .' She broke off as another spasm of nausea gripped her.

There was an oath from one of the soldiers, followed by angry mutterings that were quickly silenced by the priest.

'My lady, you must return to the castle,' Father Matthew counselled, his voice crackling with outrage. 'Owain must be put under guard.'

She looked away as one of the soldiers waded into the pool to retrieve the grisly object. Brief as her glimpse of it had been, she knew it was the bailiff's head.

'Have two men search for the poor man's body. He will be buried in full honour at Pengarron,' she said, her temple pounding relentlessly at this fresh horror. 'You, Father, must ride to the Earl and tell him what has happened. He must return!'

'I shall go at once to his lordship. The bishop must also be informed. This is a matter for the church. An example must be made of Owain for practising Druid rites. But I don't like the thought of leaving you at Pengarron, my lady.'

'I am safe enough. No harm has come to Lady Gwyneth,' Morganna brushed aside his protest. 'Some-one must convince Lord Pengarron of the danger here. Then, your duty will be to the Marquess of Radford. Go to my brother. He's Bolingbroke's prisoner, and he needs you now, Father.'

The pain in her temple stabbed harder. Swaying, she closed her eyes against the viciousness of the pounding headache.

'My lady, you are ill!' Father Matthew was at her side. 'I cannot leave you.'

Gradually the trees stopped revolving around her, and Morganna moved determinedly towards the path leading to the horses. 'It's nothing, Father. Just shock, and I have neither slept nor eaten. You must go. My mind will rest easy knowing that soon you will be with Giles.'

'Then come with me.'

'No, Father. My place is at Pengarron. My husband's people have need of me. I must see that Owain is brought to justice. It must have been he who raided the village, probably because the peasants had defied him. Go now, without delay. Take two of the escort with you.'

The priest continued to study her worriedly as they came out of the grove. 'I see I cannot stay. You look very pale, my lady. Try and rest when you return to the castle.'

She watched Father Matthew ride off and heaved herself into the saddle. Her stomach continued to churn, and the ride back to the castle was torment to the violent throbbing of her head. When she dismounted, her legs almost crumpled beneath her. Holding on to the saddle, she steadied herself and addressed the Captain of the Guard. 'Put Owain in chains until Lord Pengarron returns.'

'He has not returned from his ride this morning, Countess.' The man's puzzled face blurred before her eyes.

'Then have a patrol sent out to find him. He's wanted for the murder of the bailiff.'

With her head feeling as though a spiked mace had crashed against her skull, Morganna entered her chambers and ordered a page to send her women to her. Her throat unbearably parched, she sank tiredly on a stool and reached for the wine-flagon Nesta had brought for her earlier. Draining its contents, she closed her eyes and laid her head against the cool stonework of the wall, her throat still feeling as though it was on fire.

At the sound of a footfall in the room, she said, without looking up, 'Bring me some more wine, Nesta.'

'It's not Nesta,' Bronwyn's unwelcome voice answered. 'But I'll fetch the wine for you.'

The footsteps retreated, and returned within moments. A silver cup was thrust into her hands and Morganna took a long draught before glancing up at the girl. The auburn hair and pale face were hazy before her swirling vision.

'You don't look well, Countess. Have some more wine. It will sustain you.'

The goblet was refilled, but Morganna made no move to drink from it.

'I thought I saw Father Matthew ride out with you. He did not return.'

The sharp edge of Bronwyn's voice pierced the torpor that was settling over Morganna. Consciously, she struggled to regain her wits through an increasing haze of pain.

'He goes . . .' She paused, unsure why, but feeling the need for caution. She could not bring herself to trust the girl. 'He returns to serve the Marquess of Radford. His need for him is greater than mine. I suppose you heard that my brother is again a prisoner.'

'Indeed! Gwyneth speaks of little else,' Bronwyn shrilled. 'Poor Ralph! His gamble didn't pay off. There seems little likelihood now that your dowry will be paid.'

A spasm clutched at Morganna's stomach. Stifling a gasp, she willed her hand not to shake as she set the goblet on a table, refusing to allow the girl to see any sign of her discomfort. Her headache was making it impossible for her to think straight.

'Are you sure Ralph married me for my dowry?' she said, resolving to put Bronwyn in her place. 'He fought Lord Linsdale for my hand—and when at first I refused his suit, he abducted me.'

'If you're trying to tell me Ralph loves you, it's a lie!' Bronwyn screeched. 'It's your dowry and Daneton that Ralph wanted, nothing more. You could not even keep him at your side last night! Where do you think he spent the rest of his time here?'

The dark eyes and fiery hair swooped forward and receded in alarming fashion before Morganna's leaden eyes. What was wrong with her? She had never felt so ill. As the room continued to swirl, she answered the girl's spite.

'I know that Ralph was not with you! And as for Daneton—he has relinquished all claim to it.'

'So you say! Nesta saw the way he stormed from your room last night. Are you so sure he was not with me?'

To Morganna's distorted vision Bronwyn appeared to preen herself like a sleek, contented cat.

'I know my husband. He had no reason to shame me by taking another in my stead,' she began, and checked. Even through her dizziness she was aware of Bronwyn's feline, assessing glare. 'It was but a lovers' tiff.'

As she spoke her defiance, she was racked by another spasm, and, clutching her stomach, she commanded, 'Leave me. Send Nesta. Be quick!'

She hunched over, unable to stop herself vomiting on the rushes. Time and again her stomach heaved. Her body was gripped in a searing fever at one moment; at the next, icy chills set her teeth chattering. Too weak to move, she collapsed on the floor.

She lay there a long time before Nesta came and helped her to the bed. There was no gentleness in the maid's touch as she lifted Morganna's head and pushed the goblet against her dry, cracked lips. Almost choking at the sharpness of the wine, Morganna feebly knocked the cup aside and fell back on the pillows. As the bed-hangings seemed to dip and sway over her head, she closed her eyes.

How long she lay there, she did not know. Nesta must have left, for the room was silent, but where could her chamber-women be? She groaned wretchedly as the nausea returned and, having no strength to rise, she sank back exhausted, the mists of sleep immediately claiming her.

When she awoke, the shadows across the room told her it was almost dusk. Her head still throbbed dully, but the fever seemed to have passed. As she lay for a moment trying to recollect her thoughts, the stench in her room was appalling. What had happened to her?

A burst of anger sent the room spinning round her, and her hand flopped weakly to her breast as she tried to roll on her side to sit up. Where were the servants? Why had no one come to her?

This time, her anger brought with it a return of strength, and tentatively she sat up. The room spun slightly, then gradually stilled. Sliding her legs over the edge of the bed, she put her feet to the floor and stood up. Although shaky, they supported her weight. She reached out for the handbell and rang it weakly to

summon Nesta, and then again, more urgently, when no
one appeared.

Her gown and kirtle clung damply to her body, and
impatient for the maid to appear, Morganna unclasped
the belt and key-chain from about her hips. Where was
Nesta or any of her chamber-women? She rang the bell
again. Growing angrier, she tore off the circlet and veil
and unbraided her hair. Unreasonably, she felt a surge
of panic.

Why had no one answered her summons? In her
present state, she could not leave the room. When she
finally managed to struggle out of her surcoat, she threw
it aside in disgust. The kirtle took longer. Her fingers
shook, and the material at her neck ripped as she tried to
free herself of the tightly-laced garment. At last, her
temper and patience frayed, she managed to loosen the
lacing at her back and pull it and her shift over her head.
The exertion left her weak and unsteady on her feet.

Drawing several deep breaths, she calmed herself
while waiting for her strength to return. Still no one
came. Did Bronwyn have something to do with this? She
would not put it past that spiteful little cat to order the
servants to stay away! Glaring at the closed door, she
calmed her temper, but her anger turned to unease at the
silence which had fallen over the usually bustling castle.

What was happening? Why did no one come? The
horrors she had seen at the waterfall returned to add to
her fears. What if Owain were still free! Had he cast a
spell over the castle? Morganna inhaled deeply, fighting
against her growing alarm. She was being foolish—
allowing her weakness to make her fanciful. By now,
Owain would be safely in chains in a guarded cell.
Nothing sinister was happening. Probably the maids
were in the kitchen, eating. What was the time? Late—it
was almost dark now.

Morganna went to the bowl of water always kept in
her rooms and splashed her face and washed her body.

Refreshed, she opened a coffer, dragged out a clean kirtle and surcoat and began to dress herself. At least she felt stronger now, but still could not rid herself of her growing apprehension. Suddenly she felt so alone— deserted. First by Giles, and then by Jocelyn and, most painfully of all, by Ralph.

'Oh, curse him!'

Irrationally, she blamed Ralph, feeling it was somehow his fault that she felt so weak and helpless. Then she caught sight of his gift lying where she had placed it on the table, and her anger towards him vanished. Picking up the brooch, she touched it to her lips before pinning it to her shoulder. No, it was not Ralph's fault that she was in this state. She had no one to blame but herself.

At last she finished dressing, but lost all patience with her hair and left it loosely braided. Her mouth dry, she poured some wine into a goblet. Halfway to her lips, her hand froze, and icy shivers trickled through her veins. The wine! Ever since she had drunk the wine Nesta had brought her that morning, her head had started to ache. Bronwyn, too, had insisted that she drink it. It was unusual for the girl to show any interest in her welfare!

Morganna sniffed the contents of the goblet. It smelt all right; a little stale, perhaps. Cautiously she took a small sip. It was bitter! Gagging, she spat it out.

Her throat and stomach twisted with fear. She had been poisoned! The goblet dropped from her limp fingers to clatter to the floor, and the sound made her jump. No—she again desperately sought reassurance —it was not poison. If it had been, she would not be on the way to recovery. Or was it possible that her vomiting had prevented the drug from working? Sweet Jesu, had Bronwyn tried to kill her, and failed?

Once formed, the thought was impossible to ignore. Bronwyn certainly hated her enough, and was jealous of her marriage to Ralph. Learning that he had not returned to her chamber last night, did Bronwyn believe she could steal him from her? It was likely! The girl spent much time in Owain's company . . . they had been together when Jocelyn saw them at the alder grove. Was he teaching Bronwyn mystic arts? Owain served Gwyneth. He would see that with the new Countess out of the way, Bronwyn would pose no threat if she married Ralph. Gwyneth would still hold sway at the castle when Lord Pengarron was away.

Fortunately, it seemed, Bronwyn's knowledge of herbs was not reliable, and whatever the girl had given her merely made her sleep. A tremor shook her body, setting her teeth chattering. Clenching them, Morganna fought down another wave of dizziness. She was so alone. Whom could she trust?

Her cold, clammy hand sought the comfort of her mother's cross, and the familiar touch calmed her alarm. She must not panic. First, she would speak to Gwyneth. If Bronwyn had tried to poison her, then she must be sent away. To a convent, perhaps, where she could harm no one with evil spells and potions. Her mind made up, Morganna felt stronger. However unpleasant her interview with Gwyneth, especially following her orders concerning Owain, it must be faced. But would the woman believe her? As Countess, it was in her own power to order Bronwyn to leave, without her consent. Even so, that would be unjust, should the girl be innocent. Gwyneth had shown her friendship, and out of respect, she would consult her before she herself acted against Bronwyn.

She looked for the fallen goblet, and picked it up. A few drops of the drugged wine still remained in it. Holding it, Morganna ventured into the gloomy corridor. Outside, her unease returned. By this time the cressets and torches should have been lit, but she peered along a dark, deserted corridor. Something was wrong. A silence had settled over the castle. Even with Ralph's troop gone, it should not be as quiet as this!

'Guards!' she called nervously.

There was no sound of running feet from the floor below, where a sentry guarded the entrance to the battlements. Apprehensively, Morganna felt her way along the wall in the now almost total darkness, the hairs on her forearms and neck rising in response to the unnatural stillness. The minstrels should be playing in the hall. Though the village servants might have been dismissed for the day, others should be busy lighting the torches, and the guards should be stamping along the lower corridors. There was only emptiness. Thoroughly frightened, she quickened her step as fast as she dared. On reaching Gwyneth's chambers, she knocked, and pushed the door open without waiting for an answer. The raven squawked and flapped around the dark and deserted room.

Morganna whirled. Fighting terror, she gathered up her skirts and fled towards the hall. Her foot caught against something in the darkness, and, biting back a scream when she pitched forward, she managed to stop herself falling by flinging out an arm to grip the wall. The goblet fell from her grasp. There was a grunt from the floor, and staring down, she could just make out the bulky shape of a soldier on the ground.

'Wake up, man!' she said, sharply. 'You sleep at your post!'

He made no move. Angry, but growing more scared by the moment, she shook his shoulder. A loud snore was the only response. He was drunk! One of Ralph's men drunk on duty? She could scarce believe it.

Disgusted, she drew back from him and, forgetting the goblet, hurried on. Within a few paces, it was apparent that he was not the only one. Two other guards sprawled at their posts. Morganna halted at the entrance of the Hall, her breath coming in laboured gasps. The single lighted torch revealed the shadowy figures of servants asleep at the trestle tables. What was happening here?

Where was Gwyneth? All the guards and servants could not be drunk. She backed away in horror. Perhaps they were drugged, just as she had been? It made no sense!

Her heart clamouring with increasing terror, she ran into the courtyard. Towers and battlements loomed sinister and forbidding, ghostly silhouettes against the night sky. Not a light showed at any window. Her glance darted to the gatehouse, and through its arch she could discern the iron bars of the lowered portcullis.

A whimper close by made her spine go rigid. Then a cold nose thrust itself into her hand. With a weak, nervous laugh, she relaxed, and absently ruffled Wulfric's ears. At least now, with the wolfhound at her side, she was not entirely alone! Her eyes grew accustomed to the darkness, and she searched the length of curtain wall for a sign of a patrolling sentry. The moon appeared from behind a cloud, its sphere flattened along one side.

She shivered. The waning moon! The time when its power was at its greatest! Bronwyn's words rose ominously to her mind. In its cold, spectral light she felt vulnerable, and edged towards the King's Tower. It was then she heard distant chanting. Wulfric growled, the deep rumbling shredding her already tattered nerves.

The voices were coming from the renovated tower. Wide-eyed, she stared at the building and conquered her terror. There must be a simple answer to all this . . . There had to be! A dart of hope soared into her mind. The chanting was prayer-like. Could it be that Gwyneth's cousin, the priest, had arrived at last? But what was he doing in the tower?

An orange glow was just visible through the open doorway. Someone was in there, and, as Countess of Pengarron, it was her duty to investigate. She strove to think clearly, but the drug-induced cobwebs still clung to her mind, so that it was unable to make sense of the night's events. She could not rid herself of her fear. A sense of menace seemed to hang over the castle.

CHAPTER FOURTEEN

FIGHTING DOWN her fear, Morganna stared at the newly painted stonework of the tower, which stood out against the dark sky. There must be some logical reason for the castle's apparent desertion. Could the priest have arrived and be blessing the tower? Morganna felt a little easier, recalling Gwyneth's interest in the building, which amounted almost to an obsession. 'Pengarron's Heart', she had called it. That must be what was happening. Her still sluggish mind seized on the notion.

A short distance from the tower, she fell against a mound of the large dressed stones used in the building work and hidden by the shadows. Rubbing her bruised hip, she straightened. Wulfric growled again. Her hand on his back, she felt his hackles rising.

'It's all right, boy,' she soothed. 'You can come in here.'

Front legs braced, the wolfhound refused to move. He whimpered, his ears flattening as he positioned himself before the door, barring her entrance. A low growl vibrated through his stiff body when she continued to urge him.

'If Gwyneth is in there, I suppose you'd better stay outside. Go on—off to your kennel,' she ordered, giving in and stepping round the dog.

Watching Wulfric slink into the shadows, Morganna felt more alone than ever. Probably Gwyneth had ordered him out of the tower, which accounted for the dog's reluctance to enter. A spark of resentment welled within her, making her step firmer as she entered the building. In this respect, Gwyneth had exceeded her duty! It was not right for the tower to be blessed in

Ralph's absence. She shook her head, her mind too foggy to fathom Gwyneth's motives. The chanting was rising to a fervent pitch, and her unease returned. It was unlike anything she had heard Father Matthew intone. She wished some guards were present.

Faint-heart! an inner voice mocked. You wanted to prove your loyalty to Ralph. Go ahead, then, prove it!

Squaring her shoulders, Morganna drew a deep breath and moved forward. Apart from a single torch burning opposite the door leading to the strong-room, the tower was in darkness. She paused, combating the instinct to flee. The air was deathly cold and filled with an acrid smell of burning incense. The eerie chanting drifting to her came from the direction of the strong-room. It was louder now. With a shiver, she forced herself to go on, until unexpectedly a thin cry rose above the chanting, setting her teeth on edge.

It was a baby. There was a baby somewhere in the tower! The chanting, building to a crescendo, was menacing, rising to a strange unearthly pitch. Why was a ceremony of blessing being performed in the strong-room? Surely the living-quarters would have been more appropriate. Morganna checked her pace as her foot rested on the first stair leading down to the underground room.

Her own hackles began to rise. Suddenly every instinct was screaming at her to turn tail . . . to run from whatever lay ahead. This was no ordinary blessing service!

It was almost dusk as Ralph sat by the camp-fire, his hands clasped thoughtfully between his knees as he stared into the flames. Tomorrow he would be with Henry Bolingbroke. How long would it be before he could return to Pengarron? Too long, he thought, suppressing a sigh. And it was not just Pengarron that called to him. In the few hours since he had left, he had missed Morganna more than his home. Several times during the day he had been tempted to turn back, but each time loyalty to the Duke had won over personal inclination. If the country was not too unsettled, Morganna could join him in London in a week or so.

It was still an hour before dark, and they had camped in the next valley to Barnaby's village. Ralph stood up as his troubadour, dressed simply in homespun, approached.

'My lord, before I leave to present Jocelyn to my family, will you hear what she has to say? She's frightened for the Countess.'

'Lady Morganna is well served by other tiring-women. Jocelyn's loyalty is not questioned,' Ralph said drily. 'She must not feel guilty that you are given this chance of happiness.'

'With respect, my lord,' Barnaby persisted, 'it's more than that. I think you should listen to her.'

Ralph beckoned the maid forward. He frowned as she began to speak, hesitantly at first, then as her confidence grew, her fears poured out.

'You say Bronwyn has tried to harm the Countess!' Ralph raged. 'Why was I not told before?'

The maid wrung her hands in distress. 'Her ladyship insisted that you were not to be troubled . . . that she could deal with Bronwyn. But until today I've always been there to watch over her. To protect her ladyship from any evil spells. Helewise, the wise-woman at Daneton, told the Lady Morganna to beware of Pengarron . . . that she would be in danger. Helewise is never wrong.'

'The Countess said nothing of this,' Ralph said sharply, quelling his own mounting disquiet.

'No, my lord. She—my lady—laughed at Helewise's prophecy. She said she did not fear any place but . . .'

'But?' Ralph snapped, stepping close to the maid to look sternly down at her. Did she not know what torture she was putting him through? 'Speak up, woman! Are you saying that the Lady Morganna feared me?'

The maid shook her head. 'Not feared, my lord. I think she dreaded what lay in her heart. That one day you would force her to choose. She loves the Marquess dearly, but for years, since you were first betrothed, she has been intrigued by you. Then you rescued her from the outlaws . . .'

The maid looked down at her hands, obviously embarrassed. 'You were her champion on that day and on other occasions. The Lady Morganna wanted to hate you—but she could not. That was the danger she believed in. She did not want to be a trophy of war. But it's more than that. There's some kind of evil that threatens my lady. You must go back, my lord, before Bronwyn casts a spell on her.'

Ralph rubbed his chin. The maid's talk of spells was nonsense, of course. As to Bronwyn? He did not doubt her capable of causing mischief, but not evil. No—if there was danger at Pengarron, it was not from Bronwyn, but from another. Perhaps he should have taken more notice of Morganna's suspicions about Druids.

Just as he was about to order his men to mount up, he stared with growing alarm at the exhausted figure of Father Matthew riding into the camp.

'Praise God, I've found you, my lord!' he gasped breathlessly. 'You must return at once to Pengarron.'

Tight-lipped, Ralph listened to the priest's accounts of the happenings at the castle since he had left. His concern deepening, he bellowed his orders. Morganna was in danger. However great the Duke's rage that he delayed, he must ride to her aid; neither horses or men were to be spared.

Cold, implacable dread gripped him as he flung himself into the saddle. He glanced up at the moon—Morganna's device. He prayed it would serve him well now. He needed its light if he was to reach Pengarron in time. They must ride through the night.

* * *

Morganna hesitated in the doorway at the top of the steps leading down to the strong-room, all her earlier fears of dark, enclosed spaces returning. Even with Ralph at her side, the confined strong-room had made her flesh crawl. The weird chanting pulsated like a drum tattoo and seemed to vibrate through her mind and body.

Had Owain returned to work his evil here? Was Gwyneth and everyone lying in a drugged stupor somewhere, except the worshippers of that old, evil goddess she had seen at the waterfall? Each thought more terrible than the last, she forced her trembling legs down the steps, convinced now that there was evil here. In Ralph's absence she was responsible for the welfare of his people. Afraid though she was, this night might be her only chance to learn the truth.

Mounting terror and the steepness of the steps made her legs wobble, and her hand stung as it became grazed from clutching hold of the wall for support. The pain was tangible proof that this was not some dreadful nightmare. The light was brighter as she neared the last steps and crouched to look through the arched opening into the strong-room itself.

A dozen or so people were grouped together, their backs to her. The chanting now seemed to reverberate off the walls. From the glow of two lighted torches set in the walls, she saw two figures in long white robes step back from one of the arched alcoves. One was unmistakably Owain. Her shock increased as she saw between the two figures the kicking legs of the baby they had placed in a niche. As the more slightly built figure turned, the full impact of horror struck Morganna.

It was Lady Gwyneth.

Incapable of movement, she watched as Gwyneth nodded to two other occupants in the room. The chanting abruptly stopped, and the men stepped forward. From their clothing, they looked like the masons

Gwyneth had brought in to finish the work on the tower. Trowels in their hands, they selected a large stone from a pile in a corner and placed it between the arches of the alcove, a third man shovelling a mix of mortar. Morganna rubbed her eyes, convinced she was dreaming. The drug must have affected her more strongly than she thought. She blinked, but still the ghastly scene remained unchanged. They intended to wall up the baby as a sacrifice!

As the masons struggled to lift a second stone, Gwyneth drank from a goblet fashioned from a skull and recited some strange words that Morganna barely recognised as Welsh. The awful truth finally dawned on her drowsy mind, and her heart started to gallop. It was Gwyneth who was a priestess of the old religion!

A hasty glance around the gathering showed her that Bronwyn was not present. Even from her scheming ward, Gwyneth was obliged to keep this secret.

Morganna knew she had to stop them sacrificing the infant, but how? Alone, she could do nothing. There were too many of them. She would be overpowered at once. The guards? Perhaps she could rouse some of them, drugged though they were. If she could get to the watch-tower and sound the tocsin bell, it would warn the whole valley that something was wrong. Surely the villagers, with her at their head, would rise up against Gwyneth and Owain?

Her mind set upon this action, Morganna eased her foot up on to the next step, but as she did so, the keys on the chain about her waist swung forward and clashed against the stone. Panic seized her. Grabbing at her skirts, she began to clamber up as an uproar of shouts broke out behind her.

'Don't just stand!' Gwyneth was screaming. 'See who spies on us.'

Tripping on each step, Morganna groped her way up the darkened stairs, terror making her movements clumsy. A hand closed round her ankle, and her scream changed to a grunt of agony as a second arm circled her waist and she fell, tasting blood as her chin banged on the higher steps. She was hoisted up and dragged backwards down the narrow stairway. Her shins were scraped and bruised as she kicked out to free herself. Clenching her fists, she pounded against the burly forearms holding her, but her efforts did not even slacken their crushing grip. It could only be Owain who held her in such a merciless grasp!

Still kicking, she was drawn back into the strong-room and swung round to face Gwyneth, who held up her hand to silence the dark mumblings of those around her. Seeing the hatred blazing from the woman's slanted eyes, Morganna knew her fate was sealed. How could Gwyneth allow her to live and tell Ralph the truth?

Gwyneth's lips curled back in a malicious sneer. 'I should have known you would ruin everything! Why couldn't you have slept the night through, as I intended? How did you come to wake? I ordered Nesta to give you enough wine to put you to sleep until morning.' She shrugged, her eyes narrowing with cunning. 'I'll have to change my plans . . . A pity! Still, all is not lost. You should have stayed away, Morganna. Pengarron is mine —I alone will rule here. Now that you have learnt too much, you must die. Bind her, Owain. Use the cord about your waist if there's nothing else.'

Morganna's head came up. All around her the worshippers loomed menacingly, their eyes large and glazed by drugs and the trance-inducing ritual. Suddenly Gwyneth's hand shot out, ripping the crescent brooch from her shoulder.

'This I need! When Ralph sees it, he'll think you made good your threat to leave him and returned his lover's gift.' She paused, her malevolent gaze raking Morganna from head to foot. 'The keys also.'

She snatched the chain from Morganna's waist, a cruel

smirk twisting her lips. 'I have a spare set, but this chain Ralph cannot fail to recognise. It will be further proof that you fled.'

'He'll never believe your lies!' Morganna flung the words, biting back an impulse to scream that she had already sent for Ralph. Gwyneth must never know of Father Matthew's mission to warn him of the evil here.

At the touch of a cord upon her wrist, her struggles became frantic. 'Let me go! I am your Countess. How dare you handle me thus!' She made a valiant effort at bravado. 'You cannot kill me and escape the consequences. I have friends—and influence at Court.'

'Which Court?' Gwyneth crowed. 'King Richard's power is waning. It is I who am ruler here. My power is absolute!'

Morganna's mind raced. Somehow Ralph must learn the truth of what happened here. Gwyneth must be stopped. She jolted back her head, catching the giant under the chin. The rope dropped away and the grip about her waist loosened slightly. Kicking and scratching, she fought like a demented fury to free herself from Owain's hold.

Blessed St Winefride, help me! she prayed. She did not want to die! There was so much she had to live for. So many misunderstandings to put right. Giles believed she had betrayed him . . . and Ralph—she had never told Ralph that she loved him. But, most important, she was the only one who knew the truth.

Her struggles were useless. She could see the other figures moving in, their faces blank masks, the more terrifying for that. They were completely under Gwyneth's power, without thought or reason of their own. Some she recognised as servants from the castle, but most were strangers. Realising that her strength was failing, Morganna knew that only her wits could save her. The steely arms about her ribs were crushing the breath from her lungs. She flopped forward over the giant's arms, and, as she did so, the cross, until now hidden beneath her kirtle, swung forward to clink against her teeth. Instantly her hand closed over it. The cross! If she could just use the cross as a sign. Ralph must learn the truth . . . must know she had not deserted him.

Her free hand still flailing to disguise her true intent, she jerked the other downwards. A sharp pain bit into her neck, but the catch gave, and the cross was firm in her grasp. There was little time. A rope was dangling before her. Any moment now, they would begin to bind her. Her arms and legs thrashing as if in rage and fear, she continued to screech out her threats, and as she did so, flung her clenched fist sideways, hurling the cross into a darkened corner.

Dear God, she prayed, let it not be found by Gwyneth or her acolytes. Because of the commotion she was making, even she did not hear where it fell.

'You will not go unpunished for this!' she cried hoarsely, still hoping that reason would yet save her. All at once, she knew with ghastly certainty that Gwyneth had murdered Edmund. It had been no fever that had taken Ralph's brother's life, but poison—Father Gregory's also! They must have discovered Gwyneth's secret.

Morganna's hair had come unbound in her struggles, and hung about her face. Defiantly she tossed it back over her shoulder, her lips drawing back in a snarl as she faced Gwyneth.

'Poisoning won't work a second time!'

Putting a long-nailed finger to her lips, Gwyneth smiled evilly. 'So you've guessed! Edmund was a fool . . . I could have given him power beyond his wildest dreams. But no—it won't be poison this time.'

The baby began to whimper, then to cry. Gwyneth's eyes glinted. 'The castle must have its sacrifice. Who better than its Countess? You will be walled up in the

alcove with the child. Your death will be slow, taking a
day, perhaps longer. All the better—for as your life
slowly ebbs, so your strength will be absorbed by the
heart of Pengarron. It will rise from obscurity. I've seen
in visions that King Richard will die. Bolingbroke will
rule England. At his side, Ralph will rise high—in the
time left to him, that is.'

Walled up! The full horror of her fate screamed
through Morganna's mind. The darkness. Unable to
move in a cramped space. The cave at Daneton, and
even this strong-room itself, had brought on an
unknown terror. But this! This would be worse.

She shuddered. The woman was insane . . . She saw
that now. Driven mad by obsession and the thirst for
power!

'You forget one thing, Gwyneth,' Morganna shouted,
using her last argument. 'Ralph has sworn to hunt me
down should I leave here. He knows I would go straight
to my brother. When I don't arrive, he'll be suspicious.
I may be dead, but you'll be destroyed. Ralph will
discover the truth somehow.'

Evil glowed in the green lights brightening Gwyneth's
eyes. 'Why should he? There might be many reasons for
you not to reach your brother and just disappear. Outlaws abound in the valleys around here. I could even
arrange for a body to be found in your clothes—but, of
course, battered beyond recognition. It may take a few
days to find a girl of your height and colouring, but it's
not impossible.'

Morganna fought to overcome her panic. She was
fearful not only of her death—but of that of others . . .
the unknown girl—the baby. If it was too late to save
herself, she must do something for the infant.

'At least let the baby live,' she pleaded. 'Enough evil
has been worked here this night.'

'You would still give orders,' Gwyneth raged. A slow
smile drew up the corner of her thin lips. 'If the child's

life is so important to you, go down on your knees and beg for it.'

It was on the tip of Morganna's tongue to refuse, but for the sake of her pride she could not let the baby die. It was not for herself she must plead, but another. She nodded stiffly, and Owain released her.

Drawing herself to her full height, she made no attempt to hide her contempt as she held Gwyneth's glare. 'How do I know you will honour your word?'

'To see you humbled, after all I have been forced to give up on your account, I willingly give my word.'

'Then swear it,' Morganna persisted, 'by whatever faith you hold. For it is not our Christian god that you worship.'

'Then I swear in the name of the Earth Mother. The child will be allowed to live—for now. There is All-Hallows Eve to come. Babies are not easy to find.'

So Gwyneth meant to sacrifice the child anyway, Morganna seethed. But not yet. It was some weeks before the end of October. By then, Ralph must surely have put an end to the oppression and terror of his people.

Morganna sank to her knees on the floor, the stone cold and hard beneath her weight. 'I beg you to allow the child to live,' she said, stiffly.

For an instant, a fierce light glowed in Gwyneth's eyes as she gloried in her triumph, then, turning to one of the castle servants, she ordered, 'Remove the infant. Care for it well until All-Hallows Eve.'

Morganna was jerked to her feet. The baby stopped its crying as it was lifted from the niche and carried out of the chamber. For a long moment Gwyneth stared after it. When she looked back at Morganna, her voice was clipped with irritation.

'This is not how I planned it. I had hoped first you would bear a child. A son for Pengarron. I needed a child! Being barren myself, it was to be my security to retain my hold on the estate.'

She laughed coldly. 'You see, I'm not selfish. I was prepared to step down from being mistress here, for a year or two, until you produced an heir. Then, of course, you would have had to die. Ralph, too, when his usefulness was over. I suppose, now, I must push Bronwyn's cause. Ralph will marry her. After a suitable time of bereavement, naturally.'

Morganna's arms were pulled behind her, the cords tightening as they bound her wrists. 'You'll not escape retribution,' she cried. 'Even should Ralph believe your lies, my brother never will. He'll discover the truth of my death, if only to avenge himself upon Lord Pengarron.'

From the lines channelling Gwyneth's brow, it was clear that she had not considered Giles to be important. 'That is a chance I must take.' She sounded less assured. 'The Marquess of Radford is a prisoner. No one yet has stopped me. If I let you live, I lose everything. What choice have I? This way, your sacrifice will benefit Pengarron. To win such power, I am prepared to take a risk or two.'

Unable to suppress a shudder, Morganna's glance was drawn to the alcove. It was the same as the eight others and certainly large enough to take her body, but surely, if the archway were walled in, it would not escape notice. 'You need not think your body will be discovered by the servants when they recover!' Gwyneth accurately guessed Morganna's thoughts, and was obviously enjoying every moment of the torment she was inflicting. 'Once sealed, several coffers will be piled in front of it. There'll be no need for them to be disturbed for years.'

Morganna kicked out as the cords were laced about her ankles until a blow to her stomach doubled her over. The room spun dizzily as she straightened to proclaim, defiantly, 'God will punish you for this!'

'I do not fear your Christian god,' Gwyneth sneered.

The bonds were tightened, and Morganna found it

impossible to struggle further. Her breath coming in hard painful gasps, she still refused to admit defeat.

'You'll never overcome Ralph. May you burn in hellfire for all eternity for this!'

'Gag her!' Gwyneth screamed. 'Get her into the alcove. We've delayed long enough.'

The strange chanting she had heard earlier began again. Powerless to resist, Morganna was lifted by Owain, and under Gwyneth's direction placed on the floor of the alcove, her legs bent up before her so that she was wedged between two arches. At the side of her feet, the large stone the masons had earlier put into position prevented her from rolling sideways. Frantically she struggled, hearing Gwyneth's cackle of laughter above the chanting and the clamour of her blood pounding in her ears.

Gradually the huge stones blocked off the ghoulish figures from her. It was growing darker. Scrape, slap, the ring of trowel against stone became a merciless tattoo upon her brain. The torchlight was fading.

She stared up at the slithers of remaining light. How long could she last until the air gave out? The alcove was seven perhaps eight feet high. Her body was wedged so tightly that her shoulders were hunched against wall and stone, so that any movement was impossible. High above, there was now only a small square of light, the surrounding blackness a beckoning void.

Then that light, too, was gone. Darkness pressed down upon her. The chanting was distant and muffled. Heart drumming, her chest felt as though a giant monster sat upon it. Already her head seemed about to burst. It was worse than the terror she had felt in the tunnel at Daneton. Then she had known that freedom was but a short distance away. This was for eternity!

She started to scream, a strangled unearthly sound, smothered by the gag. Her throat was raw. Then it seemed that an inner voice called to her from the darkness. She was wasting air. She froze, and fell silent, the only sound that of the thunderous beat of her heart. If she did not move, she would have air enough for a day.

A day! Merciful St Winefride! An hour of this, and she would be driven out of her mind!

She must not think in this way, but strive for calmness. There was still hope. Father Matthew had gone for Ralph. By now, they could be on their way back to Pengarron. Sweet Jesu, let them be returning! She did not want to die!

Ralph was coming, she told herself. She must never stop believing that. Deliberately, she conjured visions of her meetings with Ralph. He was her knight. He would save her now, as he had saved her in the forest and from Lord Linsdale.

It was as though she could hear his voice calling her, telling her to fight on. She was a Barnett—a Warrender —they did not give up. Her heartbeat slowed. She must be strong. She would not die!

Morganna tried to move, to edge sideways and brace her body against the wet mortar to push a stone aside. It would not budge. The stones we're too heavy, and she was too weak.

Exhausted, she slumped back, reality escaping her as she gasped for breath.

CHAPTER FIFTEEN

IN THE EARLY morning light, the herald sounded Lord Pengarron's arrival at the Gatehouse. Impatient at the delay, Ralph's hands clenched over his reins while his troop waited on the drawbridge for the portcullis to be raised.

A second trumpet blast brought a sleepy-looking sentry to an upper window. Recognising the riders, the man shot back inside and could be heard shouting orders.

'Raise the portcullis! Rouse yourselves, men! Lord Pengarron awaits entrance!'

Ralph's charger thundered into the courtyard. His proposed rebuke at the sluggishness of his men was left unsaid as he glared round the deserted space. The men-at-arms appearing from the battlements and the guardhouse all looked dazed and drowsy. What had happened here? Fear thrust into him. Was he too late?

Leaping from his horse, he raced to Morganna's chamber, and when he flung the door open, he relaxed slightly at the smell of fresh herbs sprinkled on the newly-laid rushes. He moved quickly to the inner bed-chamber, expecting to find Morganna asleep, but at the doorway, he stopped in his tracks. The room was deserted. His throat contracted painfully. Worse, the bed was still made and unslept in. In alarm, he ran back into the corridor, where Ifor and Emrys awaited him.

'Bring Lady Gwyneth and Bronwyn to the solar. At once!'

As his men followed his orders, Ralph ran to the chapel. There was a chance that Morganna was at prayer. Upon discovering the chapel empty, his step was heavy as he stormed through the hall. Sleepy-eyed servants, who should long ago have been at their duties, scattered in his path. What had happened here? A drunken frenzy! Even after feast-days, the servants were never in such a state as this.

Ralph ignored Wulfric as he bounded forward. Summoning the Captain of the guard, his rage exploded as he questioned him, and, red-eyed, the man looked sheepishly back at Ralph.

'The last I saw of the Countess was when she returned from her ride and ordered Owain to be put in chains.'

'Were her orders carried out?' Ralph growled.

'No, my lord. He could not be found.'

'And, since then, you've seen nothing of the Countess?'

The Captain shook his head, and winced as though every movement pained him.

When the wolfhound, who had followed Ralph into the solar, began to whimper, Ralph snapped at him to be silent. Flattening itself on his stomach, Wulfric sat by the door, whistling softly through his nose. Ralph was too much concerned for Morganna's safety to pay heed to the dog's distress. Then a low growl from him warned Ralph that Gwyneth was coming up the steps. Still in her dressing robe, and looking far from pleased at being summoned, she glided into the room.

'Where's the Countess?' Ralph demanded without preamble.

'Gone,' Gwyneth returned haughtily. 'She left late yesterday to ride to her brother.'

'That's a lie!' Ralph snarled, although his earlier doubts concerning Morganna's loyalty returned to haunt him. She had been so defiant—so set on seeing Radford. He hid his uncertainty as he faced Gwyneth. 'Lady Morganna is here. She sent Father Matthew to report the bailiff's murder. And of Owain.'

'What has Owain to do with this?' Gwyneth retaliated, but her face drained to parchment white. 'What lies has that woman spread? She's left you, I tell you. It's what she threatened, isn't it? If you need proof, these should convince you!' She flung a chain and the crescent brooch down on the table, adding spitefully, 'That's how much she thought of your lover's gift! She has gone to her brother.'

As he stared at the brooch and castle keys, a storm broke inside Ralph, his fury scalding through him. Gwyneth was lying. Or was she? A red haze formed before his eyes, blurring reason, and a sly demon nudged at his pride.

Had Morganna chosen Radford before himself? Did she think her duty here done after sending Father Matthew to report the evil deeds to him? His doubts grew—flashing through his mind at lightning speed. Morganna was capable of acting rashly. He should never have lost his temper with her over Radford—no man could win her respect in that way. But she goaded him beyond patience. Did she not know that he loved her?

With a start, he acknowledged the truth: he had allowed his rage against Radford to blind him. Morganna had attracted him from the first moment he saw her. After she had bravely defended Daneton, it had not been to get back at Radford that he had taken her hostage, but because he had not wanted to leave her behind. He loved her, and his pride had sent her from him.

Wulfric began to bark, bringing Ralph back to the urgency of the moment. The last of his control upon his temper slipping, he whirled on one of his men, shouting, 'Get that damned dog out of here! Tie him up, if need be.'

'Ralph!' Bronwyn cried, as she ran into the solar. 'You're back, and so soon. We thought you would be away for weeks!'

He rounded on her. 'From the laxness of the sentries
and of recent events, apparently everyone in the castle
believed themselves safe from my wrath. Where is the
Lady Morganna?'

Bronwyn's smile faded. 'Why, she's in her room,
asleep, my lord.'

'She is not there. Gwyneth says she left the castle to
join her brother. What do you know of that?'

Bronwyn swallowed nervously and looked towards
Gwyneth. 'I've not seen the Countess since yesterday
afternoon.'

'Where was she then?' Ralph stepped forward,
gripping Bronwyn's shoulder.

'In her room, my lord.' A sly look passed across the
pale oval face. 'But the Countess was upset. She kept
saying that her brother needed her . . . that you had
argued over her dowry. She felt she was not wanted
here.'

He thrust the girl from him, repelled by what he
had heard. Too late he admitted how much Bronwyn
resented Morganna. And Gwyneth, for all her false
friendship, would have lost no chance to make his wife
feel an intruder—a usurper to her role as mistress. If the
two women had been men, he would have ordered them
to be flogged for their insolence!

'And who made her feel unwelcome? You two will
answer for this when I've found my wife.' Not trusting
himself to remain in their presence without punishing
them, he strode from the room.

Convinced that Morganna had carried out her threat
to join Radford, Ralph marched out into the courtyard.
At seeing Wulfric bound out of King's Tower towards
him, his anger flared.

'I ordered the dog to be tied up!' he raged, pushing
him away and turning to Ifor. 'Have fresh horses
saddled.'

When Wulfric collided against his legs, he swung

round to cuff him, but with a bark the wolfhound leapt out of reach and ran back towards the tower. Swearing beneath his breath, Ralph waited for the horses to be brought forward, the dog's continued barking as it evaded capture increasing the savageness of his temper. At last, the horses were led out. Taking the reins, Ralph was about to swing himself into the saddle when the wolfhound jumped up, his teeth sinking into his sleeve as he tugged at his arm.

Suddenly the strangeness of Wulfric's behaviour struck him, and Ralph looked down at the dog. Wulfric barked insistently, and this time when he ran towards the King's Tower, Ralph followed. To his surprise, the dog ran towards the strong-room. Knowing Morganna's fear of the dark, enclosed space, Ralph whistled him away, but Wulfric remained by the stairs. Was it possible that Morganna had gone there to inspect the masons' work, and been injured?.

Snatching a lighted torch from the wall sconce, Ralph ran after the dog as he disappeared down the steep steps. His heart racing, he held the torch aloft, but its flickering light scarcely reached the darkened corners of the room. Nothing. The knife-edged pain twisted deeper into him. Just a few coffers piled up in the furthest corner. Of course, Morganna would not have come here. The dog had picked up her scent from the day before, when he had shown her the room. Heavy-hearted, he was already on the first step to leave when Wulfric, who had been sniffing about, nudged his hand. There was a metallic ring as the dog dropped something at his feet, and frowning, Ralph stooped to pick it up. As he stared at the Saxon cross, cold sweat stung his brow.

Morganna would never had left Pengarron without the cross; she wore it always. But where was she? Something had happened to her. Dear God! Had he just discovered his love only to have it cruelly snatched from him? Where could his wife be? He moved forward to the coffers, half expecting to see her body lying hidden from him. She had been wearing the cross after they had left the strong-room.

With a roar, he called the guards and began dragging the piled coffers from the corner, not knowing what he would find. Momentarily the blank stone wall puzzled him. Something was not right: prickles of heat stabbed along his spine. When the wolfhound began to whimper and scratch at the stonework, he noticed that the mortar was still damp.

Was that a dull thud? He held up his hand to halt the noise of the men-at-arms clattering down the steps.

'Be still!' he shouted, as he strained his ears.

Just discernible was the sound of a weak voice calling his name.

Bellowing with rage, his voice quaking with dread, he ordered the men to tear down the wall.

Morganna stirred, and drew a deep, searing breath. The air was almost gone. She knew she must have lost consciousness, for her limbs felt leaden, and each breath was like a fiery bellows pumping air into her aching lungs. How long had she been here? It seemed like days, but it could only be hours. She was so weak. It could not be long now, before . . .

She could not bear to think of death. She let her mind wander, thinking again of Ralph, as she had throughout the cold, tortured hours. It was as though he called to her. Her eyes filled with tears. One day they would be reunited, but she feared it would not be on this earth. From sheer frustration she drew up her legs and, using the last of her strength, kicked against the wall, Ralph's name a poignant cry from cracked, muffled lips. But the effort left her gasping. Her head spun, and the blackness pressed down like a smothering mantle over her face as consciousness again slipped from her. In her weak and light-headed state, her dreams returned, more potent than before. There was a hammering in her head. She was floating, surrounded by the male scent which was distinctly Ralph—warm skin, sandalwood, leather . . . even horses. He kept calling to her. Why wouldn't he let her go?

She had no strength left. She wanted to sleep. Still Ralph called, his voice more insistent now. In her mind, she saw a blinding light, and though she screwed her eyes up against the pain it brought, she could not banish the vision of piercing amber eyes staring down at her.

Morganna blinked. Immediately the amber eyes softened to honey gold, and the firm hold about her body gentled.

'Dear God—she lives!' Her husband's voice was cracked with emotion. 'Morganna, my love, it's over! You're safe!'

She struggled to regain her senses, but everything appeared so far off, as though she were sitting on one of the great oak roof-beams, looking at the group of figures below. Gradually she realised it was no dream. The gag and bonds were gone. She could breathe again!

Her chest heaving, she gulped deeply. As her wits returned, she became aware of her surroundings. She was lying on the floor of the strong-room, cradled like a child in Ralph's arms. The blurred edges of her vision cleared. 'Ralph!' she croaked, wonderingly. Then, over her initial joy, the need to warn him was foremost in her mind. Her throat worked convulsively as she struggled to wrench out, 'Gwyn . . . Gwyneth is . . .'

'Some wine for the Countess. Be quick!' Ralph commanded. With a curt nod, he dismissed the soldiers filling the underground chamber. As he bent over Morganna, the flickering torchlight above his head softened the stern lines of his haggard countenance. 'Hush, my love! I suspected that Gwyneth was responsible for this. I've ordered her to be put under guard.'

A servant appeared, carrying a goblet, and Ralph

took it from him, eased her head up and placed the cup against her lips. Cool and sweet, the wine slid down her swollen throat, and within moments, Morganna felt the strength returning to her stiff, cramped limbs. And, with it, a greater joy.

Had Ralph really called her his love? She tried to think clearly. None of this seemed real. Her throat eased, but at the fixed anger tightening her husband's face, she did not feel strong enough to risk his rejection. Instead, she asked, her voice stronger now, 'How did you find me?'

'By the grace of God and the help of Wulfric,' he replied in a tormented tone. 'But that witch planned her story well!' His eyes cold and bright, Ralph gently brushed her tangled hair back from her face before continuing darkly, 'When I saw the brooch and keys, I was convinced you had left Pengarron. That Giles was the one who was important to you. In my anger, I sadly wronged you.'

Sensing his pain, Morganna's hand rose weakly to clutch at his, and the strong fingers closed round hers in a fiercely possessive gesture. She was gathered close, as Ralph kissed her brow before adding gruffly,

'I was about to ride out, when Wulfric's odd behaviour led me to the tower. It was the dog who found your cross.' His voice broke. Dark circles hollowed his eyes, and with a visible effort he controlled the blazing anger in their depths. 'By all that's holy,' he ground out, 'that witch will pay for what she has done! I knew that Gwyneth coveted Pengarron, but I never believed she was so evil. It is obvious now that Edmund never died of a fever. He must have discovered her secret, and the bitch poisoned him! The chaplain, too. And God knows how many others!'

A lump, solid as granite, lodged in Morganna's throat. She drank in Ralph's beloved features, gaunt with anguish and remorse. Then, to her dismay, shudders seized her body and a sob tore from her lips. Once started, the flow was impossible to stop.

Instantly Ralph's arms tightened, his body tense as he touched his lips to her temple. His rough palm gently slid along her cheek to wipe the tears from her face.

She lifted her head, studying him searchingly. Had he whispered words of love, which had been drowned by the sound of her sobs?

'What did you say,' she asked achingly.

His expression was carefully shielded. 'Gwyneth is under guard. You have no need to fear.'

Hiding her disappointment, she saw his full lips draw back, revealing white, even teeth flashing behind a provocative smile. The dark line of stubble along his jaw emphasised his rugged, warrior's image. Her heart tumbled to the pit of her stomach. Had her ears deceived her?

Ralph heaved himself to his feet, still clasping her in his arms, and carried her towards the stairs, whence sounds of a disturbance in the courtyard drifted to them.

'I can walk, my lord,' Morganna said, as his stride quickened.

'And deny me the pleasure of carrying you?' His voice was light, but as they regained the sunlight and Ralph saw the crowd gathered in the inner bailey, his eyes shadowed with concern, his attention switching to the scene before him.

At the centre of the commotion, Gwyneth's voice, shrill with anger, rang out, 'Take your hands from me! This is an outrage!'

Ralph halted, and Morganna was carefully lowered on to one of the large stones piled before the tower.

'I'd better deal with this,' Ralph whispered. 'These people look in a dangerous mood.'

He beckoned to Emrys to watch over her, and marched forward, rapping out an order. 'Release the Lady Gwyneth! She cannot escape.' He stood in front of the indignant figure of his brother's widow, thrust his thumbs over his sword-belt, and pronounced coldly, 'The time for lies is past, Gwyneth. You shall not escape justice this time!'

Morganna saw her start visibly and her face drain of colour as her gaze swept past Ralph to rest upon herself.

'Kill her!' the gruff voice of a soldier shouted. 'Kill the Lady Gwyneth! She was caught trying to escape by the postern gate. She had our Countess walled up!'

'Ay, burn her!' Several others raised the cry, the assembled faces contorted with hatred.

Morganna looked at Gwyneth, reluctantly admiring her cool manner. The woman remained aloof, unmoved by the clamour of the soldiers and peasants as they cried out for vengeance. It was almost as if Gwyneth was confident that nothing could harm her. Many of the villagers, made curious by the commotion, had wandered into the castle. Their faces, too, were hostile, as they at last saw a way to free themselves from her tyranny and rule of terror.

'Guards!' Ralph's clipped voice silenced the assembly. 'Escort the Lady Gwyneth to her room. She will see, and speak to, no one. Her fate will be decided by an ecclesiastical court. The rest of her servants are to be brought to the hall for questioning.'

The muttering and arguments that then broke out rose to fever pitch, and Morganna saw the giant figure of Owain being pushed through the crowd, a guard on either side. There was a deep gash at the side of his head, which ran with blood, and his tunic was muddied and torn. When he was brought to stand before the Earl, his opaque eyes glittered with hatred.

'Take him to the dungeon,' Ralph ordered. 'The bishops will decide his fate along with that of the Lady Gwyneth.'

'Burning's too good for the likes of them!' A shout

went up from the back of the crowd. 'Why wait for the bishops? Kill them now!'

A thickset villager, whom Morganna knew to be a troublemaker, bent and picked up a stone. Several others followed suit, their cries menacing. 'Kill her! Stone the witch!'

Ralph barked an order, but it was lost among the shouts. The crowd surged forward, their faces sullen, many already with their arms drawn back ready to hurl the stones they carried. There came an animal roar from Owain. Then, with a heave of his massive shoulders, he threw off the guards and charged toward Gwyneth, his huge body protecting her from the threatening villagers.

'Stay back!' Ralph shouted, his eyes hardening with anger.

For an instant, Morganna saw the rebellion in the villagers' faces. They hated Gwyneth. Ralph was their lord, but he was still a stranger to them—an Englishman.

Undaunted, Ralph stood his ground, his deep voice resolute. 'Go back to your homes. Justice will be done!'

He strode forward to confront Owain. 'You cannot save the Lady Gwyneth from justice. Stand back, man, it's over. Both of you will be tried for the evil you have wrought here.'

Owain threw back his head, gave another tortured shriek and, to Morganna's horror, launched himself upon Ralph. Long black hair flying, he moved with surprising speed for so large a man, but Ralph nimbly side-stepped, bringing his hands up in a wrestler's stance. Teeth barred, Owain flung out his arms, his muscles bulging as he gripped Ralph in a vicious bear-hug. A cheer went up from the crowd. Both men's faces strained as they locked in combat.

Morganna stared, her eyes large with dread for her husband, as the two men moved crab-like across the cleared space.

The guards, swords drawn, moved forward.

'Stand back!' Emrys yelled a warning. 'You'll harm his lordship. Keep your distance!'

Unable to contain her alarm, Morganna jumped to her feet, holding to the squire's arm for support. Her stomach was a tight ball of fear: Ralph's strength was no match for the oxen power of Owain.

The velvet of his surcoat stretched tight as he strained to break the crushing hold about his ribs. Morganna could see his dark hair streaked with sweat and the veins in his hands stood out as he gripped Owain's chin, slowly forcing his head back. But, to her increasing horror, Ralph's efforts seemed to make no impresion on the larger man. She could do nothing, only witness the life being ruthlessly squeezed from her husband's body.

Then Ralph's lips curled back, the sinews of his neck cording as he applied greater pressure to his opponent's jaw. Owain staggered, and both men crashed to the ground, Ralph on top, his hands now about the giant's throat. All eyes were watching the two men. The crowd cheered for their lord, as they jostled each other to gain a better view of the fight.

Suddenly, something alerted Morganna to a greater danger. Her glance darted to Gwyneth, and she saw her stealthily draw a thin-bladed knife from her belt. Her trailing black sleeves flapping like crow's wings, Gwyneth was poised, about to plunge the blade into Ralph's unprotected back.

There was no time to cry out a warning to the guards. Before she could even think of the danger to herself, Morganna pushed away from Emrys's supporting arm and hurled herself across the intervening space. Fire shot along her arm as Gwyneth's blade nicked it. Reflexes from her childhood training with Giles made her act instinctively, and she ducked, her other hand sweeping upwards to clutch the woman's wrist, the impetus of her weight bending her struggling arm down behind her back.

Fear for Ralph sustained her strength. Her vision was filled by feral, green eyes glittering with malice.

'If I can't have Pengarron,' Gwyneth shrilled in fury, as she battled to free herself from Morganna's hold, 'neither shall you!'

Morganna held on grimly, knowing that at the slightest weakening, Gwyneth would bring her arm forward to renew her attack. Dimly she was aware of Ralph and Owain still fighting, of the cries of the crowd, and shouts from the guards telling her to step back. But she had seen the murder in Gwyneth's eyes. She meant to kill Ralph. She dared not loose her hold.

Close by, Wulfric's barks added to the confusion. There was a blur of grey, and then he was snarling and snapping at Gwyneth's legs. To avoid his jaws, Gwyneth backed towards the King's Tower, dragging Morganna with her as she refused to slacken her hold. She cried out in agony as Wulfric's teeth found their mark.

'Fiend! Get you gone!' she screamed, kicking out at the dog as she did so. Her mouth gaped in alarm as she tripped over Wulfric and began to topple backwards.

Morganna swayed, but kept her balance as Gwyneth slipped from her grasp to fall heavily to the ground. For an instant, shock widened the woman's eyes, and then her body slumped. Slowly, a scarlet spot of blood spread across the whiteness of her wimple, where her head had struck the corner of a stone block. Before Morganna's stunned stare, her green eyes glazed, and remained fixed and staring. She was dead.

Horrified though she was at Gwyneth's sudden end, Morganna's fears for Ralph overrode all else. She turned to face the struggling men, grateful once more for Emrys's supporting hold.

'The Lady Gwyneth is dead!' someone shouted. 'She

tried to kill the Earl. God bless the Countess for saving
him!'

Morganna saw Owain stiffen. All at once the fight
went out of him, and his murderous grip round Ralph's
waist loosened. Agilely, Ralph freed himself from
the giant's hold and, breathing heavily, leapt to his
feet.

More slowly, Owain rolled on his side and lurched to
his knees. Ignoring Ralph and everyone else present, he
stared fixedly at the crumpled figure of Gwyneth. His
eyes hollowed with grief, he rose stiffly to his feet and
lumbered towards his mistress's body. As two guards
moved forward to arrest him, he made a threatening
gesture towards them, an animal snarl rising from his
throat. Ralph gestured to the guards to fall back.

There was a regal presence about the servant's grief,
which stilled the villagers' mutterings. Reverently,
Owain bent his knee to gather Gwyneth into his arms,
then, rising, he turned towards the hall, his pale eyes
staring straight ahead, his strong features ashen as he
moved forward as though in a trance. Surly-faced but
silent, the crowd parted.

Numbed by what had happened, Morganna found her
arm being taken by Ralph, who guided her in the giant's
wake. When he did not speak, she looked up at him and
saw a setness about the firm line of his lips. He, too,
appeared spellbound as he watched Owain's dignified
procession to the hall. It seemed that Ralph was content
to wait. A wrong move now would be disastrous, Morganna reflected. For all her evil ways, Gwyneth was his
brother's widow—a Warrender. And, in death, must be
honoured as such.

On reaching the hall, a shocked silence fell upon
Gwyneth's servants and their guards as they saw
Owain's burden. Morganna noticed Bronwyn standing
apart from the others, a man-at-arms on either side of
her. The girl blenched as she saw her guardian's dead

body, then her stricken gaze lifted, taking in Morganna's dishevelled state.

Acutely aware of the grey dust clinging to her hair and clothing, Morganna resisted the impulse to brush it away. Yet, as she held Bronwyn's stare, the young girl for once did not gloat. Instead, Morganna saw disbelief, the puzzlement of her expression turning to alarm, then finally to horror. She looked away from Bronwyn, her own emotions of relief and horror so jumbled that little of what was happening made sense. She felt faint, and willed herself not to lose consciousness.

Her injured arm throbbed, though the scratch was not deep. But the pain was a constant reminder that this was not all part of a terrifying dream. She was free from her tomb. Ralph had rescued her. The evil shadow that had lain over Pengarron was destroyed!

The warmth of Ralph's fingers closing over hers gave her the will-power to remain standing. Owain walked with stately slowness down the length of the hall, looking straight ahead, Gwyneth's body carried with veneration, her trailing sleeves flowing behind them. He approached the dais, and stood before the high table covered by a woven cloth. Gently he laid Gwyneth's body out in state, and smoothed the folds of her black gown over her legs.

Morganna felt Ralph's arm tense beneath her hand, but his gaze remained fixed upon the strange ritual. Then he shook his head as though to clear it. As he stepped forward, Owain bowed deeply in homage to his dead mistress, and turned to face him. He stood stiffly, his pale eyes dull and devoid of life, and he held his arms out in front of him as though expecting them to be bound.

'Take him away,' Ralph commanded, 'and let a man ride to the abbot. He'll know best what is to be done with the Lady Gwyneth's body. I doubt it is fitting for her to be laid to rest within the chapel vault.'

Meekly, Owain allowed the guards to lead him from the hall.

Ralph turned to Ifor, saying heavily, 'I'll question the servants later. Take the Lady Bronwyn to her chamber. She is to speak to no one until I learn her part in this.'

At the ferocity of his tone, Morganna pulled back from him. 'Bronwyn had no part in the ceremony last evening,' she said firmly. 'I think she was drugged, as were the guards.'

'You defend her, when in the past she has done everything in her power to discredit you? Jocelyn told me of her spite.' Ralph's eyes kindled with admiration. 'There truly is no equal to you in all England!'

The respect in his rich voice eased the horror of Gwyneth's death, and Morganna smiled tremulously. 'You endow me with qualities I do not possess, my lord. Bronwyn's wildness has been encouraged for too long, but I would not see her suffer injustice for something she has not done.'

At that moment, Bronwyn broke free from the guards. Sobbing loudly, she threw herself at Ralph's feet. 'My lord, forgive me! I meant the Countess no real harm. Gwyneth told me she could get the Lady Morganna to leave Pengarron, and that you would not want her any more.'

The stiffness in Ralph's stance showed his embarrassment at Bronwyn's outburst. With an unexpected burst of pity for the girl, who had done all she could to wreck her marriage, Morganna held out her hand and helped her to rise. There were tears in Bronwyn's eyes as she spoke.

'My lady, forgive me! I wronged you. I can see that now. There were times when Gwyneth made me do things—I don't know how—but I seemed to have no will of my own.' Her voice broke on a sob.

With a kindly smile, Morganna accepted the girl's apology. She recalled far too vividly her own raging

jealousy, when she had believed that Ralph preferred
Bronwyn to herself, not to feel empathy towards the girl.

'As you seem to have realised the error of your ways,'
Ralph said sternly, 'I shall not punish you further,
Bronwyn. If you agree to have done with this nonsense
and take daily instruction from the new chaplain I have
appointed, you may accompany us to Court. There will
be no more casting spells or consulting runes. It is time
you were settled with a husband. Go now. I would be
alone with my wife. We shall talk of your future later.'

Curtsying to them both, Bronwyn lowered her eyes
demurely, and outwardly, she appeared to have learned
her lesson. For the sake of them all, Morganna fervently
hoped it was so. As the girl left them, she fastened on her
husband's words, dreading that they must be parted
again so soon.

CHAPTER SIXTEEN

'WHEN DO YOU leave for London, my lord?' Morganna asked in a low voice.

For a moment Ralph's lips twitched; then, his eyes crinkling with yearning, he drew her close. 'As soon as you're packed and ready. Do you think I would leave you again?'

More than anything, she wanted to be with him. But, in London, knowing Giles was so close and in need of her, could she stand the conflict that would tear her apart?

Ralph's arms tightened about her, uncaring that the hall had not yet emptied. He tipped her chin up with his forefinger, his expression softening.

'In London we can work together to free Radford. I should never have made you choose. He is your brother, and I'll do all I can for him, but I can promise nothing. I am certain that, once at London, the King will be forced to abdicate and the Duke of Lancaster will take the crown. I had hoped it would not go this far.'

'If King Richard abdicates, what will happen to him?'

Ralph sighed. 'What choice is there? He must remain a prisoner . . . a constant threat to the throne.'

'And Giles?' Morganna's voice broke at the fear racking her that such might be her brother's fate.

'He has but to forswear his allegiance to Richard and take the oath of fealty to Henry.' Ralph looked at her compassionately, and added encouragingly, 'He's a Barnett. They're a stubborn breed, with a strong will to survive. As you have so justly proved, my love!'

Morganna's heart soared, her eyes brimming with joy as she encountered the tenderness of his golden stare.

She leaned against him. Once in London, she would fight for Giles's freedom. Now, the light glowing in her husband's eyes beckoned her to surrender to his will.

A smile tugged at the corner of his supple mouth. 'You look surprised, my love. How so? Surely it was obvious from the first time we met in the forest that you had stolen my heart? Did I not vow then I would have you, fair Morganna of Daneton?'

Her ears did not deceive her. Ralph loved her! Only a lover could look at her in the way he did now, ignoring the mortar-dust, the dirt, even the stench of fear that still clung to her clothing. There was tenderness, respect and something far deeper than desire in that burning gaze.

She touched his unshaven jaw, her answering smile evocative. 'We Barnetts are stubborn to a fault, my love,' she breathed huskily. 'I knew you would rescue me. Though I feared you would be driven by duty, not love.'

Her hand slid over his velvet-clad chest, and she exalted in the powerful quickening of his heartbeat beneath her touch. 'I was too proud to acknowledge that I loved you, my husband. Then I thought I had lost you, and I was desperate to prove my worth.'

She swallowed against the knot of emotion in her throat. 'Oh, Ralph, tell me again that you love me! That it was not all part of my delusion and fear.'

He lifted a finely-arched brow, the gleam in his eyes dangerous. 'Never question my love, dearest heart! It is yours until eternity.'

His thumb brushed along her cheek, and he lightly kissed her eyes. 'You look exhausted, sweet wife. Our journey will be delayed until you have rested.'

'I am too happy to feel tiredness,' she answered, her eyes smiling into his. 'I can bathe while my chamber-women are packing, and be ready within the hour, unless . . .'

'Unless?' Ralph queried, desire darkening his eyes to

the colour of brandywine. He bent, gathering her close. 'Are you tempting me to delay our journey, minx?'

'Surely your Henry Bolingbroke is not such a hard master? You have ridden all day and all night. Would he not expect you to rest awhile before you rejoin him?'

Ralph laughed softly. 'Sweet enchantress, I have no mind to rest just yet! But you are right. We shall not leave Pengarron until the morrow.'

He bent his head, and all the leashed yearning of the past months was revealed in the fierce possessiveness of his tender, soul-baring kiss.

The March wind howled down the chimney of the private apartments in the King's Tower. Morganna edged closer to the blazing log fire and, as she did so, her gaze lingered lovingly upon the bent head of the Earl, who was studying plans for the improvement of the estate. She could sense his impatience for the winter to end, restless from a month of being cut off by bad weather which made the roads impassable.

In her new-found contentment, she too awaited the spring. In another two months her child would be born, and her happiness would be complete. No, a nagging thread refused to be sewn neatly into place. Not quite complete. Not while Giles was still a prisoner.

She looked up, expectantly meeting Ralph's thoughtful stare, at the sound of the herald's trumpet from the watch-tower. Who had braved the foul weather to visit them? Probably a party of strolling players. It would be pleasant to have fresh entertainment this evening.

Encountering the adoration shining in her husband's eyes, Morganna promptly forgot the players as he put his papers aside and strolled to her side.

Suddenly came the ringing of spurs upon the stone steps, and the bailiff burst into the room, looking flustered.

'Stand aside, man,' an abrupt voice snapped from behind him. 'I need no announcement.'

Morganna's heart leapt to her throat as she recognised the heavily muffled traveller striding into the chamber. Ralph started forward to protest at the intrusion. Then, as the man before them flung back his hood, Morganna was on her feet hurrying towards him, forgetting all protocol in her rush of happiness.

'Giles! Oh Giles, you're free at last!'

Beneath the cloak she saw the familiar surcoat and hose of scarlet, but he looked so gaunt! His once sparkling eyes were darkly circled, and his black hair was now touched with silver at the temples. Then his arms were round her, hugging her close, his frozen lips pressed against her mouth.

At a protesting kick from within her, Giles held Morganna at arm's length, his expression strained as his gaze swept over her swollen figure.

'Anna, I . . .' His voice cracked, and he looked over her head to where Ralph stood stiffly by the fireplace.

'Radford,' he said crisply.

'Pengarron.'

Morganna's heart sank as they sized each other up. Two men silently challenging. Linking her arm through her brother's, Morganna turned to face her husband. She made no secret of her joy at Giles's presence, and her eyes pleaded with Ralph to accept him. She knew it was more anger than pride that was the barrier between them. Since October, when the Duke of Lancaster had finally accepted the crown of England, Ralph had done all in his power to get Giles released from prison. It had been her brother's stubbornness which kept him a prisoner.

As she watched, Ralph remained stiff and unbending, his expression guarded. Morganna's eyes misted, her love for both men tearing her heart in two. She smiled beseechingly at her husband.

There was a slight relaxing in Ralph's stance. He snapped his fingers for a page to bring wine and refreshment, but his voice was uncompromising. 'Come nearer the fire, Radford. You look frozen to the bone.'

Flinging off his cloak, Giles moved closer to the fire, but did not sit. 'I cannot accept your hospitality until I have had my say,' he said haughtily. 'I came to give my blessing to your marriage. I was wrong to withhold it for so long. But in prison it seemed an empty gesture. Anna's letters make it plain that you have made her happy, Pengarron. That's all I ever wanted for her. Now I am free, I can make amends. Her dowry is below in the courtyard. You have treated Morganna with honour, Pengarron, and stood by her when she had need of you most. For that, I am indebted to you.'

Knowing how much Giles's apology must have cost him, Morganna took the goblet of wine from the page and handed it to him. His dark eyes clouded with regret.

'Can you ever forgive me, Anna?'

'You are here. Both the men I love are here. There is nothing to forgive.'

'Have you sworn fealty to King Henry?' Ralph asked, less harshly. 'What of your allegiance to Richard Plantagenet?'

'King Richard is dead,' Giles proclaimed solemnly. 'He died in prison in February. Some say the unfortunate man starved himself to death. Others—King Henry's enemies—say that Richard was murdered. Whatever the truth, he lives no more. Upon Richard's death, I was freed from my oath to him, and have since sworn allegiance to King Henry.'

Giles drank deeply from the goblet before continuing. 'I expected nothing in return, except my life. It seemed that his Majesty respected my loyalty to Richard's lost cause, when so many of the late king's friends had deserted him. My estates are restored. This is the last duty I must perform before returning to them. For the moment, England is at peace. Can there not now be peace between us?'

Giles squeezed Morganna's hands as his voice became gruff with emotion. 'After all, Pengarron, we both have the happiness of the same woman at heart!'

Ralph slid his arm possessively about Morganna's waist. Once again, he was at ease and smiling. 'Well, come to Pengarron, Radford. We are united in one cause, one love—that of the Countess of Pengarron. Let us drink to her, and let no more discord grow between us.'

Her heart overflowing, Morganna took Ralph's hand and placed it over her own and Giles's. 'Let us honour our fathers by our friendship,' she urged. 'They obviously knew us better than we knew ourselves. United, how can we fail to win greatness? And what woman was so blessed with the love of two such remarkable men!'

Her glance returned to Ralph, leaving him in no doubt of her abiding love, or that it was now to him that her first loyalty would always be given.

A SIREN'S LURE

An international jewel thief called 'Le Chat Noir.'
A former intelligence officer suspected of being a Russian spy, gone to ground in Capri.
A young woman anxious to find her father.
The lives of these characters are cleverly interwoven in this intriguing, contemporary story of love, drama and betrayal from Andrea Davidson, author of THE GOLDEN CAGE.

Available in September, Price £2.50.

W◗RLDWIDE

Available from Boots, Martins, John Menzies, W. H. Smith, Woolworths and other paperback stockists.

Mills & Boon
COMPETITION

How would you like a
year's supply of Mills & Boon Romances
ABSOLUTELY FREE?

Well, you can win them! All you have to do is complete the word
puzzle below and send it into us by <u>30th September 1987.</u>
The first five correct entries picked out of the bag after that date
will each win a year's supply of Mills & Boon Romances (Ten
books every month – worth over £100!) What could be easier?

```
M R E T T E L T W I N M
B I T T E R O O R E H A
N C L H A Y V N E E R R
O I G L R S E E E S O R
S T U O S E S S I K D I
O O H Q F A E R T A O A
R X M T E C N S Y N A G
E E N R N L U D A C I E
A F F A I R R M B R P E
L O M E T E O A L O G W
M O E H A W I S H A O E
R L N M D E S I R E S N
```

Win	Marriage	Kisses	Woman	Mills and Boon
Harlequin	Letter	Fool	Eros	Desires
Romance	Love	Envy	Woe	Realm
Tears	Rose	Rage	Hug	
Bitter	Wish	Exotic	Men	**PLEASE TURN**
Daydream	Hope	Girls	Hero	**OVER FOR**
Affair	Trust	Vow	Heart	**DETAILS**
				ON HOW
				TO ENTER

How to enter

All the words listed overleaf, below the word puzzle, are hidden in the grid. You can find them by reading the letters forwards, backwards, up or down, or diagonally. When you find a word, circle it, or put a line through it. After you have found all the words, the left-over letters will spell a secret message that you can read from left to right, from the top of the puzzle through to the bottom.

Don't forget to fill in your name and address in the space provided and pop this page in an envelope (you don't need a stamp) and post it today. Hurry – competition ends 30th September 1987.

Only one entry per household please.

Mills & Boon Competition, FREEPOST, P.O. Box 236, Croydon, Surrey CR9 9EL.

Secret message _____

Name_____

Address _____

_____

_____

_____Postcode_____

COMP 2